The Journey
of the In-Between

The Journey
of the In-Between

Kyra Coates

INFUSE PRESS

The Journey of the In-Between
Author: Kyra Elizabeth Coates

ISBN: 979-8-9855804-1-9

kyracoatesart.com / kyra@infuse.gallery / www.facebook.com/kyradeviart

To Robert, Celeste, Josie, Maya, and Isla.
Thank you for sharing this journey of life with me.

The Moment It All Changes

"I wish you would've let me go with you," Eamonn said over the phone.

"It's fine," Maji said as she turned the steering wheel of her van with one hand, her cell phone in the other. "It shouldn't be a big deal. I will let you know what the doctor says when I get home. I hope it won't take too long, but I will have to get the girls from school when my appointment is done."

"Maji, you're so nonchalant about this," Eamonn said, annoyed. "I'm glad you finally had tests done because it's clear you haven't been doing well. Don't take your health so lightly. I swear, woman, you would never stop to take care of yourself if I didn't hound you to do it."

Maji laughed, switching the phone to her other ear.

"I'm a mom! Who has time for something like taking care of myself? Gotta go babe! I'm almost there. Love you!"

Maji tossed her phone into the passenger seat. She chuckled to herself about how right Eamonn was. She always pushed herself too hard, and she was terrible at taking breaks. Gratitude swelled in her heart thinking about his words. He always looked out for her well-being, and he was the one who pushed her to go to the doctor.

Maji had been feeling off for a long time. Her health had started to go downhill years before, right after her two daughters were born. She had been married before she met Eamonn. It had been an exhausting relationship for her. She found herself doing almost everything for the family, while her husband did very little. She had worked full-time and also managed the household and made most of the parenting decisions.

When her youngest daughter was born after a very difficult pregnancy, Maji realized that if she divorced, she would actually have the chance to take breaks because her ex would have to take care of the kids at his house. It was a brutal recognition to have, but an honest one. So she took the leap and got a divorce.

Though she did get breaks, being a single mom was still exhausting. It always felt like she just never had time to take care of herself. After she and Eamonn got together years later, she felt some sense of relief and recuperation with his added support. But over the past year her exhaustion and general pain had come back stronger.

Maji had brushed it off as middle-aged parenting aches. What woman in this modern day and age didn't feel maxed out and exhausted? It seemed to be the societal norm. Eamonn insisted she go to the doctor. Maji obliged and was actually looking forward to finding a way to feel better. As she pulled into the parking lot of the doctor's office, she reminded herself of that.

"I should've done this a while ago," she chided herself. "Now I'll finally get this under control."

Maji stared at her hazy reflection in the window next to her, the doctor's voice echoing through her skull as he spoke to her across the desk. She listened, taking in his heavy words like one reads a manual to build a piece of furniture. This does this, and that goes there. Factual. Black and white. Was each individual body so standard, following all the same rules? Was a medical protocol the answer?

As she was contemplating her face in the glass, she suddenly realized she didn't recognize herself. The features were familiar, but that consistent sense of "me" was gone. Who was this face? She saw her long brown hair and green eyes. Maji saw the lines around her eyes from years of smiling, the ridges between her brows from years of stress. They reflected all those worries that came and went, the fights with her children, her partner, the work she took so seriously that piled on her one moment, then dissolved into the ethers of time like everything else. The laughter and joy they shared that etched itself around her mouth, now gone too, with just a memory left as a groove. Recollections of games and freedom, of childbirth, of lovemaking. Hours ago these lines defined her, had meaning, like a child's drawing of simple shapes. Eyes: round. Mouth: Line turned up. Nose: triangle. Wrinkles: age. But now they stared back at her like scribbles on a wall. Empty. Meaningless. Who was this stranger? Her doctor continued, speaking of treatments, speaking of statistics of survival, speaking of time, speaking of hope.

Then the moment came when, as he spoke, a spring of fear welled inside her, as if she were drowning and the fear propelled her to the surface to paddle madly, gasping for breath. She listened to him intently. *Treatments? Really? Small chance?*

In that fearful desperate paddling, she looked once again to the reflection. Now she recognized the "me" she had always known. There she was. So afraid. So desperate. Had she always been? Her brow creased, and her heart grabbed onto that line between her eyes like a life raft. Yes, the fight, the struggle to survive. Yes, this is life. This is familiar. She recognized this. She could hang on to this. She could fight. She could win! She could beat the clock.

The doctor's hand on her own broke her reverie. "You need to make a decision. There isn't much time."

Time again! This thing we are ruled by. Time for work, time for bed, time for school, time for family, time for play, time to rest, no time at all. She sighed, her mind sagging. She looked back at her reflection as her doctor waited, silent. *Did he recognize himself in the mirror?* She wondered.

She felt the fear, like an old friend she loved to hate, pushing her. She thought of the years her fear moved her, keeping her above the surface, giving meaning to her actions, knowing she would disappear under the waves if she didn't keep in motion. That constant voice of *more, more, more*! Move or die, grow or die, work or die. Now the fear screamed at her. Full panic! This is it! Everything you've fought for is depending on what you do now! If you don't fight, it was all for nothing! It will all be meaningless!

Those lines stared back at her. Circles, triangle, wrinkles, her fear desperately pulling them together to form a face in her mind. *Here you are! See! See yourself!* She sighed again, feeling her desperate paddling, her gasping for breath. It defined her; for so long, it defined her.

Outside, rain began to fall. The drops distorted her reflection in the window. The lines disappeared, leaving a globular mosaic of colors and swirls. Beauty swam in that formless mass, and she found herself engrossed in it. She momentarily forgot her fear and sank down, down below the waves. Time froze in the stillness of a held breath.

She wasn't drowning. She floated in peace, weightless. She didn't know where her lines ended and the rest of the world began. She gasped a clear breath. The floating sensation punctuated her surprise. She could breathe. She let go of her fear.

She wanted to put her fist through the glass, make it all disappear. Not in an angry punch, but to shatter the old lines, the old ideas, the struggle. She was done with it, free from it. Struggle would not define her any longer. It was time to stop the desperate paddling and just float. She raised her doctor's hand to her lips and kissed it, then stood. He stared at her in surprise and confusion.

"Thank you, doctor," she said softly and walked out the door.

<u>Star</u>

Star shoved open the front door and hurled her backpack into the corner, pencils flying out as colorful helicopters. She stormed into her room and stomped up the ladder onto her top bunk, flopping face-first into her pillow. Her curly hair billowed out around her like a silky explosion. She let the angry tears come that she had been fighting in the car. Along with them came a burst of rage, and she roared as loud as she could into the pillow.

She heard Maji step quietly into her room, pausing. The young girl sighed loudly as an invitation for her mother to be with her in her rage. Rage tore at her often, and there weren't many people who could be with her in it. It irritated them. Her overflowing emotions frustrated others. She got frustrated with her emotions, too--with the power of them. One minute she could be happily coloring, or dancing in the rain, and the next an ocean of anger or sadness crashed upon her like a tsunami, sweeping her away. It consumed her. She had no control over it. She would fight back madly, kicking and hitting at whatever or whoever had triggered her pain. Or she would collapse on the floor from the weight of her emotions, or try to run away down the street, hoping one day she would run faster than her madness and finally beat the terrible feelings that were like monsters to her, that made her feel like a monster.

Maji called her Star because she said she burned bright like a star. She appeared so small and inconspicuous, like a little twinkling light in the sky. It was true that at six years old she stood, on average, several inches shorter than the rest of her first-grade classmates. Her big eyes and brown curly hair gave her the semblance of a doll. But when anyone got close they saw the swirling fiery power that she was, like a burning red giant.

It wasn't just anger that burned in her, though. Star had all the dials turned up. Beauty could easily move her, and she marveled at the sunset in the mountains and beautiful pieces of music. She felt the pain and joy of others intensely. Her teacher told Maji that Star was one of the most empathic children she had ever met in her 40 years of teaching. Star didn't know what that meant. She just thought the world was a very intense place.

Maji often told the story of when Star was a baby and they were listening to classical music during dinner. A cello concerto rose with deep elongated notes and reached a crescendo of high overtones in a slow, hypnotic rhythm. Star stopped mid-babble when the music began, dropped her spoonful of mashed peas, closed her eyes, and swayed slowly to the music in a high chair dance. Engrossed, her two-year-old fingers waved to each note as she lost herself in the beauty of the sound. Her family, her dinner, the world disappeared, and she became the music. She gave herself to that music for the entire five minutes in beautiful freedom, until the song ended and she opened her eyes to find her family staring at her with looks of delighted astonishment.

"Never have I seen a toddler become so passionately engrossed in music," Maji would say. But that is what Star was. Pure passion, in all its forms.

Mama climbed up to her bunk and lay down next to her silently. Star felt the bed sag with her mother's weight. Mama lifted her arm so Star could snuggle in. Sometimes when the feelings were too big it just helped to be held by a grownup. An adult could hold her steady so the feelings couldn't wash her away.

"What's this all about, sweet baby?" Mama asked.

But Star couldn't find words yet. Her mind still swirled with emotion. She shrugged and buried her face into her mother's side. Mama hugged her closer, not pressing the topic. She knew she had to be patient and let Star find her words. Sometimes, when she was given that space, suddenly the feelings weren't so big anymore. Sometimes, her emotions just needed to be seen by someone else to settle. Star felt her anger soften.

"It wasn't fair," she sniffed.

"What wasn't fair?" Mama asked.

"They laughed at me," she whimpered, a single fat tear welling out of her eye and rolling down her round cheek.

"Who laughed at you?"

Star paused. She thought back to the classmates who laughed when she sang a loud song at recess, to the little boy in her class who guffawed when the counting blocks she had stacked so high fell over. She thought of her older sisters who mocked her when she got in the car, her face pouted up in anger at her school day, and their giggles because they found her cute and silly in her turmoil. In her mind, she heard all of the laughter of the day repeated and a giant wave of anger and pain rose up in her once more. The memory of their faces and laughter merged together into a giant monster, a collage of mocking smiles and snickers, who poked and teased her and made her feel small. She sobbed in staggered breaths and couldn't answer her mother's question. Mama stroked her hair, kissing her gently on her head.

"Do you remember that day I took you to the zoo, and we went and saw the tiger?"

Star had to think for a moment. She didn't understand why her mother was asking her about tigers.

"Yes, I remember," she murmured.

"How cool was that tiger? What did you think of that tiger?"

Star smiled weakly, her love of tigers pushing down some of her upset. "It was so beautiful. And so big! I remember she had these huge paws."

"Right! Tigers have always been one of my favorites. Do you remember when she roared?"

Star did remember. They were standing right next to the glass, and the tiger had been walking around her enclosure when suddenly she stopped right in front of them, stared into the distance, filled her chest, and let out several loud, deep roars. It sent vibrations through everything around them. She felt it in her bones.

"Yeah! It was so loud and cool and kinda scary!"

"It was, wasn't it?" Mama smiled. "Tigers are so big and powerful it can be scary. And do you remember what we did when we heard her roar?"

Star frowned. All she remembered was that glorious sound and the awe she'd felt of the animal's big striped face and body. "Er, no."

"We laughed, baby. We laughed at that tiger."

"We did?"

"Yeah, we did." Mama looked down at Star's upturned face. "Do you think we laughed at that tiger because she was silly? Or stupid?"

Star guffawed. "Uh, no! She wasn't stupid at all. She was awesome!"

"Exactly! So why do you think we laughed at her?"

Star felt the roar in her mind, heard the tiger's panting breath, saw her teeth, her claws, her power. Her heart beat a little faster.

"I think we laughed because she was kind of scary, and we were nervous."

"And what was scary about her?"

"She was just so, I don't know, powerful."

"Exactly!!" Mama sat up and moved Star to look her directly in the eye. "Don't you see, baby? You're a tiger, too!"

Star rolled her eyes and flopped over.

"Gaaawwwd Mama, I am not. I'm small and stupid! I am not a tiger!"

Mama scooped her up, holding her in her lap.

"Sweetheart, I'm not saying you're big with claws and teeth. Look at you! You are a cute teeny little thing!" She poked her in her belly button, making her giggle. "But you have power, my darling. Most of us walk through life with protective filters on. Did you know that? People can shut down their feelings and thoughts by creating stories about the world. They say some things are a certain way, so that's the only way they can see or feel things. That's their filter. But not you. You don't have those filters. You feel everything in its raw intensity. And you want to know a secret? Your big feelings are your superpower! Did you know that?"

Star was confused. She didn't have any superpower. All she felt was overwhelmed. She shook her head. Her mother continued.

"I know it doesn't feel that way right now. But all the greatest thinkers, artists, and musicians were people who didn't put filters on. They were courageous enough to let the intensity of the world shine through them. They couldn't help it. That's just who they were. That's who you are, baby. And when other people see that, it scares them, because it shows them their own filters. And they don't want to be shown their filters, because they want their filters to be all there is of the world. Their filters help them feel safe and comfy, and your power threatens that.

"But at the same time, they also want what you have, which is an unfiltered power of the universe shining through you. It's very confusing for them. They don't know how to handle what your superpower is showing them. So they laugh at you, hoping it makes you feel small, as small as they feel, so they can feel safe inside their filters again. So, you see, you *are* a tiger! My little Star tiger! And as you grow up, you will learn to use your superpowers in a way that doesn't feel like it's too much for you, but instead will feel like not enough, because all you will want to do is shine, shine, shine your amazing powers as a gift for the whole world to see! And they will see you, and see how spectacular you are!

"Right now, though, you are in superstar training. It takes time to learn how to work with what you've got. And it doesn't make it any easier to have those scared people laughing at you because they can't handle your amazingness, I know! But try not to worry about them, honey.

They will always be there. You can just look at them and think about how hard it must be for them to live life with these filters, unable to see and feel all the things you do. You can send them love and hope they find their way because it must be so sad to have to laugh at something so beautiful because they can't find it within themselves, don't you think?"

Star was silent, taking in everything her mother said. She didn't understand what Mama meant by filters. She didn't think she had any superpowers. Weren't superpowers just from stories, like Wonder Woman and Spider-Man? She didn't know. She lay in her mother's lap in deep contemplation until the bedroom door opened again. Mother and daughter peeked over the railing of the bunk bed and saw Star's stepsister tiptoe into the room.

<u>Cloud</u>

Cloud stepped quietly into the room, her hands behind her back. The two stepsisters shared a bedroom, but Cloud knew Maji was talking with Star, so she proceeded into the room with caution.

"Do you want to play with me? We can do makeup!" she asked, her voice high and lilting. At eight years old, she was almost half a body size taller than Star, so people often forgot they were only a year and a half apart in age. She wore a velvet pink princess dress, and a sparkly crown sat lopsided on her blonde hair. Messy hot pink lipstick coated her lips and bright blue eyeshadow hovered on her eyelids in arched swirled circles, only a few shades lighter than her own blue eyes. She held a small horse figurine in her hands.

Star stared down at her, and her brow furrowed in returned anger.

"No, I don't want to play!" she barked and rolled away from the side of the bed so Cloud couldn't see her. Cloud looked at her stepmom, who wore a pitying look. Maji mouthed the word "sorry" silently to her.

"Ok." The eight year old sighed, her head hanging low, and left the room. She peeked her head around the corner into her two older sisters' room, hoping to find a playmate.

The two girls were lying on the floor on their bellies, laughing at something they saw on an iPad in their hands. Both looked up at Cloud.

"Hi!" she chirped.

"We didn't say you could come in our room. Go away!" barked Justice, the oldest of the girls. She picked up a dirty sock that was lying on the floor and half-heartedly threw it at her, laughing.

"Stop it!" shrieked Cloud, and she turned on her heels and left, the laughter of her sisters following her

Cloud wandered outside. She saw a pile of rocks by the front walkway and decided to build a shelter for an imaginary horse. She straightened her crown, and as she stacked the rocks, she imagined she was the princess of the kingdom using magic powers to build a spectacular castle for each of her stallions. As a princess, of course, she had dozens of only the most beautiful and most magical of these enchanting creatures!

Cloud was used to playing by herself. Even though she had three other sisters now, they hadn't always been family. Justice was her sister by blood. They were five years apart in age, but to the younger girl sometimes it felt like lifetimes. She remembered moments of sweetness they shared together, but long moments of isolation separated these recollections. She didn't know if it was because of their age difference, or because they were such different people, but they never really played together much. In truth, Justice treated her cruelly for many years, and she didn't understand why. Justice would randomly say something that would deeply hurt her, or would jump out and scare her, or just be crabby and snap at her for no reason. She loved her older sister, but she didn't see her as a playmate. So Cloud discovered that playing by herself made life more enjoyable. And since she had no one to play with, she created her friends with her imagination.

And her imagination was a wonderful place to play! She favored romps with horses, fairies, or other families. Romantic relationships fascinated her, and she loved imagining her mythical playmates getting married and becoming pregnant. She didn't know how they got pregnant, just that there was kissing involved. But the power to create life in a Momma's belly seemed miraculous to her.

Cloud lost herself in the worlds she created. In those worlds, she could do and be whoever she wanted. Magic ruled, especially her own. The rest of the world didn't matter when she was playing. The child often forgot there was anything else happening around her until she bumped into someone. Then, without paying any mind to what they were doing, she would announce to them the happenings of her magical universe.

The little girl ran into the house looking for more horses. As she charged into the living room she saw Dad and Maji talking to one another. They were holding hands and sitting on the couch. Tears were rolling down Maji's cheeks. They spoke in hushed voices.

Cloud paused, hearing the words "terminal" and "dying" but not understanding their context. She didn't know why they seemed so serious, so she shrugged it off and figured it was a grown-up issue. She bounded over to them.

"Hi, Maji! Hi Daddy! This is my horse, Amanda. She can swish her tail and make flowers grow! I'm going to get my other horses. They'll be her sisters, but Amanda will only let them play with her if they're nice to her! Amanda is the queen!"

Then she turned around and skipped out.

Cloud was four years old when her daddy met Maji, and her two new sisters came into her life. Star and her older sister, Cecelia (everyone called her Wolf Girl) sat on either side of Cloud in age. Two years separated the older Cloud from Star, and Wolf Girl boasted two above her. It was the best of both worlds. For the first time she got to be a big sister, and with a new older sister who *liked* to play with her! Both girls loved to enter and build on her world of imagination. The three of them often sat side by side, dolls and animals in hand, playing out elaborate stories of mystery, intrigue, romance, and betrayal. Good magic would abound, yet so would foul play. Heroes would prevail, then be knocked down in their arrogance when it was the other girl's character's turn to be victorious.

Even better, the two new sisters became a bridge between Cloud and Justice, giving them some common ground of interest to relate to. Justice began to use her own imagination to build complex cardboard dollhouses, create elaborate games, and teach her younger sisters the art of proper Barbie Dreamhouse upkeep, complete with an impeccable doll wardrobe and spotless plastic corvettes. She grew kinder to her own sister over the course of a couple of years. Cloud was in heaven.

But then, new rivalries emerged. Star and Wolf Girl had an unusually close relationship for siblings. Before moving in with Cloud and Justice, they had shared a bedroom and even insisted on sharing a bed, often falling asleep together wrapped in each other's arms. Wolf Girl was fiercely protective of her younger sister and loved her profoundly. Star returned the love in equal favor. Often when Star's emotions overwhelmed her, Wolf Girl would wrap her in her arms, and Star would calm down.

Cloud watched all of this in envy. She longed to have a relationship like this with Justice but knew it wasn't the way they were. When the two stepsisters let her into their intimate circle, she felt loved and welcomed. They were the Three Musketeers!

But then there were those moments in which they isolated themselves, protective of their partnership. Cloud would protest her exclusion, Wolf Girl would bare her teeth, and Star would throw hateful barbs. They created a circle of play together and glared at her vindictively if she tried to enter. Then the eight-year old felt the old isolation threefold. It hurt deeply. In defeat, she would return to her world of imagination and create realms of fairies to rule where magic was the only rule. She floated through these times, her own best friend.

Now as she sat outside in her world of imagination, she made sure all her horses had magnificent palaces! The pile of rocks in front of her became several triple-tiered castles with glittering marble facades, gilded golden towers with creeping rose vines caressing the sides, and arched doorways with crystal-clear blue moats encircling each lofty chateau. Each horse transformed from plastic into a creature gifted with iridescent coats that sparkled in the sunlight. Cloud sat back, admiring her accomplishment. It was then that she realized Star was standing right next to her.

"Hi, can I play with you now?" her step-sister asked sheepishly.

Cloud's face lit up. "Sure!"

Wolf Girl

"So we have a deal then? I get three of your Tokidokis, and you get my Ballerina Barbie doll?" Wolf Girl asked, the bounty of toys laid out in front of her. Cloud looked at the trade uneasily.

"But you get three things, and I only get one." She frowned.

"Yes, but the doll is worth more than the three Tokidokis, so it's actually a better deal for you. The doll cost $16, and the Tokidokis were only $15."

Cloud's face twisted in contemplation. Wolf Girl stared at her, hovering over the toys with bated breath, her shoulder-length brown hair dangling in her face.

"Well, okay."

"Great!" Cecilia scooped up the small figurines and handed the larger doll over to her stepsister. "Thanks!"

She hopped up and ran into the house. As she turned the corner to follow the hall to the bedroom she shared with Justice, the ten-year-old ran right into her mother, coming from the other direction. As the two collided, Wolf Girl's Tokidokis flew out of her arms, along with several bottles of medicine Mama had been holding.

"Oh baby, whoops!" Mama dropped down to pick up her bottles. Wolf Girl crouched down as well, and picked up one of the brown prescription bottles, turning it over in her hand.

"Mama, what's this?"

"Oh, it's nothing." Her mother snatched the bottle out of her hand. "Really. Just something for a cough I've had."

"You've had a cough?" Wolf Girl asked, surprised. She watched as Mama picked up the other bottles, tucking them into the front pocket of her sweatshirt. Wolf Girl couldn't help but notice a tremble in her mother's hands.

"Hey, whatcha got here?" Mama picked up a Tokidoki. "You better put those away before someone steps on one."

"Yeah, okay." She watched as the woman picked up the last of her bottles. Then she turned and kissed Wolf Girl on the forehead before rushing off.

Wolf Girl took her winnings into the room she shared with Justice. On her shelf was an assortment of other Tokidokis she had been collecting for over a year now: small animal figurines that looked like the results of a genetic splicing machine gone berserk. Assorted colors and themes made up horse mermaids, green pegasi, hooved cats, and more. As much as she appreciated the value of a good Barbie doll, right now Tokidokis were her prized possessions.

Wolf Girl was born named Cecelia, but her mom had called her Wolf Girl for as long as she could remember. Her mother loved giving nicknames, and this one stuck. In truth, Wolf Girl hated her real name. She thought it sounded like an old person's name. "Wolf Girl" fit her much better. She even had her friends call her that.

The child loved her collections. Over her ten years, she had always managed to successfully gather hordes of her most favorite toys. Whether it was dolls, stickers, or figurines, she had a remarkable ability to bend the will of the universe to deliver her deepest wishes--toys. But these desires weren't fulfilled as simple gifts given to a spoiled child. Wolf Girl was not self-entitled, but clever. And she learned at a very young age that there were ways to get what she wanted.

When she was four, she made two amazing discoveries. She desperately wanted an American Girl doll, which Mama flat-out refused to buy her.

"It is ridiculous to spend $100 on a doll for a child. You could make one out of old socks and have just as much fun with it."

But Wolf Girl knew that wasn't true. Mama just didn't understand. Her face crumpled in a frown.

"You can work for it!" Mama's face brightened. "You can do extra chores, and I will pay you for each one. It may take a long time, but eventually, you'll earn enough money. If you're going to get something that expensive, you need to appreciate earning it."

"Yeah, okay! I can do that!" She immediately got to work, finding an industrious side of her she had never known was there. She cleaned bathrooms, learned to fold her laundry, helped unload and load the dishwasher, weeded the garden, and dusted the living room. She asked her grandparents for even more chores to speed up the savings. She polished their glasses, brushed their dog, and watered their plants. If her little hands could manage it, she did it.

She kept a doll catalog in her room and looked every day through the pictures to decide exactly which model she was going to get. After one month, she had almost $50 saved up, and it felt amazing! Her goal appeared in sight. And the astonishing part was that it all came from her own hard work. She could make things happen by putting her own energy and effort into it!

But the real miracle was what came next. Her best friend, who possessed three American Girl Dolls herself, had gone to a local bookstore and saw that they were holding a drawing with the prize of an American Girl Doll and its accompanying book. Having witnessed Wolf Girl working so hard for weeks now to earn her own doll, her friend thoughtfully put her name in and hoped for the best. And lo and behold, she won!

When Mom took her to the store to claim her prize, and they handed her that perfect little effigy, the toy of her dreams, Cecilia realized something powerful. Larger forces than she conspired to fulfill her desires. Yes, it was her friend who put her name in, but fate had decreed its drawing. The sight of her effort had motivated the friend, and magic that brought all these steps together to manifest this great reward. And with the money she had worked hard to save, now she could buy several outfits to go with it.

Was it truly as simple as having a wish and investing energy to make it happen? Would the universe really bring it all together? She had to test this theory to be sure.

Several months later on the Chinese New Year, Wolf Girl and her mother perused a book that described the astrological significance of the Fire Monkey, the Chinese Zodiac animal for the new era.

Maji closed the book and turned to her daughter. "Well, it seems this is a strong year to manifest what you really want in life. So, baby, what is it you would like to bring into your life for this year?"

Wolf Girl thought of her experience with the American Girl doll. Now was the perfect time to test the universe.

"I want a giant mountain of stuffed animals!".

Mom laughed. "Really? That's your biggest wish for the year?"

"Yes!"

"Ok, well, let's see if it happens." Mama sighed.

As the months passed, Wolf Girl focused all her energy on manifesting her stated wish. Asking, of course, was the first step. She targeted her parents first, expecting a denial nevertheless. They were pretty minimalist in their parenting style and rarely gave random toys. Holidays and birthdays always came with gifts, though, so for her fifth birthday, she received multiple stuffed animals from friends. But long periods separated these special days.

The next step was to work on her grandparents. She realized that if she asked often enough, it planted the seed. Enough requests wore them down. They caved in, and she received numerous little stuffed animals from the old couple here and there after asking, but soon this tactic started backfiring. The grandparents complained of her greediness to her parents, and her whole system shut down. She had to devise a new tactic.

So she tried again but with a finesse to it, a gentle nudging here and there, an exclamation of a deep desire dropped in a silent room like a ping on a piano key, leaving a subtle vibration in the mind. And as predicted, one day her grandma just "magically" decided to buy her an oversized lion she had seen at Costco, claiming that something had told her it was meant for Wolf Girl. Wolf Girl knew exactly what that something was!

She received more stuffies as party favors from birthday parties. She even got one from the free box at the dentist's office. Stuffed animals started showing up from all corners of her life. Wolf Girl was thrilled, and it further confirmed that if she put a bit of her energy into it, some greater force out there dictated that her wish be met with opportunity. At the end of the year, Mama stood in the door of Wolf Girl's bedroom, shaking her head at the pile of stuffed animals.

"Well, sweetheart, you certainly got your wish for a mountain of stuffed animals, didn't you?" Maji said. Wolf Girl grinned.

As the young girl matured, she learned that patience was key and to trust that she would get what she wanted. Yet as her desires grew and changed, so did her experience. She began to comprehend that as much as she wanted it, her desire for certain people to change wouldn't happen. No matter how much she focused on that annoying boy in her class to stop being rude to her and her friends, he wouldn't. She couldn't wish her way out of chores, or get out of school, as hard as she tried. She would even try to muster a fever or a sore throat, proclaiming to her mom that she felt awful until she nearly believed it herself. But Mama saw through her trick, and off to school she went. These events undermined her understanding of the nature of reality. Why didn't it work like it did with her mountain of stuffed animals?

She noticed time had something to do with it. There was no instant gratification from her manifesting powers. It took time for the universe to register her order. Like a fine meal, all the ingredients had to be put together in just the right way, and then, voila! Perfection. So she started to appreciate that this was a long game she had to play, but like a wolf stalking its prey, she knew the wait was worth the reward. So Wolf Girl learned patience.

In 2016, at six years old, she had a shocking experience. The presidential election was in full swing. She didn't know much about what that meant but was extremely curious. Mama explained to her that the president was the person who was in charge of the whole country. She said that for its entire history our country had only men as presidents, but that this year, a woman had a really good chance of winning the vote. When her mother spoke about it, she had tears in her eyes and her cheeks would flush red, so Wolf Girl knew Maji was very emotional about this.

"It's time to let women rule. Women are more compassionate. A woman will focus on peace, not war. A woman will take care of those who are suffering, not just try to take more for herself. It's time to let some feminine energy make a difference."

This amazed Wolf Girl. She grew very interested in the election. She sat with Mama one night watching the Democratic National Convention. So many amazing people came out in support of Hillary Clinton. Musicians...actors...other people she didn't know, but people who thought her pretty awesome. They played beautiful songs and gave powerful speeches that made everyone, including Mama, clap and cheer. At the very end, Hillary herself came on the screen. She sat with several women and girls. Wolf Girl listened as the presidential candidate spoke, thinking that perhaps this woman could make the world an amazing place. Then she said something the child would never forget.

"To all the little girls out there watching tonight, I want you to know something."

Wolf Girl's ears perked up. Hillary's eyes gazed directly into hers.

"I may become the first woman president of the United States, but if you want to, you could very well become the second."

The six-year-old's heart leaped. Was that true? She had wanted her stuffed animals and she got those. Could she become president too?

"Mama, is that true? Could I become president?" She looked up at Mama, perched on the edge of the couch. Maji's eyes were bright with pride.

"Baby, I think you can be whatever you want when you grow up. Even the president."

From that day forward, Wolf Girl ran downstairs after school and turned on the news, hoping to learn more about the election. The excitement and to-do of it all fascinated her. She learned that Donald Trump, who ran against Hillary, said some really mean things about people. She saw him make fun of a disabled reporter and thought of the bullies at her school. She thought he was very rude.

Then one day, when her mother was out of the room, she turned on the news and heard a recording they had taken of him on a bus talking about grabbing women "by the pussy." She didn't know what that meant, but it deeply upset the news people talking about it. Mama came downstairs after a few minutes and paused to catch what her daughter was watching. Wolf Girl watched as her mother's face turned an angry red.

"Mama, what does that mean? Why was he grabbing women? What is their pussy?"

Maji looked down at her young daughter, pain etching extra lines in her face. Tears brimmed in her eyes as she paused.

"It means he was touching them without their permission. He was touching their private parts. This is called sexual assault, honey, and it's a really terrible thing. No one, and I mean *no one* is ever allowed to touch someone else without their permission. It was a horrible thing that he did, and he should not become our president."

Mama sat down on the couch as tears began to flow down her cheeks. She pulled her tiny daughter into her lap. Wolf Girl felt her throat tighten at seeing her mother so upset. *Why was someone who had done something so bad allowed to run for president?*

"Mama, has that ever happened to you? Has anyone ever touched you without your permission?" she asked. Her mother blinked rapidly as her tears flowed, and she buried her face in Wolf Girl's hair.

"Yes baby, that has happened to me. And it made me so sad, and so mad."

She heard her mother's voice break into sobs. She reached out with her little hand and stroked her mother's hair, her own eyes spilling over.

"I'm sorry, Mama." Her heart pounded with her mother's pain and she felt scared at the intensity of her mom's emotions. This election was more important than she thought. Anger welled inside her. "He can't become president. He won't. Hillary will win!"

Mama chuckled through her tears. "I hope you're right, baby. That man has done many terrible things. He can be very cruel to people. All he cares about is money, and it's greedy men like him that are hurting our planet."

"How do they hurt our planet?"

Maji looked into her daughter's eyes, blinking.

"They take, baby. Just like he grabbed those women without permission. They take and take until there is nothing left but ruin. They take the water. They take the trees. They take the oil out of the Earth and burn it so everything is heating up. They take all the money and don't want to share. They just keep taking."

Wolf Girl's eyes filled with tears and her throat tightened. *Are these greedy men going to take everything? Are we going to be okay?*

After that day, Wolf Girl decided she would wish Hillary into winning the election. She didn't want a greedy man like Donald Trump to win. She thought it was time for a woman to be in charge, too. Mama wanted it, so she wanted it.

She drew pictures of Hillary winning and made sure to watch the news for at least a few minutes each day, wishing as hard as she could for her to win while she watched. She knew she was too young to vote, but she told every adult she knew that they should vote for Hillary. *Surely this will work*, she thought. It worked for most of her other desires, and this one was so important. And now she had time on her side. They were months away from the election.

The night of the election, Wolf Girl was beside herself with excitement. She couldn't keep her eyes off the news. She would eat a few bites of dinner, then run downstairs to check if any new results had come in from the vote, running upstairs to share updates with the adults.

"We just got Colorado! But they are still waiting on Pennsylvania!" She didn't even know where each state was, but the news people did. They had a big digital map that kept changing colors as they announced who each state voted for.

As the night wore on, Wolf Girl tried her best to stay awake. Her mother didn't have the heart to send her to bed, so she let her stay up as long as she could. They watched as the map on the screen turned more and more red. By 11:00 they still hadn't called the election, but it was clear what was going to happen. Wolf Girl's head was nodding against Mama's arm. The woman scooped her up and carried her to bed, snuggling her in next to two-year-old Star and kissed her head.

The next morning, Wolf Girl burst into her mother's room at 6:00, and leapt onto the bed, as excited as if Santa had come the night before.

"Did we win, Mama? Did we?" She bounced on the bed.

Her mother's face looked wrecked and tired. "No baby, we didn't win."

Wolf Girl stopped bouncing, confused.

"So, Donald Trump won?"

"Yes, he did." Maji breathed heavily. "I'm sorry."

. Wolf Girl sat still, staring at the wall. Her heart pounded in her chest. It didn't work. Everyone was so excited, and she wished so hard, and it didn't work. She slid off the bed, silent, and went upstairs.

After that day, Wolf Girl realized that the universe contained greater machinations that she didn't understand. Not everything was fair. Good people didn't always get what they wanted. This was very different from what she read in her storybooks. Suddenly to Wolf Girl, the real world wasn't so black and white anymore.

<u>Burning</u>

Colorado burned. It was late August and four separate wildfires raged throughout the state. One, less than 40 miles away, had now been named the largest wildfire in Colorado history, burning close to 185,000 acres. Smoke and haze filled the air. The mountains, which usually stood tall, clear, and majestic in their view on the daily commute, had disappeared behind a wall of brown. The sun blazed an eerie neon pink, leaving the sky unsure if it was day or night.

Maji drove her minivan with Wolf Girl and Star, taking them to their father's house. They had split custody of the girls and this was his weekend with them. Even with the windows rolled up, they wore N95 filtered face masks across their mouths and noses. All three were asthmatic, and the masks helped filter out some of the burning smoke that found its way into the car through invisible cracks.

These masks had been a part of their daily life for months. The previous March, the world had awakened to the global pandemic of COVID-19. As schools shut down, and social calendars transformed into empty spaces of contemplation, Maji and her family learned to face the daily unknown and fear of impending illness with some semblance of routine.

Now, as the fires burned, leaving a visible orange in the mountains north of them, it felt as if they were driving through an apocalyptic wasteland. The isolation of quarantine, and now the inability to even enjoy a walk outside, weighed heavy on them. They lived in a double quarantine, and the attempt to cram all of their lives inside enclosed walls sometimes made it difficult to even speak.

Maji looked in her rearview mirror at the girls in the back seat. They stared silently out the window. She could see the pink sun reflecting in the pupils of Wolf Girl's eyes that peeked over the top of her mask. A flaming skull embellished the mask's mouth, and Maji couldn't help but feel how appropriate it was for the current condition of the world.

Wolf Girl's gaze flitted to Maji in the mirror. Maji thought she saw her eyes crinkle in a smile but couldn't tell with the mask on. But as Wolf Girl's eyes began to glisten, Maji realized instead she was fighting tears.

"Are we going to die?" the child asked abruptly. Maji jumped at the question in surprise.

"Why are you asking that, baby?"

"Because of all this." Wolf Girl waved her hand to the outside world.

"Oh no, honey, the fire isn't close enough to hurt us. We are safe."

"No, no, I mean because of what caused this. You know, climate change! Are we going to destroy the Earth? Are we *all* going to die?"

Wolf Girl pulled her mask off and looked hard at her mother. A tear spilled down her cheek as her face turned an anxious red. Maji felt her own face burn, her heart quickening. Her mouth opened, but she couldn't find the words. This was one of those moments, those big motherhood moments she knew would shape Wolf Girl's life, and it terrified her to think she might screw it up.

She looked at her daughter's face and saw that impending fear of mortality that she herself struggled with now, facing the nearness of her own death with her newly diagnosed illness. But this was different. This was a child afraid of having no future. This was a child feeling the world and humanity blowing itself up. Star sat next to her sister, her eyes big with terrified wonder to mirror the size of the words Wolf Girl left hanging in the air.

Maji looked out the window at the orange and pink atmosphere. She felt the mask that had lived on her face for months. It was all so dire. It felt so hopeless. It was the hopelessness that gripped Wolf Girl now, at 10 years old.

When Maji was 10, she had asked that same question. It was 1990. The world was much more innocent then. No Google, YouTube, or other online services bombarded you with information. Maji lived in the safe bubble of a beautiful home with a duck pond and a high enough affluence to keep her comfortably bored in her suburban life.

One evening they turned on a television program that was celebrating the 20th anniversary of Earth Day. Entertaining, well-known celebrities filled the screen. She was excited to see a star-studded production to celebrate the beautiful, natural world.

Maji had never heard of Earth Day before that TV program. But she was already a deep lover of nature and animals. At that time in her life, she dreamt of being a zoologist, so she could study lions on the African plains. She envisioned weeks spent under a sprawling sky, surrounded by her companion prides, each cat with a familiar name, rubbing up against her like oversized house pets, accepting her as one of their own. She wanted to be the Jane Goodall of the savannah and live in harmony with her four-legged brethren.

Now she sat and watched as Bette Midler portrayed Mother Earth, dressed in a gown with earth-toned splotches that represented continents. Maji watched in shock as the actress cried for help to be saved and saw her collapse on the floor dramatically. As the ambulance rushed Mother Earth away, hooking her to oxygen machines, statistics of deforestation, pollution, and global warming flashed across the screen. Maji read them all in horror. She had never heard of endangered species. She had no idea about global warming. She didn't realize the family car they drove was contributing to the temperature rise on the planet. She was devastated, gutted. Maji had become Dorothy in Oz, seeing the incompetent Wizard behind the curtain for the first time. She had been so comfortable, so complacent when all around her the world was falling apart. And it was their fault. It was all their fault.

When the TV program was over, she was inconsolable. She cried angrily for hours, baffling her mother.

"Why didn't anyone tell me? Why isn't anyone *doing* anything?! Are we all going to die?" she wailed. Her mother tried to console her but spoke only empty words. The poor woman, whose generation had flourished on the American Dream of profit and prosperity for all, now stared down the consequences of their greed and neglect in the devastated face of her daughter.

"Maybe you could write a letter to the president and tell him how you feel?" she suggested in desperation.

Yes! That Maji could do. She would proclaim her passion to protect the environment and pledge her allegiance to join forces with the government to end the danger to the planet. Surely the president would be inspired by the passions of a young child hoping for a better future for them all. The girl had visions of international leadership meetings, of rallies calling for change, of corporate leaders turning off their factories, of massive tree-planting ceremonies. She imagined her small, impassioned voice rallying thousands to the cause.

Maji fervently penned her words and sent the letter the next day. She anxiously waited for a response, and after three weeks, one came. The White House sent her a generic, kindly-worded letter thanking her for reaching out, accompanied by a shiny brochure explaining to her the virtues of staying in school. Maji was crushed. At ten she was savvy enough to recognize her letter had been disregarded, and they were placating her with frivolity. She felt something inside of herself die. Her safe world was shattered. She realized then that the adults and leaders of the free world probably wouldn't do anything at all. It was up to her, and all the other kids.

Maji caught Wolf Girl's eyes in the rearview mirror.

"Honey, there are so many people out trying to fight for this world. There are so many amazing technological breakthroughs that have been made for conservation!"

"I know that, Mama!" Wolf Girl spat her words. "But look around! The world is *on fire*, and it looks like it's only getting worse! If so many people are fighting, why aren't things getting any better?"

Maji's heart pounded as she struggled to find words. She knew exactly what her daughter was feeling. It was all too familiar to her.

After she received the hollow letter from the White House, Maji spent the next few years researching as much as she could. She single-handedly cleaned up her neighborhood pond from the careless litter left behind by the residents. She started a school environmental group. Whenever she could, she sent her meager allowance to the World Wildlife Fund. She learned about the pesticides in the food she ate and the devastating effects they had on the ecosystem, so she asked her mom to buy organic. She learned about the incredible waste and emissions from the meat industry, so she became a vegetarian. She learned about the desperation of the farmers in rural Africa and South America, and the clearcutting that happened so they could graze cattle to feed their barely surviving villages. She learned about the fossil fuel industry and the vast amount of wealth it supported around the world. She learned about the leaders of the world who profited from this lucre. She read about oil spills, and the dying coral reefs, and endless burning for more land, more building, more cash crops. She learned that it wasn't ignorance that kept the wheel of planetary destruction spinning. It was greed. The kind of greed that was first born from the need to survive by those who were struggling to do so but inflated into the desire of those in power to increase it. It was this greed, she realized, that would send humanity spiraling into its own destruction.

Her efforts to save the world evolved to address the flaw. She joined her high school Amnesty International group to fight for basic human rights and spent weekends writing letters to governments, begging them to view with compassion the pain of those they hurt and imprisoned and the devastating global results of those actions. She protested on the lawn of the White House with an upraised fist about the genocide the US government supported in Rwanda that no one spoke of. She joined fundraising programs and did tabling sessions in her cafeteria during lunch hour.

In her senior year of high school, her group was invited by the Washington, DC Amnesty International chapter to come as student lobbyists and meet with their state congressman. Maji dressed in her finest business wear. As she and her seventeen-year-old companions walked the halls of the Capitol, the power that was housed between the walls of this majestic building overwhelmed her. The people who worked here shaped the world. In her innocence, the teenager felt each clack of her shoes on the marble floor was one step closer to changing the world.

When they entered the office of her state senator, they discovered they would be meeting with one of his aides instead of the senator himself. Upon hearing that, Maji felt that the same flash of disappointment hit her that she'd felt when she received the skeleton letter from the White House at the age of ten. They weren't taking her seriously.

The aide graciously welcomed them into the office and ushered them to a large round table. He was a young man of about 28 years old. He sat directly across from the seven students gathered around in a semicircle.

Each teenager offered their arguments that, as constituents, they wanted the senator to support. The aid diplomatically countered with points of success the senator had achieved in his career, a plastic smile never leaving his face. Maji felt her frustration growing. She could tell this man was on his way to be a successful politician. He never directly addressed the topics they brought up. From their plea for support of a women's rights treaty to an entreaty to speak out against the Afghani suppression of female education, the aide pleasantly avoided each topic with a carefully curated list of all the ways the senator was the most amazing man at his job.

When it was Maji's turn to present an issue, she sat tall, but had to keep wiping her sweaty palms on her skirt. Calling on her passion for a better world, she spoke of the need for the senator to speak out against selling weapons of war to Saudi Arabia. These weapons were being used to kill innocent civilians in Iraq, and the US government profited from their murders. The leaders of the free world had blood on their hands and cultivated an atrocity to the very principles of freedom the US stood for.

But Maji knew the senator had supported the weapons sales. Saudi Arabia was one of the largest buyers of US-made armaments, and three of the largest manufacturers donated large amounts of cash to the Senator's campaign. Her words fell on deaf ears. Once again, the aide began listing off the great achievements of the man he clearly believed was the most amazing politician that ever lived.

"Well, in 1993 the senator successfully stopped the sale of weapons used in Somalia, and-_"

"We are very grateful for the Senator's work on that issue," Maji interrupted, "and we are encouraged that he will continue to support such efforts to put human lives above profit."

The aide's Ken doll smile waivered, and he cocked his head.

"Let's be honest here." Maji's restraint broke. The entire cordial conversation sickened her. These were people's lives they were discussing. Families, children, people who loved each other and just wanted to be safe.

She glanced at her friend, Nia, sitting next to her at the table. Nia's family had fled Iraq when she was a toddler, and she'd grown up as a US citizen. It was her people they discussed. The humble teenager had elected to speak on girls' education instead of the more painful issue that hit too close to home. Nia's eyes were on the floor. This smug little aide didn't even know there was an Iraqi sitting in the room with him. Maji felt an ache in her gut and persisted. Surely there was an element of compassion that was bigger than the political game.

"We can acknowledge the fact that the senator has done many good things." Maji placed her hands palm-down on the table to steady herself. "But we also need to acknowledge the fact that he has taken contributions from some of the largest weapons manufacturing companies on the planet. We know they have been major contributors to his campaign. Is he going to continue to trade his conscience for money? Because in the end, money shouldn't be as important as innocent lives and the basic human right to feel safe in your own home. Money shouldn't matter as much as that. But I'm not sure if the senator agrees with me."

Maji stared at the aide pleadingly. *Please let him soften.* The aide didn't move in his seat, but his poker face slipped. His eyes narrowed slightly, and his smile curled almost imperceptibly at one corner of his mouth. She knew this look. It was the same look some of her teachers gave when they looked at a student they knew was hopelessly lost. It was an expression of disgust at such extreme naivete. She could read it like a book. He cocked his head to the side in a gentle, mocking way.

"Yes, the senator supports human rights, of course." He clapped his hands together, rubbing his palms. "OK then, I will be sure to pass on what you said. Thank you all so much for your time."

In a whoosh of self-importance, he leaped up, shouted "best of luck", and rushed out the door, leaving it open behind him with clear implications.

Maji's classmates turned and looked at her with surprised faces. She had blown it. She knew it. But she just couldn't play the diplomatic role anymore. It made her feel dirty. Speaking with the aide felt like playing some twisted, sleight-of-hand game. Politics were like a southern debutante ball. Only the shiniest won the prize, and the prize was simply to keep being the shiniest.

After her lobbying experience, something changed in Maji. She realized that for as much power as they had, politicians would always be playing "Battleship," trying to sink someone else to win whatever war occupied their agenda that day. They suffered the sickness of greed just as much as the corporate conglomerates. She committed then and there not to buy into a life based on the never-ending quest for more. She would find some other way.

Maji brought the van to a stop at a red light and swiveled to look Wolf Girl in the eye. "Do you remember when Trump was running for president, and we talked about the greedy men taking everything? The problem is they don't want to stop. That's why it isn't getting any better yet. It's a fight. But that doesn't mean it always will be. People are really trying!"

Wolf Girl threw her mask on the floor. "Well clearly the good guys are losing!"

"I wish it was just about good and bad, baby. It's so much more complicated than that."

"Mama," Star asked sheepishly, "why do greedy people feel like they have to take so much? Why are they so greedy?"

Maji turned back around, contemplating her question as the traffic light turned green.

"I think people are afraid. We all have this animal instinct in us to survive. For greedy people, that survival instinct is on hyper-drive. They feel like if they stop, they will die. So, they keep taking."

Star's eyes grew wide with fear. "What if they don't stop taking?"

"Yeah, Mama," Wolf Girl barked angrily. "What *if* they don't stop taking? Are we all going to die?"

In the winter of her 20th year, Maji went on a late spring skiing trip with some friends and had a bad accident. She fell on a green slope, twisting her knee underneath her and tearing her MCL. She had been waiting tables full time while trying to put herself through school. The accident devastated her financially. Stuck on crutches, she could no longer work and couldn't cover her bills. She scraped together just enough to pay her rent for her one-bedroom apartment. When her tuition payment came due a few weeks later for the fall semester, her student loan wouldn't cover all of it. She burned through her savings to keep a roof over her head.

She broke down into angry tears on her bedroom floor one day, her piles of bills and letters scattered around her. She buried her face in her hands and screamed an angry roar. As much as she knew her unfortunate circumstances were a result of her skiing accident, she also knew them to be caused by the greed that created a society where she could barely survive at poverty level, where getting a college education was like trying to pay a mortgage on a house, and the meager insurance that cost her a fortune each month wouldn't cover the physical therapy she needed to get off crutches.

She looked around the room, tallying everything she owned in her head: a couch, a television, a DVD player. A couple of chairs around a cheap table in the kitchen. A bookshelf. A small desk. Her computer. A futon and dresser in the bedroom and camping gear in the closet. A few cooking and art supplies. A photo album. A Subaru station wagon outside.

She came up with a plan.

The next day, she called her landlord and told him she was subletting her apartment. She phoned her school to withdraw from the next semester's classes. She put an ad in the paper to find a tenant, then rented a moving truck. Two of her friends helped her drop every stick of furniture she had at a consignment store, then drove two boxes of art supplies, dishes, and photo albums to her parent's house an hour and a half away.

Hobbling on her one good leg, Maji piled boxes in the corner of the garage. Her mother stepped through the door with a crinkled brow. "I don't like this plan of yours. It's dangerous. It's reckless. A young lady like you shouldn't be out alone living in a tent in the woods. You could be attacked. You could be raped! You know you can come and live here." She crossed her arms across her chest in a fluster.

"Yes, Mom, I know. But that isn't the point. I don't want to be stuck in this cycle. I already feel like a slave and I'm only 20 years old. All I do is work, so I can go to school, so I can get more work, and keep doing that until I die. I had one accident and suddenly I'm buried in debt. How is anyone satisfied with this?"

Her mother shook her head slowly.

"It's the way of the world. It costs money to live, honey."

"Yes, I know--but how much, really? We keep accumulating all this stuff. We're the richest country in the world, but we keep wanting more, wanting something different, wanting, wanting, wanting. It's like we're at a buffet and never satisfied with what we eat. And we're eating this planet alive in the process. I have to try something else, even just for a little bit." She saw the tears her mother held back and wrapped her arms around her. "I will always have mace and a knife with me, OK? And I won't be far. If I ever feel unsafe, I will come crash here for a few nights. Deal?"

Her mother nodded silently in resignation.

The injured twenty-year-old was able to pay off most of her debt with the sale of her furniture. She found a place to set up camp near a state park, just outside the boundary. This way she didn't violate any permit rules. It was a small location, not far from a populated suburban area.

She knew she still had to work to pay for food and gas, so Maji found a part-time job as a summer camp art teacher. She would shower at a local recreation center before work at 10:00, then make a trip to the store for her provisions once her four-hour shift was complete.

It was an incredibly happy time for Maji. After one week, she found herself going to sleep and waking up with the sun. After two weeks, she no longer missed her bed. At first, she was restless. With no movies to watch before sleeping, she read by lantern light in her tent. But soon even the need for that stimulation fell away. She often just sat in the silence of the night and stared at the stars, listening to the movement of the trees around her in the breeze, or to the stillness on windless nights punctuated by a fellow cohabitant of the land in a chirp, caw, or squeak.

Her knee healed up, and she could walk comfortably again. She became sensitive to the forest, feeling it as a living, breathing organism. Deer passed by her campsite on several occasions, and she learned to hear the birds announce their arrival before they came, like a game of telephone being passed from tree to tree. Her life slowed and simplified. The sense of always hustling to get ahead disappeared into the gentle peace of the moment. Yes, Maji still saw friends on occasion, and after a late evening, she would crash on their couches. Sometimes she placated her mother and spent a night at her parents' house. But most days she returned to her camp long before dark, savoring a life unplugged from the traffic, artificial lighting, and continuous sense of doing.

One day, she was cooking a late lunch on her tiny stove and a group of five deer crept within 20 yards of her site. They walked slowly, stopping to munch foliage, and looked up only when Maji turned her head. She had seen this group before. It seemed they remembered her as well and decided she posed no threat. The woman watched them, contemplating the freedom there must be in being a deer. They had no agenda. Their life was to simply *be*. She laid her bowl with care on the ground. *I think I'll be a deer for a while.*

She stood slowly and tiptoed closer to the deer. Once she stood within twenty feet of them, their heads sprang up as if pulled by the same string and their ears swiveled forward on full alert. The largest deer, clearly the matriarch, flared her black shiny nostrils, catching Maji's scent. She stomped her hoof once with a huff as if to announce her authority to this intruder. Maji stopped and turned her gaze, trying to appear submissive. The deer pondered her for a moment more, then relaxed, returning again to graze. Maji looked up, caught their disinterested eyes, and moved closer until she was about twenty feet from the deer. They didn't flinch but instead continued their slow meander through the trees, stopping only to snack on a patch of greenery. They had accepted the human's presence.

Maji followed them on their slow journey for several hours. They wandered for miles. As they grazed, she would break off pieces of a granola bar she had in her pocket and pop it in her mouth to join them in their meal. She followed their every move, trying to learn what it meant to be a deer. Whenever the animal would pause to listen for a sound, Maji would listen, too. She heard the shuffle of animals she never would have noticed on her own. When they lifted their noses to smell the breeze, Maji would sniff as well, occasionally catching an odd scent. She tried to have her feet crunch the leaves as gently as theirs but found feet far more cumbersome than hooves. Peaceful ease filled her. She felt a connection to the rhythms of the world around her that everyday life never gave her. .

After a few hours, they emerged from the trees into a large clearing, which opened to a hillside covered in pine. It had been many hours since Maji left her campsite. The sun was just beginning to touch the treetops in its descent. As her new "friends" moved down along the clearing's edges, Maji stayed behind, realizing she would soon have to turn back to her campsite or try to find her way home in the dark.

She sat on a boulder and took a moment to look up at the sky, fading into a dark blue with just a hint of orange. To her left, the sun appeared balanced on the tops of the trees on the horizon. Directly across from it in the sky hung a full moon, also grazing the tree tops. Maji had caught them both in that brief liminal moment when the sun and the moon shone equally as bright, when neither light nor dark dominated, and she stood between them both. The sky itself became a large Yin-Yang, a perfect balance of opposites.

Maji's breath caught in her throat, and in a flash, like a light switch turned on, something expanded in her awareness. A sail had been unfurled in the wind. Her sense of self grew bigger than what she perceived through her five senses. Suddenly the filters of sight, smell, touch, hearing and taste were revealed as unbearable limits.

A deep longing blossomed in her heart to reach out to something she couldn't see but feel. She knew it was there, just outside the perimeter of what she could take in, but she didn't know what "it" was. She wanted to pop her eyeballs out of her head so she could see around herself in 360 degrees. She wanted to rip all her clothes off so every inch of her skin could feel this mysterious force that ached for her to connect with. But the fear that movement might break this sacred spell paralyzed her. Her heart pounded faster and faster in her chest, and tears spilled out of her eyes. Beauty itself pushed her from the inside out, aching to merge with the outside-in. She panted from the overwhelming grace of it all, and a small cry escaped her lips.

Then, just as the sun sank below the tree line, her body sucked her awareness back in. Maji looked around, blinking, expecting the world to be different. But everything appeared the same. Only she had changed. She had touched something, had a peek at some great mechanism, some force of the universe bigger than anything she'd ever imagined.

She watched as her deer friends began to walk into the woods on the opposite side of the clearing. The matriarch lifted her head and looked back at Maji. They locked eyes. Through the steady gaze of those black pearls, the woman felt a final confirmation that yes, indeed, she had just received a powerful gift. This gift left her with a sense of peace, knowing that there was a perfect balance, an order, to everything as it unfolded. Her heart swelled with gratitude. And as the deer turned and disappeared into the forest, Maji laughed at herself and waved goodbye to them. Then she turned and made her way back to her camp.

Wolf Girl repeated her words, then coughed lightly in both impatience and distress from the heavy air.

"Are we all going to die?"

Maji took her mask off.

"Yes, baby, we are all going to die." She swiveled in her seat to look Wolf Girl in the eyes. "But everyone and everything dies. That is the only thing in life we know for sure. What we don't know is how, or when." Maji turned her gaze back to the road.

Tears flowed freely now down Wolf Girl's face. Star stared in shock at her big sister, and reached out her small hand, placing it on Wolf Girl's forearm in comfort. Her own eyes glistened in tears.

"But look, everything is burning!" Wolf Girl cried, the avalanche of stress and frustration from the past few months exploding out of her. "We can't even see our friends because of this stupid virus! The air hurts to breathe. I feel like people are screwing everything up!"

Maji's heart pounded, feeling her daughter's pain as her own failure, as a failure of humanity.

"I know exactly how you feel. It's really hard, especially now. And yes, people are screwing things up badly. But you know what? There are those of us that can see where we went wrong. We can try our hardest to create a world where people are living in harmony with the planet. It's our job to do that, girls!"

Both kids stared back at their mother with big shining eyes, blinking.

Maji wiped her own tear away before her daughters could see it. "I really don't know how. I won't lie. But if we don't try, if we don't keep imagining a world where harmony is possible, then there will never be a chance of something changing."

Maji looked around at the orange sky. The gas pedal of the fossil-burning car pressed back against her tired foot. She saw the big box chain stores out her window, endlessly going on as they drove, filled with consumers. Consumers of goods, consumers of resources, consumers of life. For so many years, so many like herself had tried to fight this mentality, and things got worse, not better. She knew the science. She knew they had already passed a point of no return. Already, too much carbon filled the air, and emissions grew worse every year. Forests died at an exponential rate. Then the dead forests burned, adding to the carbon. This was one of many feedback loops their world was caught in. And they made no progress to stop it.

Her heart ached in her chest for her children's future, and panic fluttered in her stomach at the thought that she had little preparation time left to give them. She was dying. What would it be like for them when she was gone? What would they be left with? She knew she wanted them to have a sense of power, of courage to shape their own lives. There was a perfect balance and order to everything. Maji knew that. It was that perfection they had to have faith in.

"There is something beautiful about the way everything rights itself," Maji said. "All this is just one way nature is righting itself. If we can respect that, find the intelligence in it, then perhaps we can find our balance with the process."

She turned her head again and looked at both the girls. They smiled weakly at their mother. Their heads tilted toward one another, and their hands clasped together between their seats, creating a heart-shaped space between their bodies. It was a vision of perfect balance. Maji smiled back at them. Another reminder to her that everything unfolded as perfectly as it needed to be. Her only job now was to trust in that.

Justice

Justice walked into the kitchen, glimpsing the sky through the window. The heavens glimmered with the purple light of early morning. The clock showed 6:30, and her body moved slowly, heavy with sleep. Every morning she woke up instantly, her eyes popping open with clarity whether she wished it or not, an inner force driving her body against her will. But she was like her daddy, a morning person. So, most mornings she came into the kitchen for breakfast before anyone else had gotten out of bed. She knew her dad was awake behind his closed door, but he often lay in bed reading the news on his phone before he made an appearance.

Justice savored the silence of having the kitchen to herself. It was one of the few moments of "alone time" she found in the crowded house. She appreciated the newness of the day, the stillness pregnant with possibility. Yet simultaneously, she resented the fact that she preceded everyone else out of bed. Her younger sisters started school much later than she did. It seemed like a downright spoiled-girl luxury that they could squeeze out almost an hour more of sleep than her.

But today was a Saturday. She had promised herself she would sleep in, but once again, her body betrayed her mind. So, with a growl at her current state of contemptible consciousness, she grabbed a pan and quickly fried up some eggs.

Justice was used to things feeling unfair. Like all firstborn children, she shouldered more responsibility than the others. She was the one who had to babysit when Eamonn and Maji had to go places. When the girls had shared chores, she was the one who had to keep the little ones on track. She had to accommodate their desires on movie night because the younger girls couldn't handle the more mature, exciting movies she preferred. She had to wash her own laundry, while the younger ones only had to fold theirs. She cleaned the kitchen faster after dinner but had to wait to be done until the other girls finished their share, which took F-O-R-E-V-E-R. She lived a very unfair life.

After finishing her eggs, she washed the pan and her plate, then unloaded the dishwasher as quietly as she could. She did this most mornings now. In the past, determining who had this chore always led to a small domestic battle. Her sisters would argue it out until her dad or Maji intervened, and inevitably in their frustration with the battle, made them all do it together. When she turned 12, she decided it was easier just to get it done herself. That way, there was less bickering between the girls, and it didn't take as long. She didn't mind doing it to keep the peace. But again, she felt that tickling resentment in the back of her mind as she placed each plate on the shelf. The other girls were just as capable of doing this, too. They just didn't. So Justice took the burden.

It did come with its rewards, however. Her extra responsibility was noticed by the adults. So sometimes when they were assigned chores, Maji and her dad let her off the hook while the other three had to do extra. It helped balance the scales a bit. Just not enough to temper her resentment.

Justice wiped her hands on a towel and went into her room. She shared a room with Wolf

Girl, her polar opposite. Justice was very organized. Cleaning her room wasn't a chore; it was an opportunity to recreate her space. When things stayed in their place, her world made sense. The simplicity and structure allowed her thoughts to flow in a direction that could be relied upon without distraction. Order provided a sense of stability and meaning. When she organized her space, putting her books in order on her shelf, her jewelry placed in their drawers by color or size, her shoes stacked by style on the closet floor, she created a world she could depend on. When she decided to reorganize things, she rewrote her own story. The meaning changed, creating something exciting yet still dependable. In general, Justice hated change, unless it was change she initiated in her own space, change she commanded herself. She controlled her own world when the rest of the universe felt like chaos.

Wolf Girl, however, was a lot like her mother. Her thoughts floated around in spirals of emotion, spontaneous and without order. Wolf Girl embodied that chaos, and it showed up in her space. Justice looked over at her dresser, stacked high in a haphazard pile of papers, books, and dolls shoved between each layer. There were multiple drinking glasses half-filled with water on her shelf. Under her loft bed lay clothes scattered about with half-finished drawings. Justice sighed. Her stepsister's slobbiness irritated her to no end.

She remembered what it was like before Wolf Girl had moved in. She had the whole room to herself. The organization gave it a beautiful flow. A person's eyes could follow it around the room in a 360-degree composition. It was like a picture in a magazine. But now that flow ended on Wolf Girl's side of the room. The choppy, jarring, nonsensical feel of that sudden change stressed her.

With her foot, she pushed the scattered papers out from the middle of the room to her stepsister's side, sighing deeply. She heard a squeak of metal as Wolf Girl stirred in her bed. Justice couldn't see her due to the height of the loft bed, but she watched with frustration as one of the many stuffed animals her stepsister kept piled up in bed with her popped out between the side rails of the frame and bounced onto the floor over to Justice's side of the room. She snatched it up and hurled it, unintentionally knocking the pile of papers and toys off Wolf Girl's dresser, sending them spilling to the floor. Wolf Girl popped up in bed, her hair a spiky disheveled mess, her eyes droopy with sleep.

"Whatwastha?" she asked, only half-awake. Her movement knocked another stuffed animal off the bed.

Justice clenched her fists in frustration. "It was all your crap! Keep it off my side of the room."

Wolf Girl paused. She peeked over the railing of her bed, seeing the papers that had been piled on her dresser scattered on the floor. Her brow furrowed. "Hey, why did you do that?!"

Justice felt a momentary pang of guilt, which she stuffed down inside with her anger. She felt like she was always accommodating her stepsister's mess, always the one forced to carry the burden. Why didn't the younger girl ever just clean her stuff up without being asked? Why couldn't she just bring some peace and order to their room so they could enjoy it together? The constant battle over the issue overwhelmed her.

Justice had gone to her father about it before. Her father only nodded in understanding,

53

then patted her on the back with an air of resignation.

"I get it, kiddo. I'm in the same situation." He nodded at the pile of books and jewelry stacked up on the bedside table on Maji's side of their shared bed. "But it's her space, and you can't demand she keep her space in a way you want. As parents, we can keep asking her to clean her part of the room, but she just doesn't work the way you do. It's something you have to understand in your relationships: acceptance of who the people are in your life. You can't change people to be the way you want them to be."

Justice scowled. She had never asked for a relationship with Wolf Girl. She did love her. She did enjoy their shared moments together, especially at night when the younger girls had gone to bed. They would put on music and laugh at TikTok videos together, or break out the iPad and film themselves acting out characters with silly voices, in outlandish jokes about farting that only kids could enjoy. There was a shared camaraderie in being the oldest of the four girls. In those moments, she felt like Wolf Girl was her best friend. But those days came less and less.

When they first met each other, Justice was nine and Wolf Girl was seven. In their shared play dates, they discovered quickly that they loved all the same kinds of dolls and played together for hours on end. Then, one day, Maji and Daddy left Star and Cloud with Maji's parents, and the adults took Wolf Girl and Justice to the Women's March in downtown Denver.

When her dad explained to her that they were marching in protest of the new president, Donald Trump, because of how he viewed and treated women, Justice understood. She paid enough attention to the adults around her to know it was really bad news this man won. But for her the real excitement of the march was going with Wolf Girl. She was a new friend, and she knew Maji was a new friend of Daddy's. She didn't make new friends too often, so she cherished this relationship like gold.

As they walked, both girls carried handmade signs covered in glitter announcing their rights as women. Justice looked around in awe at the massive crowd of people surrounding them. She saw people in pink knit hats with pointed cat ears. She saw outrageous costumes, people in tutus, and several signs that made her blush for the language used. It was a sea of color, diversity, and joy!

The girls cheered and clapped and laughed. In their pockets they had brought small dolls that they held up next to each other, the dolls joining them in protest.

"Women are people too!" Justice squeaked in a playful doll's voice as she held her tiny figure aloft to see the crowd.

"Yeah, you can't grab *my* pussy!" shouted seven-year-old Wolf Girl, lifting her doll as well.

Justice's mouth fell open in shock. "I can't believe you said that!"

Wolf Girl laughed. "Trump said it first!"

As they moved slowly down the street, the crowd fell silent. Suddenly, Maji jumped up onto a bench they passed and cupped her hands around her mouth to amplify her voice. "Show me what democracy looks like!"

"This is what democracy looks like!" Hundreds of voices rose up around them in response to Maji's call. Goosebumps rose on Justice's arms.

Daddy jumped up next to Maji on the bench, clasping her hand and thrusting both fists in the air. "Show me what democracy looks like!" Daddy and Maji shouted together.

"This is what democracy looks like!" The crowd roared.

Justice and Wolf Girl looked at each other and scrambled onto the bench with their parents. Their small voices rang out in unison. "Show me what democracy looks like!" Justice yelled as loud as she could. The strength of the crowds' shouts sent tingles up and down Justice's spine, and she felt power she had never felt before in her nine years. Her voice was causing this!

She looked over at the adults and saw her dad lean over and gently kiss Maji on the lips. It was easy and casual, and Justice could see this wasn't their first kiss. Her heart leapt. She turned and looked at Wolf Girl and saw her mouth open in shock, staring at her mother.

Justice leaned in close to Wolf Girl and grasped her hand. "Maybe we'll be sisters!!"

Wolf Girl's face melted into a smile, and she enthusiastically returned Justice's squeeze. "That would be amazing! Maybe we could share a room!" The two girls spent the rest of the march holding hands.

As the girls got older, Justice started getting tired of playing pretend all the time. She began to find more interest in her books. Within her books, she could go on adventures without ever having to leave the comfort of her own sanctuary. As Justice's interest became more mature, Wolf Girl turned to the other girls for play.

One Sunday morning, Justice was awake and reading in her bed. Wolf Girl sleepily sat up on her bunk. Justice turned to her as she started to climb down her ladder from the loft. "Now you're awake! I've been waiting for you all morning! Want to watch some PewdiePie on YouTube?

He just put out a new video!"

"Nah, I want to see what Cloud and Star are doing. We said we would play with our LOL dolls today."

Justice's brow furrowed. "But you played with them all day yesterday!"

Wolf Girl turned, a surprised look on her face. "So?"

Justice felt anger bubble in her stomach. "Whatever! Do what you want. Play with your stupid LOLs."

Wolf Girl jumped at her anger. "Uh, do you want to play LOLs with us?"

"No! I told you they were stupid!"

Wolf Girl blinked, her mouth puckering in a look of disgust. "Fine, whatever!"

"Yeah! Whatever!"

Wolf Girl stomped out of the room, loudly slamming the door behind her. In her bed, Justice fought back hot tears that stung her eyes. She was losing her best friend.

Now she glared up at her stepsister, who looked confused and angry at Justice's attack. The division hurt worse than ever. The burden of being the most responsible of the four girls weighed upon her, amplified by the fact that she didn't have anywhere to go that felt like her own. The fury bubbled up in her like a simmering pot about to boil over. Strength and power flowed from the anger in an avalanche of emotion.

"You are such a slob, and you don't care about how frustrating it is for me! You're so selfish!"

Wolf Girl balked. "My God, I'm not even out of bed yet. What the heck?"

Justice's eyes grew hot with tears.

"Whatever!" Justice picked up the other stuffed animal on the ground and heaved it at her younger stepsister. She ducked out of the way.

"Hey!!"

Justice grabbed a book off her bedside table and stormed out of the room. This was one heck of a way to start a Saturday.

The Building Blocks Of A Person

Maji sat on the couch, her legs pulled up underneath her. The sun had set and the rest of the family had gone to bed. This was her usual routine: to stay up late and have some quiet time to herself. She loved the stillness the night brought, when the rest of the family had retired for the night and the hustle of everyday living was behind her. During the day she rarely had time alone. Her thoughts and movements would flit between the disciplined drive of self-employment, the endless needs and interruptions of the kids, the desire to share space and the ache to share touch with her man, and the consistent nagging of her phone rattling off notifications demanding her attention. Time passed like a flock of birds startled into flight, an endless chaotic movement that found its way into the murmuration of a thousand moments dancing in an unpredictable order.

But her nights were hers. When she was alone, in the stillness of the dark that made no demands, she belonged to herself. She breathed only to hear her own breath, not to know how her exhalations sounded next to someone else's. She rested in the freedom of solitude, when she could reach into her mind to fill the space around her without obstacles. She spoke only for her own ears, moved only for her own body

Most thought Maji was a fairly extroverted person. But her need to experience all her senses without being filtered through a relationship to another was fundamental to her mental wellbeing. She could too easily lose herself in her relationships with those close to her. She forgot herself and became instead a form that shaped itself to fit the lives of those around her. She didn't disappear entirely, but shapeshifted into whatever filled the space between her and them.

So, at night, when she was alone, she would sometimes dance with her headphones on in the living room just to feel the exhilarating freedom of her aloneness, allowing her energy to take up all the space in the room. At other times she would simply sit still, observing how her mind filled the silence. Then there were nights where nothing changed. She was then as she always had been: just there, living, with no need for anything else. Sometimes then she would pick up her phone to see how she felt about the rest of the world when hers was quiet.

This night she had done just that. Her brow furrowed as she stared intently at the device in her hand. She gandered at Facebook, and specifically at a photo of a dark-haired man staring back at her from his profile picture.

The man was an old coworker of hers, from a nonprofit based in Guatemala. He was a good friend; someone she had enjoyed talking to and spending time with on her trips down there. They had taken several road trips to the rural areas of the country to film interviews with clients and their families. He had taken her to dinner multiple times and gone to hundreds of meetings with her. Although they had not worked together for a few years now, he always reached out to her on occasion to see how she fared, a practice born of the interconnected culture he came from. She had often shared stories and thoughts with him in a refreshing ease of acceptance, someone who felt familiar even on their first meeting.

The name listed on his profile was John Michael. But Maji knew that wasn't his name. He had recently changed it for some reason. To shake things up? To appear exotic? *Who knows why people make the choices they do in their personal presentation to the world.* A name resembles a shirt, selected for its color and design, until it no longer fits and is discarded on the floor. Whatever the reason, it didn't matter why he changed his name on his Facebook profile. What mattered was that she couldn't remember what his real name was.

This was no momentary brain-lapse. She had gazed at the photo for almost 30 minutes, trying to remember. She scrolled through his profile hoping something would spark some recognition in her mind. But it didn't. She remembered he cherished mountain biking. She remembered he loved to speak English instead of Spanish with her, much to her own frustration (she'd wanted to practice her second language). She remembered he gave her the first sip of Zacapa Centenario, the most amazing rum from the Guatemalan highlands that tasted just how silk felt to the touch. She remembered his laugh, unobtrusive, as if he didn't want to disturb the equilibrium in the room. She remembered the night he walked her back to her hotel and a raging storm unexpectedly moved in. He jumped in front of her in an act of chivalry to shield her from the waterfall of sparks that rained down when a branch cracked and fell, severing onto the electrical wire above them. She remembered the musty smell of his aftershave and the story he told about his ex-girlfriend and her daughter, whom he missed terribly. But at that moment, as hard as she tried to stretch her mind, she couldn't remember his name.

Her doctor had warned her this might happen. As her health slipped away, so too might her mind. Was this it? Maybe she was just tired. Maybe it wasn't a big deal. She gripped the phone more tightly, as if squeezing it would somehow force the memory to drip from the crevices of her brain back into her awareness. She felt the old familiar fear grip her heart, pounding in her chest and ears. It was one thing to be told she would experience a fast decline. It was another thing to actually live it, like being paralyzed while watching ice crack beneath her feet. She had so many memories. Surely this one slip-up didn't mean...

When Maji was 22 years old, her grandfather died in a hospice center, suffering from advanced dementia. The hero of her childhood, he spoke softly and used his voice only to crack a joke or say something beautiful and deep. His marriage to her grandmother had lasted for 65 years and encompassed an unwavering devotion that spoke more to the integrity in his heart than to the ease of their relationship.

The deeper truths of existence drove him as they did Maji. His life had been lived as a success story out of the American Dream handbook: a successful career, beautiful homes, loving children, beautiful wife. But beneath this surface, a greater truth lay. Once someone got to know him, it was clear his depth of mind, his profound inner exploration to the larger machinations of the universe was what made his heart continue beating in his chest. He often remained silent because there were no words to express the profundity of what he experienced in everyday mundane life. No ears could comprehend the great well of wisdom that lived within his mind. Beauty often moved him to shameless tears. He could be playful and simultaneously exude stillness in a natural way.

His presence comforted Maji like no other man's. And as she watched his mind unravel over his last years, it was as if she watched him dissolve, one tiny particle after another, until only a shadowy remnant remained of his former self.

She only visited him a handful of times before he passed. Half a country away separated them. But when she went and visited him, she was so moved by the love and compassion the caregivers had shown her grandpa.

On her last visit to see him, Maji watched as her grandpa grew confused. He kept asking, "Are we going home now?" Maji repeated to him over and over, "No, Grandpa, you have to stay here," only to see his bafflement reflected back to her each time. Janet, the caregiver, came in to bring him some dinner, heard him repeat the question, and saw the pained look on Maji's face.

"Now, Clyde, why would you leave when we've been having such a good time? I would miss you so much!" She swooped in and kissed him firmly on the cheek.

Grandpa laughed his sweet soft laugh. That laugh always reminded Maji of the end of a rainstorm when the air is fresh and clear and the last drops splash onto the leaves of the trees with enough separation that one can make out each individual, gentle plop. Her grandpa laughed like soft rain.

"Awww, shucks," he said, feigning embarrassment. He didn't ask again about going home after that.

Maji was so moved, so grateful for her grandpa's soft laugh at that moment. His laugh bounced in her heart, spreading a sense of levity in the face of mortality. As life happens, so too does death. She would realize later it was the last time she heard Grandpa's laughter before he died. As she watched the caregiver with her grandpa, she knew she had to do for others what Janet was doing for her grandpa.

When she returned home, a local caregiving company hired her and discovered she had a gift for working with the elderly. She kept in mind the love Janet had shown. She always remembered that each client was someone's grandparent, parent, or child.

One night, her company sent her to a hospice center for an overnight shift with a woman named Inez. Inez suffered from very advanced Alzheimer's disease and faced her last days of life. Maji's job was to sit with her throughout the night in case she woke up in need of anything. She prepared herself for a fairly simple, yet sleepless night.

Maji walked into Inez's gently lit room to see a rail-thin woman with violet-splotched skin propped up in a hospital bed. Two nurses were attempting to change the IV in her arm. Inez swung her arms wildly and rocked her head back and forth.

"No! No! No! *No!*" she wailed, sounding more like a small child than an old woman.

"Inez, we have to change your IV!" an exasperated nurse shouted. "You keep ripping it out. You have to hold still!"

"No! No! No!" she continued, her white hair a frizzy cloud around her head. She opened her eyes and glared at the nurse, then swung her fist as hard as she could into her shoulder. It landed with a dull thud, her weakness inflicting minimal damage. But the nurse shouted, and took a step back, throwing the needle onto her cart. "My God!" she hissed, flustered. Maji sensed the weariness in the nurses and guessed this was a regular occurrence.

The young woman froze, unsure where to put herself. She knew people who had Alzheimer's and dementia could get aggressive, but this was far worse than she had ever seen her grandpa get. Inez thrashed back and forth like a toddler in a tantrum.

Maji sucked in her breath, chucked her purse and coat on a chair, and leaped forward to take Inez's flailing hand. The old woman froze, turned and looked at Maji with big round eyes.

"Inez, you're angry! You're so angry!" Maji said loudly. "You're scared too, aren't you Inez?"

The patient blinked in surprise, her face a picture of confusion. Her eyes searched Maji's face, hoping for recognition.

"Inez, you don't know who these people are, or what they want to do to you, right? It makes you mad. Why won't they just leave you alone?! It makes you so mad!"

Inez stared at Maji, her mouth open, her head nodding slowly. Inez had never met Maji before but stared at her with a flicker of understanding. "Yes, I just want them to leave me alone."

Maji took a breath, letting Inez digest her words. She knew she couldn't pause too long or she would lose her again. Maji was using a mirroring communication technique to reflect back to Inez her own emotions. It had worked with other clients before, so she thought it wouldn't hurt to give it a shot.

The young caregiver had learned through her grandfather, as well as a few clients, that people who have memory issues can slip so far into a demented state of mind the world around them becomes a swirling experience with no linear continuity, experience after experience standing alone, no reasonable context to explain the "now" moment as their minds have left them nothing to hang on to. Normal minds create a storyline bridging moment to moment: *I'm in the living room because of this; I feel this way because this happened.* But with no memory to carry the story forward, a person is faced with the stark experience of the now without any context. They become rudderless boats tossed on the sea of life, a terrifying naked experience of reality. Many people in this state lash out, frustrated at their own spinning emotions with no understanding as to their causes.

Maji stroked her hand, then gently turned her arm over. "Do you see this, Inez? This hurts!" she pointed to Inez's bloody IV tube, dangling from her arm. Blood oozed out of her wound, and the tape hung on by a corner.

"Yes, this hurts," she whined. "I want it out!" Inez reached over to rip it away from her arm.

"Wait, Inez! This nurse here," Maji pointed with great exaggeration to the nurse who took the punch in the shoulder. "This nurse wants to fix it so it doesn't hurt anymore. It's scary when it hurts, Inez. She wants to help you so it doesn't hurt."

Inez looked at her arm, then at the nurse, who weakly smiled at her, then at her arm again.

"Scary. Okay," she said softly, her eyes distant. The nurse moved in slowly while Maji held Inez's hand.

"Good. Inez, I'm just going to take this tape off. It may pinch a little," the nurse said calmly. Inez nodded, flinching slightly as she removed the tape, her eyes glazing over, losing themselves in a faraway place that existed only in her mind. The nurse continued to narrate each step, and her patient lay there, unmoving. Once the process was finished, the nurse smiled a silent "thank you" to Maji.

Inez closed her eyes and fell into a shallow sleep. Maji settled into the chair beside Inez's bed. She brought a book to read, preparing for a long night.

Around 2:00 am, Maji startled awake in the chair, her book resting on her leg, her neck stiff from dangling to the side in sleep. Inez stirred in her bed, also waking. She lifted her arms weakly, like a baby bird testing her wings for the first time after hatching. She lifted them from the bed, unsure of what to do with them, and looked bewildered at the wires that hung off her in a dangling web, hooking her to the machines. She turned her half-open eyes to Maji, who was blinking herself awake.

"You're here!" Inez said with joyful surprise. Her eyes opened wide, bright with recognition.

"Yes Inez, I'm here," Maji said through a yawn. "They asked me to come sit with you tonight in case you need anything."

Inez reached out her hands, taking the young woman's into her own. Maji felt the patient's frail, bony fingers fold themselves around her hands with a determined strength she didn't think the old woman could muster. Her skin crinkled like a dried-up used teabag.

"I'm so glad you're here!" she breathed, her eyes beginning to glisten with tears. "I've missed you!"

She thinks I'm someone else! Maji knew this happened with people with Alzheimer's, but she had never experienced it herself with clients. She didn't want to upset the poor woman any further, and she knew if she told Inez who she was it would just confuse her and probably agitate her more. She decided to play a character in the memory that was playing out in Inez's mind. Maybe it would merge the scene in her mind with what was happening around her. Maji could only imagine the relief that sense of normalcy could give her.

"I've missed you, too." Maji stroked the withered hand. "I'm so glad I'm here."

A tear spilled out of Inez's eye and rolled down her cheek, lodging into the wrinkly folds around her mouth. Her lip quivered.

"I'm so sorry," she whispered, before beginning to sob. "I'm so, so sorry. I could've been a better mother to you. I know this. I want you to know that I love you."

Maji felt her face flush hot. She didn't know anything about the woman's daughter. Would she be here in the morning? Were they fighting? Clearly, Inez was seeking forgiveness. Was it for something that happened recently, or was Inez living out a long-ago recollection, something her mind pulled out of the recesses of her subconscious, something that had left a deep enough groove in her memory record to rise now?

"I love you, too," Maji stammered. "I always have."

Inez continued to sob. "I love you so much. Please forgive me. I tried my best. I know it wasn't good enough."

Inez's pain pressed into Maji, this pain that was so real at that moment, even if it had been lived half a lifetime ago. She felt the silent wail in her words. The young caregiver's heart sped up and she blinked back her own tears.

"I know you tried your best," Maji's mind scrambled. Was this okay? She spoke for someone else, someone she didn't know, about an intense situation of which she knew nothing. But here was this woman, lost in the inner universe of her own untethered memories, begging for forgiveness from her daughter. Would she remember what her "daughter" said? Would her family be angry? But she was giving her final bow on the stage of her life. And Maji hoped that on the day of her own death she would be able to feel forgiveness for her mistakes too.

"I forgive you," Maji blurted. "I forgave you a long time ago. And I love you! You were a good mother to me. We all try our best."

The old woman continued sobbing, but a grateful smile spread across her face.

"Oh, I love you! Thank you, my dear! You are so precious to me." She reached up and touched Maji's face. The young woman smiled back, kissing Inez's fingers, feeling the warmth of her joy rush through her. Her fingers smelled like a combination of old books, hand sanitizer, and lavender lotion. They had freshly painted nails, the color of soft pink roses. Maji wondered who in the elderly woman's world had taken the time to perform that simple act of love, painting a dying woman's nails. "You rest now," she said. Inez chuckled lightly but kept her watering eyes on Maji.

"Yes," she said softly, her eyes beginning to fade into a faraway look once more. But she held Maji's hand and continued to say "I love you. You're so precious to me. I'm so sorry," over and over, never turning her gaze from her caregiver's face.

Maji answered her with "I love you, too," and shushes to help her relax.

This continued for 20 minutes. Inez stroked Maji's hand, her eyes filling with tears until they spilled over like a glass left under a running faucet. The waterfalls would stop, Inez would go silent. Then her hand would stroke Maji's once more, and the words of love would roll from her lips, her eyes spilling over again. It was like the ebb and flow of a tide: the tide of a dying woman's emotions. The smile never left her face, until finally, her eyes closed and she drifted back into sleep. Maji waited until her breathing came deep and steady before freeing her hand from Inez's still-tight grip. She took a deep breath, feeling heaviness and lightness all at once.

Inez slept straight through the end of Maji's shift. As the morning nurses came in to relieve her, Maji stood over the patient's bed. Her mouth lay open, and her deep breaths rattled like she was sucking air through a thin hose. Her eyes looked far sunken into her head, and Maji fancied she could make out the sockets in her skull.

"Goodbye, Inez. Have a good journey home."

The next day Maji received a phone call from Inez's son. She had passed away a few hours after Maji had left her side. She never awakened after her emotional plea for forgiveness. Her son had been told the young caregiver was the last one with her while she was awake and wanted to know if she had said anything in her last moments. She shared with him the story of their conversation.

"I didn't want to lie to her," Maji confessed, her heart pounding. "But I just wanted to give her some peace. She thought I was her daughter."

"Oh, yes." He sighed over the phone. "My sister passed away from cancer sixteen years ago. She and my mom were always fighting. They had a terrible relationship. My mom had so many regrets after she died."

"Oh my." Maji touched her face where Inez's hand had stroked cheek. "I hope this conversation helped. I truly didn't want to deceive her."

"Yes, I'm sure it gave her peace at that moment. Truth be told, my mom has been gone for so many years already. There really hasn't been anything left of her, so I don't know if she could even hold on to any of it. But thank you for giving her those last moments of love."

When they ended the call, Maji stared at the phone in her hand. *He said his mom had been gone for so many years.* Who was it that was gone? Her consciousness still inhabited her body, feeling, experiencing. But he said *she* was gone. So, what was it that made her *Inez* which had vanished? The memories went and took the person with them? Someone was there, she knew. Someone had cried with her the night before and expressed love, fear, pain, and forgiveness. So, if it wasn't Inez, who was it?

Maji thought of her own grandfather who left his life with only pieces of who he had once been there. He was clearly not the same person he was when Maji was a little girl, so vibrant and aware. But neither was she the same person she had been as a child. So, what is it then that remains, that makes us who we are?

That question lodged itself aggressively in her mind, leaving her little room to think of anything else. At every encounter she had with someone over the next couple of days, she always asked herself: what makes this person who they are?

A few days after Inez's death, Maji went into her bathroom and stared at herself in the mirror. She recognized herself clearly. The way she styled her hair, the smokey eyeliner she applied around her green eyes. All temporary. She took a tissue and wiped it all off, then stared again at the plain face, smeared and red from her abrupt makeup removal. Maji was pretty by all social standards of beauty. She had petite features, bright eyes, and a graceful, long neck. This beauty she saw in the mirror would fade, she knew.

She remembered when, as a teenager, she'd gone into her grandmother's room and seen the old woman staring at herself in the mirror. Her grandma had been a runway model before she married and even played a small role in a movie alongside Douglas Fairbanks, Jr. when she was 20 years old. She was a shockingly gorgeous woman.

Now in her seventies, Grandma stared at her own wrinkled face with sadness in her eyes. Maji sidled up beside her, putting her face next to her grandma's. She saw the same dark features, heart-shaped face, petite nose.

"I can see our resemblance, Grandma," Maji chirped. The former model looked between the two faces, then pressed her cheek back, trying to smooth out her wrinkles. Her granddaughter took her hand and pushed her own cheek back, making a silly face as her mouth stretched wide. Her grandma's brow furrowed.

"Ugh, at least you still have your youth," she growled and stormed out of the room. Maji felt her sting of anger in surprise. Why was she so upset? As she contemplated it staring into the bathroom mirror, she wondered, did her grandma not recognize herself as she thought she was? Was identity such an intangible thing?

Now as Maji stared at her 23-year-old face, she realized how easy it was to take for granted the sense of "self," the labels we put on ourselves, and the things we claim to be. Right now, she was a beautiful, young woman who could get the attention of any man she wanted. Was this really who she was, though? What would it be like to be someone else? What would it be like to be Inez and not remember who she was? Would it be freedom or a prison?

Maji pursed her lips. She dropped to her knees and pulled open the bathroom cupboard, finding her roommate's electric hair clippers. Before she could think her way out of it, she plugged them in, flipped on the switch, and with one ferocious stroke, shaved off a strip of hair right down the center of her head. Her long, brown hair floated delicately to the floor. Maji watched it in shock, expecting it to land with the same thud her heart had set off in her chest.

Maji sucked in her breath and stared at herself again in the mirror, her stomach jumping at the sight of her Mongolian-esque hairstyle. She already looked like a different person. In one fast swoop of her arm, her traditional beauty had vanished.

"Alright. No turning back now."

She meticulously applied the clippers to her head, shaving off one strip at a time as if mowing a lawn. Her roommate walked by the open door, then did a double-take as he saw her.

"Oh my god! What are you doing?" He gawked.

"I'm shaking things up," she said with a tremor in her voice. "I want to see what it's like to be someone other than a pretty girl."

He cocked his head to the side, contemplating her words. "You know you are more than just a pretty girl."

She stared at him sideways in the mirror. "Yeah, I know that. And you know that. But maybe I need to see what else there is without the distraction of being beautiful, you know?"

He raised an eyebrow. He didn't know. "What happens if you still look hot with a shaved head?" He laughed.

"Well, then I embrace a new look I guess."

He shook his head. "Girl, you crazy." He wandered off.

Maji finished the work of removing her old, familiar self and put the clippers down. She stared back at the girl in the mirror. Except for a short fuzz, no hair graced her scalp. Smearing off the makeup had left her eyes red but the rest of her skin appeared paler without her dark locks framing her face in contrast. She looked harder, more masculine. Her jawline seemed sharp. She looked like a different person but still felt like Maji.

"Well, this should be interesting."

She looked at the clock, realizing it was time to get ready. Every Tuesday night she went Salsa dancing with a few of her girlfriends. She loved to dance and had practiced her moves enough to hold her own on the dance floor. Dancing with a stranger was, for her, a safe way to feel the unique intimacy of each person she was with. They each had their own unique style, energy, and flavor to the way their body moved with hers. Some of her favorite dance partners were people she never would have given the time of day if they hadn't been dancing, but who met her in that shared space between their two bodies. It opened a new world for her.

Typically, at the club, a line of men waited to dance with her. As she pulled on her skirt and strapped on her heels, she wondered nervously how different the night would be with her newly bald head.

At the club, Maji sat nursing a cocktail, her cheek resting in her hand, her own solitude keeping her company. No one asked her to dance. Not one man. She sat in the vacuum of the corner of the room, watching her friends enjoy themselves. Even the men she knew by name who she partnered with every week didn't ask her. They looked past her as if they didn't know her.

"So, this is what it's like to be a different person," Maji huffed.

Though she still felt like herself, she was unfolding from her cocoon of limited perspective into something else entirely. She recognized that the men in the dance hall saw her as an object easily passed over because she dared to violate society's concept of "sexy." In that recognition, she became every woman who questioned her worth due to size, shape, and color. She became a stereotype of unconventional gender flexibility and felt the sting of society's distaste for it. She became the embodied injustice of the female form. She became the anger of an entire oppressed gender. She became the universal archetype of the female.

Maji unfurled into empathy and compassion that opened her heart to every woman. And she realized that she was, indeed, much more than a pretty girl. She was the daughter of Artemis, Kali, Medusa, and Tara. She was the avatar of Joan of Arc, Gloria Steinem, and Athena. And she seethed in all her feminine power and rage, she became aware of how intangible an identity is after all.

Now forty-one, sitting on her living room couch with her phone in hand, she experienced that same loss of self. Was her memory loss like shaving her head? When her mind had unraveled too far, would everyone else see her as a different person while she still felt like herself on the inside? Or would she lose her sense of self altogether?

Suddenly the name of her dark-haired friend in the photo on her phone rushed back to her.

"Matias!" Relief exploded in her. She dropped the phone next to her and flopped back onto the couch, the tension washing out of her in grateful laughter. *I'm okay, for the moment.*

But the heaviness in her chest did not subside. Instead, it lingered as a reminder that she was standing on the edge of a cliff, staring at the vast space of the unknown in front of her. She wondered if she would fall, or if she would fly.

Stepping Sideways Toward A Mirror

After dinner, the four girls worked on their evening chores: doing the dishes and cleaning up the kitchen. Justice stood at the stove with a scrubbing pad in her hand, trying to scour off the orange spaghetti sauce that had baked onto the burner in a stubborn crust. Her face crumpled into a scowl. Wolf Girl busied herself at the sink, washing off plates to go in the dishwasher. Her chin jutted out in an angry frown.

"Why do I always have to rinse off all the dishes?" she muttered with a pout.

Justice rolled her eyes. "Because I always do them in the morning, *and* I unload the dishwasher, *and* I do most of the pots and pans at night." She looked over at Cloud, who spun in circles in the middle of the kitchen, her arms spread wide, humming a tune. "What are you doing?! Finish the table!"

Cloud stopped spinning and turned her head to the table, still filled with condiment bottles, glasses, and salad plates. Justice had placed a few books on the corner earlier so she could wipe down the counter. Her sister's chin lifted, and her eyes closed as her voice lilted into a high whine. "Those books aren't mine, so I can't wipe down the table until you move them!"

Both Justice and Wolf Girl stopped what they were doing, their faces frozen in a look of shock and annoyed anger.

"Are you freaking kidding me?" Wolf Girl shouted.

"Just pick up the stupid books and put them back on the counter!" Justice shouted. "Oh my god, you are such a whiny baby."

"I am not!" Cloud shrieked.

"Haha, yes you are!" piped up Star, her voice carrying out from under the table where she used a hand broom and dustpan to sweep up the floor.

"I am not! You are! You're the biggest baby of all of us!"

Star sat silent under the table for a moment. Then in one swift movement, she reached her arm out and slapped Cloud with the dustpan across the back of her leg with a loud thwap. Cloud's wail grew in a slow crescendo from a low "Oh" into a high howl as she realized her pain. It was quickly followed by the clatter of cups that dropped out of her hands, spilling all their contents into a grotesque swirl of milk, water, and tea onto the counter.

"Oh, my freaking god!" Justice barked, throwing her scrub pad down. "I just cleaned that! What the hell!"

"She hit me!" Cloud cried.

"What did you hit her for?" Justice put her hands on her hips and glared at Star.

"I don't know, and I don't care. She's the worst stepsister in the world!" Star smirked as she crawled out from under the table. Her quivering lip and tear-filled eyes betrayed her nonchalant words.

"I'm telling Daddy!" Cloud shouted.

"No!" screeched Wolf Girl. "We'll *all* get in trouble, and you know it! Just shut up and do your stupid chores!"

Cloud crossed her arms, whimpering. Star stood glaring at her.

"Both of you!" shouted Justice. Star looked at the broom and dustpan in her hands and hurled them across the room. They clattered noisily against the wall.

In their bedroom just off the kitchen, Maji and Eamonn lay on their bed. Eamonn had headphones over his ears as he watched a Youtube video on his phone. Maji had tried to read a book but couldn't avoid hearing the arguments outside their bedroom door. She sighed heavily and rested her book on her chest.

She ached everywhere that day. She felt like an elephant was sitting on her chest instead of a paperback. Her body was accelerating in its breakdown. Each day she grew weaker. Each day her dread of telling her children about her illness rose. She knew she couldn't avoid it for too much longer. But she wanted to savor her time. She knew the news would devastate them, and she wanted to squeeze in as much joy together as she could.

As she listened, she felt the fragility of joy in their shouting voices. She contemplated how happiness was this state of mind we all yearn for. We reach after it through ideas that represent it, whether it be a perfect relationship, a perfect home, everyone treating us the way we want, more money, or more stuff. But when all of this is obtained, happiness shatters like porcelain from one small tap of dissatisfaction. Intangible and fleeting, like life itself. She recognized that the basic human condition is to chase after joy relentlessly as if it were money we can hoard in a bank. Or we try to fix ourselves until that thing we think is broken within us is gone. Instead of joy, we continually find perpetual suffering and a sense of wrongness in the world.

Maji grew up in a typical Christian American society that believed in a merciful God, a God that loves all his children. But if God is love, why would he create a world filled with so much pain?

Maji pulled her legs over the side of the bed. The sound of the girls arguing pounded in her head. She could hear how they riled each other up, their own stories stacking on top of the other in a domino effect of anger. She lifted herself wearily and walked to the bedroom door, opening it to hear their arguing amplified.

"Girls, why all the fighting?"

All four kids raised their voices in a garbled cacophony of complaints and accusations. It sounded like pure noise in Maji's ears, and she lifted her hands for silence.

"Stop, just stop. Forget that I asked."

The resentment pulsated in the room. The girls looked angry and defeated. Maji leaned against the door frame, her body sagging. The weight of her limited time pressed on her. Arguing over dishes and counters felt like such a waste of what little time when she had left.

Maji recognized how thin the line was between differing perspectives. The girls were so young and felt life and the world as a big daunting experience that went on forever. As far as they knew, they had no control over life. They felt they were victims to parents, to teachers, to friends. They didn't see how easily they could choose not to lay blame, but instead make a small shift in perspective, like stepping sideways toward a mirror to get a different angle. A situation could be seen in so many various ways. Maji knew this was a learned skill that came with time and maturity. But Maji didn't have time. Something had to shift their view now.

Maji walked into the kitchen, looking at what was left of their chores. On the counter sat a half-filled bowl of salad. On the stove was a pot of cooked spaghetti, next to it a pan of red sauce.

"There isn't too much left to do," Maji said quietly. "Who is taking care of this spaghetti?"

"Me," grumbled Wolf Girl.

"Oh yeah? Come here, I want to show you something."

The girl lurched over toward her mother, looking down at the floor, her expression sour. Maji picked up the pot and held it down for Wolf Girl to see inside.

"Do you see all that spaghetti still in the pot?"

"Yeah." Wolf Girl groaned.

"Well," Maji's eyes danced. "I think it belongs on your head!"

Maji swiftly lifted the pot and dumped the spaghetti onto her daughter's head. Wolf Girl gasped, her eyes and mouth round with surprise, spaghetti framing her face and dropping off her shoulders like a rag doll's wig. The other three girls froze, their faces mirroring their sibling's shock. Their silent surprise was cut by the sound of Maji's laughter.

After a moment, Justice joined in Maji's laughter, followed by the other girls.

"Oh, you think it's so funny?" Maji teased. She scooped some spaghetti off Wolf Girl's shoulder and hurled it across the room, hitting Justice squarely in the face. Justice's laughter lifted an octave in delight, and the other girls jumped up and down in joy.

"Oh, you two aren't off the hook!" Maji shouted. She picked up the salad bowl and tossed the contents all over Cloud and Star, who danced around in circles as if in a refreshing rainstorm instead of a shower of romaine and tomatoes.

The kitchen was filled with joyful laughter. The girls all scooped up the food around them and began to gleefully throw it at one another.

"Nothing for me?" Maji asked, jutting out her lower lip in mock sadness. "Oh wait! Here's something for me!"

She reached down and picked up the saucepan of spaghetti sauce. Taking one last mournful look at her clean pajamas, she lifted the pan over her own head and with a flourish of her other hand poured the entire contents all over herself, covering her hair, her face, and most of her shirt with the chunky red liquid.

The girls howled in ecstatic disbelief.

"Mama!!" Wolf Girl shouted. "Oh my god!"

Maji dropped the pot with a clang onto the floor, then began rubbing the sauce into her cheeks as if it were a facial scrub. The girls doubled over with uncontrollable laughter.

Suddenly Eamonn opened the bedroom door, his face a picture of confused surprise as he saw the remnants of dinner scattered across the kitchen and his family members. He balked when he saw Maji's red-stained face, clothes, and hair.

"Oh my god, what are you doing?" he gasped. Maji's eyes twinkled.

"Get him!" she shouted, rallying her troops with the point of a finger, and the girls all scooped spaghetti and salad into their hands and pelted him with the food in squeals of delight.

He took a moment to register the food fight he had walked into. Then he shouted in mock surprise, ducked playfully, and fell to the floor, curling up in a ball as the kids attacked him on all sides.

"Ahhhhhh, you got me!!" he shouted, then collapsed onto his back as if dead. Star and Cloud pounced on him in a fit of giggles. Wolf Girl and Justice danced around him in circles. Everyone's faces lit up with delight.

Maji smiled. "Thank you for playing with me." Her eyes brimmed with joyful tears. The girls flocked to Maji and encircled her in a hug. Eamonn lifted himself off the floor and threw his arms around them all. The laughter burst out again as they squished together in the group embrace.

"Well, now we have to clean this mess up!" Maji chimed. The girls let go and returned to the chores they were doing before the food fight. But this time they had smiles on their faces, and small giggles escaped their lips as they worked.

Maji washed her face at the sink and peeled off her pajama top, throwing it in the laundry room. She turned back to the kids. "Well look at this! Here you are doing the same chores, but now you have happy faces! Why is that, do you think?"

The girls smiled sheepishly.

"Because we had fun first." Justice smiled.

"But the fun is over, and now you're working. In fact, now you have more work, but you're happier! What difference does the fun before make for right now at this moment?"

"Well," Wolf Girl said, "we are remembering the fun."

"Oh, I see. So before when you were angry doing the same chores, why weren't you remembering something fun then?"

The girls were silent, thinking.

"Can you see, girls, how easy it is for our minds to change? In one moment, something can seem horrible, and in the next moment, it's wonderful. It's so easy to let what is happening to us control how we feel when really, you can just look at it from a different point of view, and suddenly, the entire experience is different. And you can do that at any time."

They slowly nodded their heads in understanding.

"Please always remember that. The world is just a mirror of your own mind. It isn't as intense as we often think it is. We can shift our perspective in the blink of an eye and see the world in a totally different light. Everything you experience comes from how you choose to look at it."

"Well, right now I'm looking at you." Wolf Girl laughed. "And you look pretty funny!"

The kids burst into laughter as Maji looked down at herself, naked from the waist up, her hair and face crusty with red spaghetti sauce. She laughed at herself along with the girls, then turned to go hop in the shower, her heart full.

<u>Visions</u>

Maji was 24. It was one year after she had shaved her head, and her life looked entirely different. After realizing how intangible an identity was, she found herself spending more time alone, quietly contemplating this feeling she now lived within constantly, of having a flexible persona. She walked between two unseen realities to either side, more solid than this in-between she was living in. One was who she had been, and one was who she was becoming.

The other realities held an intention, a purpose, and a clear direction for all the movements that happened within them. In Maji's in-between, she floated, tossed in the wake of those that passed her by. It wasn't a bad feeling per se, but one of openness, spaciousness, that left her neither happy nor sad. She waited in this space, but she didn't know what she was waiting for.

Maji spent much of her time hiking through the mountains in Colorado. There was a rhythm to life in the natural world that allowed her to breathe. She could move through the woods on a trail with a destination in mind but never felt the need to arrive as quickly as possible, as she did when driving a car. She took the time to observe the symbiotic relationships around her.

In particular, she loved finding animal tracks. She created stories in her mind of each creature she came across. Perhaps the rabbit that left this footprint in the snow was searching for food for her babies? Or perhaps she ran from a predator and had made a narrow escape?

Maji began to read tracking books to try to understand the subtle language between earth and animal. She was particularly inspired by the Native American tracking techniques she read about. Their profound connection to nature and its flow struck her with awe. Their worldview reminded her of the experience she had in the woods with the deer when she was 20. She ached to feel that sense of beauty again. Perhaps by learning to read the tracks she could find a deeper sense of connection with the rhythm of Mother Nature.

Diving deeper into Native practices, she read about their tradition of a vision quest undertaken by individuals to find their next step in life, their purpose moving forward. The vision quest took three days. The seeker would hike out into the woods with only the clothes on their back, which would then be removed completely. They would stay in one spot for three days without food. The discomfort of the fast and the brutality of the elements would break through a person's pervasive need for comfort and open them up to receive a vision. According to the tradition, the vision would be whatever the individual needed at the time from the spirit world.

Maji loved this idea. The potential to receive a message from something greater than herself felt like exactly what she needed as she walked through her current space of persistent non-reality.

She found a location within Rocky Mountain National Park on the map where she wanted to pursue her own quest. She decided to bring a zero-degree sleeping bag for warmth at the high elevation. Even in the dead of summer, nights could drop to freezing above 8,000 feet, and hypothermia didn't sound like an effective approach to receiving spiritual enlightenment.

Maji woke early on the day she was leaving for the vision quest. She hopped in her car, singing joyfully as she drove the two-hour journey to the trailhead she had selected. It was in the more remote western side of the park, and she was relieved to see an empty parking lot when she arrived. She didn't know where exactly on the trail she would stop for her quest, but trusted the perfect spot would present itself to her. She parked her car and hopped out, grabbing a backpack that held nothing but water, a map of the park, and her sleeping bag.

As she turned to start her journey, she paused to look up at the silent peaks of the Never Summer mountain range before her. Snowfields glistened a brilliant white from the eastern sunlight above the treeline. The aspen trees were a brilliant lime green of early summer, and the sky was a startlingly clear blue with only a few small wispy clouds hovering around the mountain tops. Maji smiled and took her first steps onto the trail.

Immediately an image struck her mind: two creeks flowing in to meet one another, and a cluster of tall ponderosa pines at the apex of the meeting point. The image flashed like a photo negative, where all colors were inverted to their opposite. Maji shrugged as it drifted from her mind.

She hiked for about an hour before deciding to leave the trail behind. At a hairpin turn in the path, Maji continued straight, parallel to the slope, opting not to gain any more altitude. She was already at about 9,000 feet and knew a chilly night lay in front of her. The underbrush was fairly sparse, so bushwhacking posed little challenge as she carefully stepped through the forest.

After she had traveled a few yards off the path, the same inverted image of the two creeks joining and the tall cluster of trees appeared in her mind once more. This time Maji paused, contemplating its meaning. Had she seen some picture of this before she left? Again, it faded away. The young woman shook her head and moved on.

After another hour of bushwhacking, Maji began to hear the sound of rushing water. She liked the idea of being near a river. They were easy to locate on a map in case she needed to orient herself. So, she pressed on, allowing her ears to guide her toward the sound.

As she scrambled over a small ridge, she caught her breath. In front of her was the mental image made real--two creeks joining together. At the apex stood a cluster of ponderosa pines towering over the water.

"Oh my god," she breathed, as goosebumps rose on her arms and legs. It looked exactly like the image that had shown up in her mind, but without the color inversion. Maji's heart pounded. She had already been given her first vision. She remained still for several moments, taking in the surroundings. The water bubbled and rushed. In the trees, a bird tweeted, loudly blurting out one chirp repeatedly as if he was yelling for the world to hear him. Maji felt exhilarated, but confused. Why was she shown this specific place?

She moved closer to the water. The merging creeks weren't very large, and Maji was able to hop across the water with relative ease by stepping on a few exposed rocks. Her last leap landed her in the middle of the cluster of trees. She looked around, realizing the largest tree was the one right at the point where the rivers met. Its roots created a mat holding the earth in place in a large swath around it, preventing the water from washing it away over time. The other trees grew around it in a near-perfect circle.

Right in the middle of the trees was a small circular clearing about 5 feet in diameter. Soft pine needles blanketed it, giving it the appearance of an oversized bird's nest. Maji laughed. It was truly perfect. She had shelter in the trees, a resting area, and water. She couldn't have asked for a better location.

She dropped her bag and began stripping off her clothing, gently folding each piece and placing it in her bag, until she stood in the forest completely naked. A gentle breeze sent goosebumps up and down her back from the unusual exposure, and she giggled at the sensation. She spread out her sleeping bag underneath her and took a seat.

Hours later Maji found herself incredibly bored and ached to move around. It would be different if she could get up and explore, but that wasn't what a vision quest allowed. She had promised herself to follow through, to sit with herself, no matter what. She let herself move around inside her 5-foot diameter nest, but nothing more. She only left the nest to pee, then quickly returned. She was committed, and she continually reminded herself that boredom and discomfort were part of the process.

As the sun set behind the ridge, it took all the warmth from the summer air with it, leaving Maji shivering in her bare skin. She heard the forest come alive around her with the sound of crickets and locusts. As the night carried on, at one point she heard the crunch of leaves of some large animal walking just on the other side of the creek. She could make out the shadow of a large form but couldn't tell what it was.

Maji held her breath, reminding herself that she had the safety of the water between her and the creature. But she also knew there were moose, bear, and mountain lions all over the Rocky Mountains. She had not brought any knife or bear spray.

"This is all part of the practice," she whispered to herself as she held her knees tight to her chest. "It's all about trusting in spirit."

The animal slunk off into the night, and Maji allowed herself to curl up into a little ball inside her sleeping bag. She was cold enough to feel uncomfortable. As committed as she was to the quest, she did mentally take note to allow herself to put her clothes back on if it got much worse. She then spent the next several hours in an internal battle about what determined that point. She pulled her sweatshirt out of her jacket four times before shoving it back into the bag with a huff.

"I can do this, dammit," she growled through gritted teeth.

Her eyes closed and she drifted into a fitful, pained sleep, waking up with a chill rushing up and down her body a few hours later. The circle of ponderosa framed the brilliant stars above her. She could see the golden haze of the Milky Way across the sky. The stars looked sharp in the cold. Maji lay there, counting them, contemplating why she was stupid enough to take this ridiculous vision quest. She was cold and tired, and miserable all over. Her mind drifted into a garrulous whine of all the ways she suffered, naming them off to herself instead of counting sheep. She felt her eyes close again, lulled by her inner monologue. When she opened them again after what felt like only minutes later, the sky had begun to lighten into an indigo blue and the stars were fading into vague splotches.

Maji kept herself curled in her sleeping bag, unwilling to come out until the sun warmed the dampened exterior of her bag to a suitable temperature. She felt her stomach growl in protest of her fast. It had been almost twenty-four hours since her last meal. Her body felt hollowed out.

The sun broke over the horizon and beamed through the trees, warming her. She could see all around her steam rising from the ground as the heat evaporated off the night's dew. The sight of it gave Maji a renewed sense of spirit. She crawled out from her sleeping bag, feeling the warmth caress her skin like a hug, feeling like a solar panel charging in the sun's rays. She closed her eyes, watched the red behind her eyelids that resulted from the new sunlight.

Maji placed her hands onto the ground into the grass shoots that sprouted up through the pine needles in her nest. She brushed her hand across the top of them, then felt an unusual sensation. As she raised and lowered her hand over the grass, she felt a slight resistance, as if she were trying to push two positive ends of a magnet together. It reminded her of an interesting trick a yoga teacher had shown her. She placed her hands about six inches apart and imagined a glowing, warm ball of energy throbbing between her two palms. As she tried to push her palms together, she was met with a gentle force.

"This is the energy that makes up everything. That's what you're feeling," the teacher had told her.

Now, Maji placed her hands back down toward the grass and felt the same thing. She laughed in delight as she swirled this feeling around her fingers with the grass.

"Haha, wow!" She laughed, delighted at this symbiotic experience.

Then in a sudden massive rush, like being hit by an ocean wave, Maji felt her entire body go stiff. All noise around went silent, and her ears filled with a low rushing sound that welled up from deep inside her paralyzed body. Instantly, she felt a massive force shoot up like a geyser from the center of the earth through her body. All her nerve endings exploded, and her body convulsed uncontrollably. She yelled out at the force of it.

Immediately another rushing sensation exploded into her body, this time coming down from the top of her head and smashing its way down through her into the center of the Earth. The spasms rocked her as the two opposing forces rolled up and down within her body like crashing waves in a storm. She orgasmed in every cell, every blood vessel, at an intensity greater than she had ever experienced before.

She felt like a windsock in a hurricane and plunged her hands into the dirt around her to try to ground herself, to gain some control back. The convulsions deepened as wave after wave thrashed through her.

Her cries at the intensity of the pleasure were the only noise she could hear. The world around her remained peacefully silent. Her mind raced, unable to pull together a cohesive thought. She was overwhelmed and confused at what was happening to her, but surprisingly, she felt no fear. Was this that feeling she had been so close to tapping into when she was in the woods with the deer? Slowly, a deep sense of trust filled her, and she allowed herself to let go of the ground, surrendering to the force that rocked her. She fell backward onto her sleeping bag.

Maji didn't know how long the convulsions continued, but it felt like a very long time. Once her quivering subsided and she regained control of her limbs once more, the sun had already moved higher in the sky. She looked around as she sat up, realizing something was very different. She had no idea what had happened to her.

She felt a movement brush near her head and looked up. Overhead in the sky, a falcon soared above her. Maji gasped. She could *feel* it flying in the sky a hundred feet above!

The clouds drifted by on a breeze, and Maji felt every swirl of their water droplets as if her entire nervous system had extended hundreds of feet in the air and all around her in every direction. As the falcon flew, she sensed waves of energy coming off him, much like the wake of a boat in the water.

A gentle breeze blew through the trees all around her, and Maji felt a cascade of motion all through her, and she knew she was feeling the leaves of the forest dancing in the wind.

Maji's eyes filled with tears. She had imagined before she left that the vision she would receive on her quest would be dreamlike, a hallucination, more like an epiphany. But this was the most real thing she had ever felt in her entire life. It consumed and expanded every part of her. She brought her hands to her mouth and began to sob in an overwhelmed sense of gratitude.

"Oh, thank you, thank you!" she cried, unsure of who or what she was thanking. But she felt the entire world move around her. Each bird, each squirrel, was an extension of herself. She could feel their hearts beating in their chests and the breeze on their fur and feathers. She felt her own heart pounding and realized it was doing so in rhythm to the splashes of water coming off the rocks in the creek.

With shaky legs, Maji stood and began to dress. Her hands shook as she unfolded each garment. She had thought she would stay for the entire three days of the quest, but at that moment she couldn't imagine needing more. It would be greedy to stay, to demand more gifts when all she felt was overwhelmed gratitude.

She packed up her sleeping bag and made her way out of her nest. She turned and gave the space a small bow in thanks before she stepped across the water.

As she walked through the woods, her own wake of energy expanded behind her. She felt it flow around the trees in swirls as she passed and their own slow, steady energy reached out to connect with hers. She could sense the slow movement of sap in the tree trunks and the even slower push of growth through their branches into the leaves like a patient, unstoppable urge. She felt the movements of everything around her and marvelled at the simple order in the way life moved around itself.

Everything flowed gracefully around everything else, as if there was an infinite amount of space in the smallest areas, so as two entities met, they danced in this size-less space with no competition. Maji felt the space between the very molecules themselves. *The essence of grace.* She fell to her knees, again overwhelmed with tears. She paused there for some time, allowing herself to feel. An energetic tether emanated off her, a million strands of lights reaching off her body and connecting to every other living thing around her, illuminated from pure life force.

Eventually, Maji made it back to her car. She was happy to see that the parking lot was still empty minus her own vehicle. She climbed in and started the engine, her hands shaking on the steering wheel.

As she turned out onto Trail Ridge Road, she looked up at the mountains looming in front of her. Her heart caught in her throat as she felt the powerful upward force of their imperceptible movement. They only appeared to stand still. In reality, they exploded out of the ground at a rapid speed. She slowed the car in response to the feeling of an earthquake. Inching her way through the passes, she hooted out loud at the thrill of the drive, feeling more like she was on a rollercoaster than a road.

Maji returned home a different person. The walls of her basement apartment felt like a steel cage. She couldn't connect with anything down there, and she found it too painful to cut off that experience. She set up a tent in her backyard and slept there for over a week. Her ability to feel the energetic connection to everything around her remained for almost a month before the intensity began to lessen.

Her friends and family noticed her difference. As she explained to them with joyful tears what happened, many of them were moved and astonished. They held her hand, sensing the depth of her experience.

Then there were the few people who shut down, the people who couldn't process what they heard as something real. No one questioned how real the experience had been to Maji. The authenticity in her words was too apparent. But they did question the truth of it compared to their own reality and considered the one Maji now lived in too far away from what they could understand.

One friend told her, "I don't think my reality is big enough to fit your reality in it." She then stood and walked out of the room. She never spoke to Maji again.

Maji learned over time that it was best not to share her experience. When she was met with resistance or confusion, she didn't know what to say. It created more difficulties than expected, and she found many of those who had been close to her grow awkward in her presence. So, she moved on with her life and rarely spoke of her vision quest at all.

But she was still determined to understand what had happened to her. This experience felt like a beginning, not a conclusion. Surely there were others out there that had similar experiences. Maybe she could find someone who could teach her more about what had happened.

Several months later, Maji swam laps at the gym. As she jumped out of the water her eye caught a man across the pool, pulling himself out at the same time. He was tall, perhaps in his mid-thirties, and had tattoos covering both his arms. There was something about him that intrigued her, but she couldn't place her finger on it. He glanced at her, then turned his back to pick up his towel. Maji turned and made her way into the sauna. She always enjoyed sweating the chlorine out of her skin after a swim.

Several minutes later, the man joined her. They were the only two people in there, and he smiled pleasantly at her as he sat down. She felt the awkward tension that always came with sitting in an enclosed space with a stranger, the sound of their deep breathing from the heat echoing off the walls.

Suddenly, the man burst into a long, drawn-out sound of "Aaaaaaaahhhhhhhh" like a one-note song. Maji jumped at the sound.

"I love the acoustics in here!" he said between breaths. "Ooooooooooooooohhhhhhhh!"

Maji had to smile at his brashness. His pitch dropped low, and she felt the vibrations of his voice in her legs as the sound reverberated throughout the small room.

"Ooooooooooooooh." he rumbled. "If I drop it way down in my belly, I can sound like a Buddhist monk chanting."

Maji laughed out loud. She reached out her hand. "I'm Maji, what's your name?"

"I'm Tye; a pleasure to meet you."

"You, as well."

Tye opened his mouth and began making the sounds even louder. He started slapping himself in his belly, flexing his muscles.

"This one kind of tickles me here," and he began a high "uuuuuuuuuu" sound. Maji laughed, opening her mouth, and began the same sound at a higher, harmonizing pitch.

"Haha, yes!" he said.

They continued for several minutes, harmonizing their voices in a bizarre concert of melodyless sound, sweat dripping down their faces. Then, suddenly the sauna door opened to an older man with a round belly and white hair. He stopped dead, his mouth open in confusion as he encountered the loud pair with mouths open, their voices echoing off the walls. They stopped and stared at the man in surprise.

"Uh, sorry!" He slammed the door.

Maji and Tye looked at each other and started laughing.

"I'm famished!" Tye exclaimed. "Let's go get some lunch. Indian is on me!"

He jumped up and headed to the door.

"Uh, sure!" Maji stammered. She never did things like this, but she felt some odd pulling in her to explore this person more. It wasn't sexual attraction. It was something else. Like an intuitive nudge that pointed her to something deeper.

"Great! I'll meet you out front after a shower."

Maji decided to drive separately from Tye and followed him to a delicious local Indian restaurant. As they sat and talked, the nudge continued inside her. He talked about his music business. She talked about her art. They talked about their favorite hiking places. Then, suddenly, a flash came across Tye's eyes and his face lit up. "You should meet my teacher!"

"What kind of teacher?"

"A teacher of life! Of spirit!" he swirled his hands in the air like a magician.

"Like a life coach?"

"No, like an enlightened master! She is amazing. A true embodiment of the divine."

Maji's eyes widened. "Oh, yes, I do think I would be interested in meeting her. I recently had this experience that maybe she could help me with."

With some hesitation, she shared with her new friend the experience of her vision quest. His eyes went wide as she recounted her story. When she finished, he clapped his hands together with a large smile.

"Well, it all makes sense now. We were destined to meet so you could meet Chandra. Your experience will make perfect sense once you see what she is all about!"

Two weeks later, Maji found herself walking into a small conference room at a hotel in Vail. The room was dimly lit by the warm glow of candles. About fifty people sat and walked around in silence, with more coming in behind the curious woman. The only sound besides the shuffle of feet and clothing was a low recorded "om" playing on repeat over the speakers. It reminded her of Tye's sounds in the sauna.

Large sculptures of elaborate geometric shapes made from copper tubing decorated each corner of the room. They were large enough for a person to stand inside of, and Maji noticed a small line of people waiting to take turns inside the shapes. One by one they stepped inside and held their arms out as if standing under a shower.

Everyone wore flowing, light-colored clothing and had gentle smiles on their faces. Many people greeted each other silently with a bow and their hands together at their hearts in a prayer position. It felt very "New Age." But Maji loved the sense of peace she experienced in that atmosphere. There was a softness to the room that made her feel warm and cozy.

She spotted Tye as he waved to her across the room. As she walked closer to where he sat among several rows of chairs, she noticed one singular seat facing the others on a raised platform at the front of the room. It was a white Victorian chair with swirled armrests and a white satin cushion. On either side of it sat two massive glass vases filled with towering spectacular bouquets of lilies, roses, and babies' breath. The bouquets themselves stood about four feet tall, and the scent of the flowers filled the space.

Maji sat next to Tye in a folded chair. He wore a smart suit and tie that made him look very sophisticated. He reached over and wrapped his arms around her in a firm embrace.

"So amazing you came! Your life is never going to be the same again!" he gushed in an enthusiastic whisper. "It was lucky I could get you in. This retreat is only supposed to be for Chandra's long-time students. But she allowed it. She must see something about you!"

Maji pondered that. Chandra had not even met Maji yet. How in the world could she see something about her?

Over the next few minutes, the chairs around them began to fill. Then the Om recording stopped playing and a gentle flute song played over the speakers. Everyone in the chairs turned to face the entry door with jubilant smiles on their faces, all hands immediately coming to a prayer position in the center of their chests.

Maji turned as well to see a small woman who looked to be in her fifties glide through the door. She wore a flowing white gown fastened at her throat and a long strand of pearls around her neck. Her skin was a caramel brown, and Maji guessed she was of Indian descent. Her black hair was piled high on her head in an elegant cascade. Chandra was short, only about 5-feet tall, but her presence was as commanding as royalty. She walked slowly down the aisle between the chairs, her hands at her heart as she smiled at the faces staring up at her adoringly. Occasionally she reached a graceful hand out as if to touch someone, but never made contact. The faces gushed up at her in star-struck wonder. As she neared, Maji could smell the distinct aroma of sandalwood and roses wafting off her.

When Chandra spied Maji, she beamed at her with a dazzling smile.

"Welcome! I'm so happy you are here!"

Maji was surprised to hear a French accent. She nodded a "thank you" as Chandra continued on, until at last she finally reached her satin throne. She took her seat, and a man in a white suit hurried up to her, helping to fasten a wireless microphone behind her ear. The pink tip of the small mic that was now sitting next to her mouth bore the same color as the roses in the bouquets next to her. Maji wondered if that small detail was intentional.

Chandra spoke a few hellos, nodded to her sound guy, then took a long deep sigh and smiled out to the crowd.

"I love you so!" she exclaimed. The crowd responded in a blend of "ahhhs" and "I love you too's." The energy of the crowd surged through Maji. Longing looks painted the audience's faces. It felt like a crowd of children eager to crawl into their mother's lap.

Chandra smiled silently for a minute, then closed her eyes as if thinking.

"Devotion," she purred, her eyes still closed, her voice ringing sweetly over the speakers. "We are here today because of your devotion--your devotion to the divine. For all of you, there came a time in life where what you experienced on the material plane was not enough. You felt this longing, this desire deep inside you for something more. Life is much richer than your job, your partner, your hobbies. You felt suffering, no matter what you have done. Always thinking you need this, or you need that, when what you need is inside you."

Chandra placed her hands on her heart, a pained look coming over her face.

"The majority of the people in the world--they are like zombies. Sleepwalking, chasing one addiction after another. Addiction to food, addiction to money, addiction to sex, addiction to work. Always needing more. This is because they have failed to wake up to the truth that they are the divine! They are the divine in action! They have perfection inside them, as you have perfection inside you!"

The faces beamed joyfully at Chandra again, hands coming to hearts in an expression of gratitude once more. Chandra reached over to the small table next to her and picked up a small blue glass candle votive, the small flame dancing inside.

"Our light inside--it is like this candle. The light is the same in you as it is in me. We just see it differently because of how it shows through this form and this personality. Our thoughts and bodies can be clouded, not allowing the light to get through. This happens when we are in negative states of mind and when our bodies are in poor health. We must purify our minds and bodies and turn our minds and hearts to devotion. When we surrender to the master who has realized true enlightenment, then the light gets through. Your devotion is the purifying force that allows you to experience the divine that you are! It is this pure desire that cuts through the most convincing illusion that there is anything but the divine!"

Maji felt intrigued by Chandra. Her words were beautiful and spoke of truth, but they were nothing Maji had not heard before in her own explorations of spirituality. There was something else, an atmosphere the teacher created around herself, an energy that seeped into Maji, pulsating, like the throbbing deep bass on a speaker. But this energy had no sound.

Chandra spoke for quite a while longer until she slipped into silence. She took a breath.

"I'm going to access all the divine beings of the fifth dimension. I'm going to call them in to merge with your light bodies so we can accelerate the process of purifying your DNA for ascension. Close your eyes."

Maji raised an eyebrow. She really didn't know if she could believe Chandra would be accessing "beings" in the 5th dimension. And ascension? Did these people actually believe that stuff? It sounded like a tremendous amount of New Age "woo" but Maji closed her eyes to see what would happen.

A penetrating silence slowly filled the room. Maji couldn't even hear her own breathing. The outside world fell away, and she felt herself dive deep into the darkness behind her eyelids. She saw dark, swirling colors moving around without order. Then they pulled together in a swirling whirlpool, disappearing into a black center. Maji felt the throbbing energy in every cell of her body.

Then, in a very subtle way, she felt the same energy she had felt on her vision quest begin to move through her as if something descended from the sky and simultaneously rose from the center of the earth through her body. This time it wasn't violent and wildly out of control. It rolled gently, as if massaging her from the inside, opening her. It filled her with a profound sense of peace and delight. Was this really happening again? She felt her body begin a gentle rocking motion, much different from the jerking spasms she felt in the mountains. Why was this happening now? Was Chandra doing this?

Maji opened her eyes. Chandra stared right at her with a big smile, a knowing look in her eye. Was she doing this? Was this what spiritual masters did? Maji felt a spreading sense of amazement in her heart at what she was experiencing. She began to understand why Chandra spoke of devotion to the master.

"Close your eyes," Chandra said to Maji, her voice sounding like thunder through the silence. No one else seemed to notice. Maji shut her eyes again, saw the swirling patterns behind her eyeballs, felt the rocking in her body. She let herself float in these sensations. She disappeared into the dark space behind her eyes.

Maji didn't know how long they stayed in meditation, but she did remember a song penetrating the silence, rising gradually in volume. It was an orchestral blend of violins, sitars, and pianos. A soft female voice began to sing words of love and devotion to the master.

"I want you to sing," Chandra crooned over the microphone. "Through your voice, sing to the divine, sing to the master. Show your devotion! Show your commitment to your own mastery!"

The voices in the crowd lifted. Everyone clearly knew all the words. Blurry, delighted drunkenness infused Maji, though she'd had nothing to drink. She began to sing along with the words she could pick up, once she realized the voice repeated the same refrain over and over again.

She looked around the room and saw people singing their hearts out, hands steepled again in prayer position. Most people sang directly to Chandra, clearly channeling the words of devotion to her. Everyone had a blissful drunk look on their face similar to the one Maji knew was on hers. Chandra sang as well over her microphone, moving her arms in sweeping gestures toward the crowd. Suddenly a few rows of people stood up and began forming a line in the center of the room leading to Chandra.

"What's happening?" Maji asked Tye.

"It's time to meet Chandra. She meets everyone for a moment to give them a blessing."

Maji saw the first person step up toward Chandra. Chandra smiled, and they spoke a few words to each other that were inaudible over the music. Chandra then placed her hand on each petitioner's head and spoke a few words more. In turn, each blessed individual moved on to the left and was given a piece of chocolate out of a basket by a young woman standing next to the guru. The next person stepped up.

"Hurry, get in line!" Tye gently pushed her to move.

As Maji watched the people in front of her approach Chandra, she saw many of them bow to her feet. She saw one woman burst into tears as the small, elegant woman held her in a hug. She saw Chandra get visibly angry with another man and chastise him. He left the conversation with bows of gratitude. Then it was Maji's turn. She shuffled up to Chandra, insecurity and intimidation gripping her heart. She placed her hands at her heart and bowed.

"Thank you for allowing me to come today." She wondered if Chandra could even hear her over the music and the crowd's singing. "I thought you could help me. I had this experience….."

Her words trailed off, unsure of even what to tell the woman. Chandra smiled and looked at Maji wordlessly for a moment.

"What you experienced was yourself, your higher self. It is always there. You are just beginning to learn to open to it. You will find what you are looking for. Don't worry."

Then the teacher reached out and placed her hand on Maji's head. Maji looked into her face, still feeling awkward at this unusual posture, like a child being patronized by an older adult. Chandra turned to the young woman next to her, giving out chocolate.

"I like this one," she laughed, then nodded to the young woman as if to indicate some action required on her part. The young woman returned a confirming nod. Chandra released her hand from Maji's head and indicated with a sweeping arm that their time was done. Maji collected her chocolate and walked back to her seat. Tye followed her after his own greeting with Chandra, looking giddy and blissful.

The singing and meeting went on for at least an hour. Maji watched with fascination as the lines and lines of people approached Chandra with profound reverence. They were all star-struck by her presence. After experiencing what she did that day, Maji could understand why. It was apparent that Chandra had access to some deep spiritual gifts that she could use to affect those around her. Maji wished she had more time to ask the woman questions.

When the last people in the line returned to their seats, the music faded out. Chandra addressed the crowd once more with words about devotion to the guru and accessing their own mastery. This idea of being devoted to a "guru" was foreign to Maji. She understood learning from a teacher, but what she saw in this crowd was an unquestioning devotion, reverence, and loyalty. It stirred up some alarm in her, but also intrigued her deeply.

The music started again with the high, lilting melody of a woman singing her love to the divine, and Chandra got up, walking slowly out of the room. The crowd began to get up and leave. Tye turned to Maji. He laughed and playfully jabbed her in the shoulder.

"Haha, see! I told you! What did you think?"

"I think this was a lot more than I expected. I don't know if I'm more confused or have a lot more clarity."

"Well, time will tell, my friend! This is just the beginning."

The Beginning Of The End

It began with Justice noticing how skinny Maji was becoming, and how slowly she moved. The woman always seemed tired, and they went out on fewer and fewer adventures.

"I've noticed you're taking a lot more supplements than usual. Are you sick, Maji?" Justice asked one day in the kitchen, a tremor of intuitive knowing in her voice. Maji jumped, thrown off by the unexpected question.

"Oh, yes, I've been under the weather," Maji focused her gaze on the tea bag in her mug. "But I'm working with my doc to figure it out."

"Oh, okay."

Justice wasn't convinced, and Maji could feel it. She was almost fourteen years old. Maji knew she could see beyond the surface of the empty words.

Then Wolf Girl complained one day in her characteristic blunt way.

"You don't look so good. I think something is wrong with you. Have you gone to the doctor?"

Maji nodded, smoothing her daughter's hair lovingly.

"Yes, I have some new supplements. They'll help me feel better."

"But what's wrong with you?" Wolf Girl demanded, folding her arms across her chest impatiently.

"I've had some things going on. I'm figuring it out."

"You didn't answer my question," she said in exasperation.

"Don't worry, baby." Maji walked away, afraid her daughter would guess the truth.

Then, another day in the park, the mother walked hand-in-hand with Cloud and Star. The three of them swung their arms jubilantly as the two girls skipped along either side of Maji, causing her to jog along with them. Suddenly she couldn't catch her breath. She let go of the girls' hands, trying to steady herself from the breathlessness and wave of dizziness that rushed over her. She dropped abruptly to the sidewalk, panting. The girls gasped.

"Are you okay, Maji?" Cloud asked, her eyes big with worry.

"What happened? Why are you breathing so hard?" Star rushed to Maji's side and took her hand. Her face crumpled into a frown.

"Oh my," Maji panted. "I think I did too much. I just need to rest here for a moment."

The young girls stared at Maji in concerned silence. Star wrapped her arms around her mother's shoulders. "I will take care of you, Mama," she said, her sweet voice lilting in sadness.

Over the next couple of weeks, Maji realized the memory loss that she had feared so much was beginning. She would often forget why she walked into a room. Sitting in front of her computer, she would forget what she was working on. These momentary lapses of memory she wrote off to stress and fatigue, pushing down the gnawing concern that it might be more.

One evening the family talked and laughed at the dinner table. The conversation centered around who in the family liked specific vegetables. Maji had a strict rule about vegetables.

Everyone had to eat anything green on their plates, no matter what. Maji and Eamonn struggled to serve green vegetables each kiddo liked to eat. Cloud loved peas, Wolf Girl and Star loved kale, and Justice was slowly learning to like both of those as well, but only if they were steamed without any seasoning. However, everyone could handle broccoli. So that evening, the family celebrated their mutual enjoyment of broccoli with a hearty helping for each.

Maji looked down at her plate and saw the small broccoli heads. She stuck them upright into her mashed potatoes, giving the impression of trees in a snowy hillside and pointed them out to the family. Everyone laughed, and the kids followed her lead, creating mini landscapes on their dinner plates. Maji ceremoniously plucked a broccoli tree from her hill of potatoes and popped it in her mouth, closing her eyes. When she opened her eyes after chewing, they felt heavy, as if she was waking from a long sleep.

Maji was startled to find herself standing in front of the bathroom mirror, her pajamas on and a toothbrush in her hand.

"Wha-what happened?" she stammered, looking at Eamonn in the mirror as he walked up beside her.

"What do you mean?" he asked, circling his arm around her waist.

"We were eating broccoli. I made the trees in the hill of potatoes. What happened after that? How did I get here?"

Eamonn's face went pale. He shook his head. "That was hours ago," he said quietly. "You don't remember what happened after that? We watched a movie. Do you remember the movie?"

Maji felt her stomach drop, and a fluttered panic filled her chest. She took a deep breath, fighting tears. "N-no," she whispered.

Eamonn said nothing. They looked at each other in the mirror, the heavy acknowledgment of what this meant passing between them. Maji let out a stuttering breath and her husband wrapped his arms around her, pulling her close, holding her tightly to him.

Conflict raged in her. She wanted to explode into sadness and pain and have Eamonn hold her and protect her. But she also wanted to clasp him to her and tell him everything was okay, do whatever she could to alleviate the sadness she knew he felt. The divided feelings paralyzed her. She was left with a vacuum, a sense of emptiness. Soon, she knew, she would have to choose what she would fill that emptiness with.

Maji pulled out of his embrace, pausing to look into the eyes of the man she loved. What she'd built with him was the most amazing relationship of her life.

Both of them had been divorced for several years. Both of them had given up on ever finding someone else to love. Burned by the drama of divorce, Maji decided she wouldn't compromise on anything in any relationship ever again. There would be no imperfections. It was to be all or nothing, and in her skepticism, it seemed *nothing* was the option that remained to her.

Then she met Eamonn. It was a fluke meeting in the park where their kids played. They chatted as Star and Cloud climbed the terrifyingly high monkey bars. The two girls had found each other and teamed up as instant friends. Now they raced each other up the bars as Maji watched with bated breath, not trusting her youngest daughter's ability to navigate the bars without a slip. Eamonn stood by watching.

"How old is your daughter?" he asked, keeping his eye on Cloud.

"She's only two, but she is completely fearless. It scares me to death!" Maji laughed.

"I can see that." He laughed, watching Star scramble past Cloud, who carefully navigated each step with precision and caution.

"I'm Eamonn." He reached out his hand.

"Maji. A pleasure to meet you." She shook his hand. "That's Star, my daughter."

"Mine is named Cloud." Eamonn chuckled. "Seems we both like out-there hippy names, right?"

"Yeah, guilty as charged."

They spent the next hour chatting while the kids played and discovered they were both single parents and lived only a couple miles apart from one another. They proposed having playdates with the kids, as Star and Cloud seemed to have become best friends for the day.

It was another month before they saw each other again, this time for a planned meetup at the park. Maji had no interest in Eamonn romantically. She already assumed he lacked several important qualities she would even consider for a relationship. But as a single-parent friend, she found him to be quite nice.

They ended up having dinner together with the kids one night at his house a few weeks later. Then, one evening, he invited Maji over for a late-night drink after she had a stressful workday.

What could it hurt? she thought. *He knows we're just friends.*

They spent several hours together, laughing and talking about life. She didn't hesitate to tell him about her vision quest and various spiritual pursuits. She had learned at that point in her life it was easier to be completely open than to hide any aspect of herself. Others' reactions to her were their issue as far as she was concerned. She was surprised to find out he'd also had many profound spiritual experiences. He was versed in the Eastern philosophies and had done vision quests as well. He was the first man she had met who truly understood her experiences when she shared them. Her mind was blown. Suddenly, Eamonn became interesting.

He invited all of them over for Valentine's Day dinner. When Maji, Star, and Wolf Girl arrived, they were met with a dozen roses and individual boxes of chocolates. Maji was officially charmed.

Then, about a month later, Eamonn offered to babysit Star and Wolf Girl for a couple of hours while she worked one Saturday. Maji was impressed he was willing to have four screaming little girls in the house and told him so when she dropped them off.

"Oh, the kids? That's the easy part," he laughed as the girls rushed off into the playroom. Then, he stepped forward, and grabbing Maji by the back of her neck, he pulled her in close for a passionate kiss.

Lightning struck her. Her knees almost buckled underneath her as he held her close, and she heard a small moan escape her lips. His arms pulled her in closer, supporting her weight. She pulled back, shocked and delighted.

"That was the hard part," Eamonn said, smiling wide. "But it didn't end up being as hard as I thought."

When Maji got out to her car, she slid behind the steering wheel and slammed the door.

Instantly, she exploded into giggles, pounding the steering wheel in excitement.

"Oh my god! Oh my god! Oh my god!" she squealed. She had never experienced such a powerful kiss in her life. The universe opened up and poured itself into her. It felt almost like the vision quest.

After that kiss they fell in love. With Eamonn, Maji felt the most like herself she ever had with anyone. She was relaxed. She was passionate. He understood her and could meet her in her deep philosophical states of mind. And that kiss was just the beginning of the profound explorations their physical intimacy offered. He turned out to be the complete package after all.

As their relationship grew over the years, Maji learned so much with him about what it meant to have a partner. Sometimes they fought bitterly, and her heart filled with pain and the fear that it had all been too good to be true. But then they reconciled, able to step back and see where they had acted out from old patterns of trauma and recognize where they could grow. Maji learned to trust him. It was a new form of love for her that left her vulnerable. But learning to trust opened her up to a profound experience of deep intimacy with him she had never known with anyone else. She felt grateful for every day with him.

Now as Maji stood, looking into Eamonn's eyes in their shared home, she remembered that first lightning kiss and leaned forward, pressing her lips to his.

"I will never forget what we have, or you," she whispered. "I love you. Thank you for being my love."

Eamonn smiled and tenderly brushed the hair out of her face.

"I love you, too." He smiled. Then he reached down and scooped his wife into his arms and carried her over to the bed.

Over the next couple of weeks, she had more episodes of forgetfulness. One evening she sat on the couch with Star in her lap and Wolf Girl leaning against her arm. Maji blinked and suddenly found herself sitting on the toilet in the middle of the night.

Another time it happened more slowly. Maji looked out the window in the kitchen while talking with Justice. Suddenly, Justice's words sounded garbled. Maji couldn't understand what she was saying. She turned and looked at her.

"What did you say?" Maji asked. Justice repeated what she said, but again her stepmother couldn't make out her words. White noise in her brain blocked out all other sounds. She stared at her stepdaughter.

"I...I don't understand."

Justice stared at her, confused concern crossing her face. Maji turned to sit down at the table. As she sat, drowsiness overtook her. She nodded her head for a moment with her eyes closed, then opened her eyes to find herself in her bedroom, sitting on her bed and leaning against the headboard. Eamonn sat next to her, his hand on her leg.

"Hi," Maji smiled. Eamonn took in her greeting with a flinch. Maji realized they had probably already been talking, and the memory had gone. The sadness on his face told Maji how difficult this must be for him.

"Oh, God, I'm sorry! I don't know what to do."

Eamonn rubbed her leg in a show of support.

"We have to tell the girls, Maji. You really just freaked out Justice there. She was talking to you, and you just floated away. It was like you weren't there anymore. She was trying to shake you and you just stared into space and hardly said two words. She came to me in tears. The other girls have mentioned to me that you aren't doing good. They know something is going on. The girls need to know the truth."

A wave of emotion crashed through her, and she burst into tears. She knew what he said was true, but she didn't want it to be. She wanted to preserve her children's innocence. She wanted to preserve their joy. Everything would be different after this.

Conflict pulled at her once more: the desire to protect those she loved versus the desire to be held and protected. The tears fell, the dichotomy tore at her, and the sense of emptiness inside her grew, but she recognized again that a choice lay before her. Her life was coming to an end. That, she couldn't change. It was those she loved who would have to live without her and live with the emotional fallout of that truth. Her children's lives were just beginning.

She remembered back to the day she sat in the doctor's office and accepted the fact that she was dying. She chose not to fight it, but to surrender, and she found a well of peace inside herself, and trust in the bigger picture. Though she had been following all of the doctor's instructions to prolong her life, she had resigned herself to her fate. But until that moment, she hadn't been able to face the fact that everyone else would have to accept her fate, too. Now she knew that she would have to paint the picture of her death's meaning to her family. She could approach them in pain and sadness, the feelings she expected them to feel, or she could approach them with the peace she had found within herself.

She wiped the tears from her face and leaned forward, planting a kiss on Eamonn's lips, squeezing his hands tightly. "This is the beginning of the end, but let's make the end something beautiful!"

He gave her a pained, confused smile. Maji stood up and went to her closet.

"Give me a few minutes to change. But can you bring the girls into the living room? Let's light the candles, too."

"Ok, however you want to do this." Eamonn sighed and stood up, squeezing his wife's shoulder before leaving the room.

Maji selected a long, flowing, sleeveless Bohemian dress with pastel rainbow splatters of color, one of her favorites. The kids called it her "fairy dress." She went into the bathroom and put makeup on, brushed her hair into a half-up-half-down style, and added earrings and a necklace to the whole ensemble. Looking at herself in the mirror, she smiled. This was the beginning of the end. But it was going to be a beautiful end. She would make sure of it.

Maji turned on a beautiful, ethereal Tibetan flute song over the living room speaker. She glided into the living room. The girls and Eamonn all sat together on the floor. Eamonn had lit the candles as well as the string of Christmas lights they had across the top of the windows, which faded in and out of a deep yellow. The room glowed with warmth and color.

"Wow, Maji, why are you so dressed up?" Justice asked.

"You're in your fairy dress again!" Cloud rolled onto her back and kicked her feet in the air. "I love your fairy dress!"

"So do I, sweetie! That's why I wanted to wear it tonight. I have some things to share with you girls. And I wanted to be in my best dress for it. I think first, though, I want to tell you a story."

Justice and Wolf Girl groaned, rolling their eyes.

"Shush!" Eamonn barked, and they reluctantly straightened up to listen.

Maji walked to the window and plucked off a crystal star prism that hung from a suction cup hook. She sat on the floor, her dress billowing around her. Star scrambled into her lap and started playing with her mother's long hair.

"Since I'm wearing my fairy dress, let's make this story about a fairy, and let's call her Ray."

"Isn't that a boy's name?" scoffed Wolf Girl.

"It's a fairy's name--*this* fairy's name!"

Wolf Girl rolled her eyes.

"Before we tell Ray's story, we need to hear about how Ray was born. You see, fairies aren't born from mommies' bodies like humans are. Fairies are born in an entirely different way."

She held up the crystal prism, then picked her phone up with her other hand, turning on the flashlight. "Fairies are born when someone imagines them into existence. So, someone had to think a specific thought that has all the amazing qualities that make up each specific fairy. When the thought is made, it pulls all the creative powers from the center of existence and filters it through that one thought."

Maji shone the light from her phone through the crystal prism. Several small dancing rainbows appeared on the wall behind Wolf Girl and Justice's heads. Cloud and Star jumped up and ran to them, trying to catch the rainbows with their hands, only to find them appearing on their skin. They erupted in giggles.

"It's just like this light shining through the prism. The light divides and makes a rainbow. When someone thinks a fairy-thought, the creative power of the universe divides like a rainbow, and a fairy is born!"

"But HOW are they born? I mean, you said no one is giving birth to them," said Wolf Girl.

"They just appear, like a dream appears when you sleep. Where do you think dreams come from?"

"My mind?"

"Right! As do fairies."

The girls paused, pondering.

"So, Ray was thought into existence. And she was a wonderful fairy! She loved flowers and trees; she loved playing with her animal friends. She spent most of her days planting seeds so new plants could grow in the spring and would make wonderful food for all her fairy friends. Ray lived a happy life.

"And as time went on, and Ray saw many more of her fairy friends thought into existence, she began to wonder, what was she before she was Ray? What was she before that first fairy-thought brought her into the world? She knew she didn't come from nothing, so what was the 'something' she came from? She always asked herself that.

"One day Ray sat on a daisy, and she began to think about how wonderful it would be to have a fairy daughter she could be with. She imagined her as kind and funny, with a love of singing, and creative enough to make up wonderful games. She imagined what it would feel like to hold this fairy daughter in her arms. She felt how deep her love would be for her. And as she thought this fairy-thought, the flower next to her began to glow. Suddenly, a beautiful little fairy girl appeared on the flower, curled up in a little ball! Ray realized with surprise that she had imagined her daughter into existence!"

"I thought you said fairies didn't have mommies?" asked Star.

"I said they weren't born from mommies. That doesn't mean they didn't have them. Someone has to think them into existence, don't they?"

The girls all nodded in agreement.

"Ray was so happy, and she felt so much love for this new little fairy! And as she watched her appear, Ray discovered the answer to her question about what she was before she became a fairy. She was love, pure and unfiltered! That was what she was and that was what she was born from. The light of Love. And it was her love that birthed her new fairy daughter. Ray named her Sprout because this little pixie was the birth of so many amazing dreams and adventures, like the sprout of a plant bringing new flowers.

"Sprout was a happy fairy and loved Ray very much, too. They spent the years of their life together growing and changing and discovering so many things about the world they never knew was possible.

"Then one day, Ray began to feel tired. She had lived many, many years. Fairies don't grow old like people do. Their bodies always look the same. But like a candle burning, their fairy light eventually goes out. Ray knew she was close to her time to leave this world. She brought Sprout to her and told her that her mother had to leave. Sprout was very sad. She didn't want Ray to leave.

"'I know you will miss this body, and this voice. That's ok! It was the only one of its kind. But I'm returning to the center of existence which makes up everything, so really, I'm not going anywhere. All you need to do is feel the love in your heart, and I will be there!'

"Sprout understood. They held hands, and as Ray smiled at her daughter and laughed one last time, she began to glow brightly. And just as Sprout had appeared to her mother in a bright light, Ray too returned to the center of existence in a bright light. And as she disappeared, a beautiful rainbow appeared in the sky over Sprout's head, and she knew her mom was home."

The girls stared at Maji, contemplative faces resting on hands, slight smiles on their faces.

"So girls, I'm telling you this story, because I'm like Ray."

Cloud laughed. "You're a fairy?!"

"Well, I certainly feel like one when I'm in my fairy dress!" Maji laughed. "But what I mean is, like Ray, soon it's going to be my time to return to the center of existence, to Love. My body is wearing down, and I will be moving on soon."

The smiles dropped off the girls' faces, replaced by looks of confusion. Justice's face flashed understanding, and she began to breathe heavily, clearly fighting emotion. Maji's heart raced and her stomach grew queasy. They sat in silence for a full minute. Behind the girls, Eamonn lay on the floor, his fingers pressed against the bridge of his nose. Maji saw the glint of a tear on his face.

"What does that mean?" Wolf Girl glared. "You're going to disappear?"

"It means she's dying," Justice whispered, her eyes spilling over.

The other girls turned and looked at Maji with shocked confusion.

"What?" squeaked Wolf Girl, overcome with emotion. Her eyes filled with tears and spilled like a faucet turned on. Silent sobs shook her, and she reached out around her for something to grab onto. Her hands found a blanket and pulled it close to her, and she clutched it with white fists, pulling her knees up close to her chest. "What?" she repeated.

Maji felt herself begin to shake, realizing how delusional she'd been to think that this could be a beautiful, inspiring experience for her family. She felt like a fool. This was just pain, pure pain.

Cloud and Star stared at Maji in confusion. A painful, confused smile flickered around Star's mouth, but she said nothing.

"Do you mean dying like our grandpa died?" Cloud asked Justice.

"That's the only dying there is," Justice growled, a waterfall of tears flowing down her cheeks. Cloud balked, looking like she'd been punched in the gut.

"But why?" she began to cry.

"Well, my time has come." Maji's voice shook. "My body is sick and can't go on anymore. We never know when our time is to die, girls. But we know it will come one day. Mine is coming soon. So you see, I'm like a fairy! I won't grow old, and I will return to the center of existence, which is pure Love."

No one responded. The only sounds in the room were sniffles and sobs. Then suddenly, Star jumped to her feet, a deep guttural scream exploding from her mouth. She ran at Maji and jumped on her, pounding her shoulders with her fists as hard as she could.

"No! No! No! No!" she screamed through kicks and punches. Maji curled up, protecting herself from her daughter's blows, but felt she deserved every one of them.

"Star!" Eamonn yelled, jumping to his feet. "Leave her alone!"

Maji lifted her hand. "No, let her!" she yelled through the dull thuds of Star's little fists. Tears and hair flew in every direction as Star screamed and kicked and hit in a ferocious explosion of emotion. Finally, she stopped, panting, and stepped back to look Maji in the face. Her own visage was red and angry, and snot smeared across her cheek.

Maji stared back at her youngest daughter, her own eyes wet with tears, her heart aching. She opened her arms, inviting her in. Star's face crumpled, and with a wail, she threw herself into her mother's arms. The dying woman held her close as her daughter's cries echoed through the room. She wrapped her hand around Maji's hair. As a baby, Star had always loved playing with that hair, a source of so much comfort. Maji made a note to cut some off and save it for her to keep.

Wolf Girl scooted across the room and lay down next to her mother, dropping her head into the woman's lap by Star's legs. Cloud did the same on the other side. Finally, Justice and Eamonn moved closer too, the girl leaning her head on Maji's shoulder and Eamonn sitting behind her, supporting her weight. They all held each other tight. Maji tried to reach out and touch each girl, but she only had two hands.

"I know this is hard," she said, choking on her tears. She still hoped beauty and peace could come from this. But she realized that stories and pretty dresses wouldn't provide it. She felt angry and stupid for even trying that tactic, and recognized it was her own denial of the pain of it that made her think it could be anything but hard for them. She saw now that the only way it could become something else was from acceptance of the pain, and that had to include her own acceptance of their pain. She had been trying to circumvent it, to dress it up, to camouflage it. But that isn't how pain works.

"We all feel sad. And it's okay. You can feel as sad as you need to. We can be sad together right now."

The family lay on the floor, wrapped up together. Maji felt their breathing, heard their sniffs and sobs. Her own heart pounded. She felt Eamonn behind her, strong and supportive. This was living. Facing dying was a part of it. She swore to herself to make her last moments of this life the best she could. And gratitude overwhelmed her for each moment she had with her family, even the sad ones. In that moment, she was deeply, painfully, beautifully alive.

__Renunciation__

Four months after Maji had gone to Chandra's retreat, she found herself back at the same hotel in Vail. After the first meeting, Maji knew she had to explore further working with Chandra as a teacher. The young woman had gone to six more retreats with the charismatic leader, even driving out to Santa Fe for one.

Tye introduced her to the local community of students. Chandra had a surprisingly large number of followers in Colorado, despite her residence's location in France. She learned Chandra was indeed of Indian descent but had actually been born in Tahiti. She moved to Paris as a teenager and grew up to become a psychotherapist. She had two children in their early twenties. She left behind her psychotherapy practice to become a spiritual teacher about 15 years before Maji met her and amassed thousands of students all over the globe.

Chandra's family was a blend of Catholicism and Hinduism, so she presented herself as interfaith and "beyond religion." But after spending more time with her, Maji could see that Hinduism and New Age philosophy influenced her more than any other spiritual viewpoint.

Within Chandra's community, there was a tremendous focus on energy and "vibration." The constant question being asked was "what kind of vibration are you in right now?" There was a strong focus on positivity and averting negative emotions, as well as on health and products that helped purify the body. According to Chandra, having a pure body was optimal for reaching higher states of consciousness.

At her events, Chandra offered all sorts of tonics and remedies for sale in the gift shop area. She sold numerous photos of herself that people bought to put on altars at home. She stood in some of them with the Dalai Lama, with Desmond Tutu, or with other religious leaders around the world. She sold crystals, malas, specific beads that she and other holy teachers had blessed, and even bottled water that had been filtered through a crystal technology that caused it to vibrate at a higher level. Chandra called it "enlightened water" and sold it as a concentrate for $20 a bottle. Maji was amazed when one day at an event Chandra told the crowd that everyone needed to buy a bottle of this water for a specific blessing she was about to give, and within 15 minutes the entire audience bought every bottle of it, over $8,000 worth.

None of that in particular resonated with Maji. It was what she felt in Chandra's presence that kept her coming back. A probing depth of experience and energy awoke a powerful sense of connectivity in Maji. It kept her continuously diving deeper into her own inner exploration. She was a flower just beginning to blossom, with epiphanies unfolding as each petal of herself opened.

After Maji had gone to a couple more events, Chandra invited her to be a part of her A/V team and travel with her. This wasn't a paid position, but a volunteer one, and considered an act of selfless service that was a common practice in Chandra's community. Maji quickly learned the big international machine composed of her thousands of students created Chandra's retreats and videos, and it was built on members as devoted to their selfless service work as they were to their own livelihoods. Based on the Hindu practice of *Seva*, it was considered a spiritual practice to purify oneself from the effects of harmful past actions. By doing selfless good, you counteracted the negative consequences of past patterns.

Maji embraced her new position and quickly found herself in Chandra's "inner circle" of students in close contact with her. So, for the last four retreats, Maji sat behind the A/V desk during the events, learning how to control sound levels, select music, and take subtle, almost imperceptible cues from Chandra during her events.

She learned how much of Chandra's retreats were actually very dramatic productions. Chandra had specific songs and lighting she requested during specific parts of the program. Many of these were planned for, while others were spontaneous. She learned from her fellow A/V workers to read the atmosphere in the room and listen for specific words Chandra spoke in her guided meditations to know which music to cue up. If Chandra was doing a dramatic invocation of the Divine Feminine, there were two or three songs they would have to have ready to fade up into the room at the nod of Chandra's head. If she was doing a meet and greet, they played songs that spoke of devotion to the guru. She had a list of over 100 songs or sounds that were accessed at any point during an event, and similar lighting cues to create an atmosphere in the room.

Maji realized by watching the crowd that this production level drastically shifted the emotional response of people. And as much as she recognized Chandra's spiritual gifts, she saw too that Chandra was a performer that adored working the audience like an actress on stage. The audience adored her spiritual theatrics, which seemed to inspire a deep sense of devotion and loyalty in them.

Maji's drive to keep coming back was her now-obsessive desire to dive in as deep as she could to unravel the mystery of her own profound experiences, and proximity to Chandra seemed like a practical way to do it. The other students in the community seemed to equate being close to Chandra to being close to God itself. This star-struck sense rubbed off on Maji, and she found herself giddy whenever she could be close to this divine figure.

She saw that Chandra had spiritual insight and powers that boggled Maji's mind. Putting all her theatrics aside, Chandra was tapped into a greater power that Maji had only tasted.

During a small retreat that took place at a church in Boulder, Maji watched as Chandra led the crowd into a silent meditation.

"Be very still now. Close your eyes. I'm going to evoke powerful energy and I need you to be still."

As the crowd closed their eyes, Maji kept her's open. It was her duty as the A/V person to wait for Chandra's cues. A deep silence descended over the crowd. It became so still Maji couldn't even hear breathing or movement from the 150 other people in the room. A low hum sounded in her ears. The brightness in the room dimmed, and as Maji watched Chandra, she saw diamond-shaped prisms of light emanate from her body. The light was soft, as if she had just looked into the bright sun then turned her gaze away. It pulsated and spread from Chandra's small form like concentric rings in a pond. Maji blinked several times and shook her head, but the light continued to beat in a silent rhythm.

At another retreat, Chandra stood on stage and invited people to ask her questions. A round, red-headed woman in her fifties approached the microphone. Her shoulders stooped, and her eyes were circled dark like a raccoon. Her pain was written clearly on her face.

"My son," her voice broke as she leaned toward the microphone. "He was killed two months ago in a motorcycle accident." Her tears flowed down her cheeks. "He was all I had. My whole life I lived for my son, and now he is gone!"

Chandra's face fell and her hand came to her heart. "I'm so sorry. Please, come up here."

The woman moved slowly up to the stage, sobs escaping her lips. She came and stood next to Chandra, her face contorted. "If there is only love, as you say, how can I f-feel so much pain? My baby is d-dead, and I wish it was me who had died!"

Chandra watched her, her own eyes filling with tears. "My love, it is only the body that dies. The essence of your son cannot die. It can't! It is the light that makes up all of creation. He has merely shed a skin. Do you miss a coat when you take it off at the end of the day? No! Your son has left behind a garment and will soon find another."

The woman doubled-over, holding her stomach as her tears came faster. "I feel like my heart has been ripped out!" she wailed and pulled on her shirt. "I can't live with this pain anymore. You say his essence can't die, but my son is gone! He's *gone!*"

The woman brought her hands to her face, sobbing loudly. Maji felt her own tears brim her eyes. She watched Chandra study the woman, her tan face crumpled in the same painful expression as the woman, her hand still resting on her heart. She sighed deeply, then reached out and firmly planted her hand on the top of the crying mother's head. Immediately the woman's sobbing stopped, and her hands flew into the air, trembling. She yelped and fell to her knees, her entire body quivering. The crowd gasped in surprise. The grieving mother jerked and convulsed under Chandra's hand as if ten thousand volts coursed through her. For a brief moment, the only sound in the room was her stuttered gasps.

"I have cut through her pain," Chandra announced, her voice strong and booming. "I have awakened her kundalini energy." The woman stared up at Chandra, her face frozen in shock as she continued to convulse. Chandra stared at her intently as she spoke, never turning her gaze from the mother's watery eyes. "Now she will see through her pain." The guru leaned closer to the woman's face. "I couldn't let you suffer anymore, my dear."

Chandra released her hand and the woman fell forward onto her hands, breathing heavily. Chandra stood over her for a moment, the crowd silent in shock. The teacher then motioned to Maji to come to the stage and help the woman to her chair.

As Maji helped her to her feet, she walked her slowly down the aisle with all eyes on them. By the time they reached her chair, Chandra had started speaking to the crowd again. Maji leaned in close to the woman as she sat panting.

"Are you alright?"

The round face in front of her slowly looked up at Maji and broke into a broad smile.

"Yes, thank you!" she cried, tears filling her eyes once more. But as she watched her smile grow and small giggles escaped her lips, Maji realized they were now tears of joy.

One month later the same red-headed woman came to another retreat. As Chandra announced she would take questions, the mother strode up boldly to the microphone.

"I just want to thank you for the gift you gave me, Chandra." She clasped her hands together in gratitude. "I thought I was going to die of a broken heart. But you awoke something in me, something so powerful I have never experienced before. I feel like I have been reborn. I can now say that my son's death has been a blessing to me!"

Maji's mouth opened in shock. She never imagined she would hear a grieving mother say those words. *What did Chandra do to her?* The mystery of it only intrigued Maji more. She was all in.

The attention she received by being close to Chandra gave Maji a boost in her self-confidence. Her closeness to the teacher was a gift and maybe it had to do with the distinctiveness of her own spiritual experiences. Maji began to think that maybe she had some special spiritual gift that Chandra perceived in her, and that was why she pulled her close so quickly. The elegant teacher spoke of each student finding their own mastery. Was Maji meant to be a master like Chandra?

She started to compare herself to the other students close to her teacher. If Chandra spoke of someone's clarity of mind, Maji imagined that surely, she had this as well. Why else would she be there, so close? If Chandra spoke to Maji during an event, her student felt an inner flicker of pride at the singular attention she received. This had to indicate something special about her, didn't it? Maji was never able to speak directly to Chandra about her vision quest, but surely such an experience meant that she, too, had access to spiritual gifts.

During one of the retreats, Chandra had Maji play a video she had received from India from a group of devoted students that had been living out there for the past year. The students were all young, in their twenties and thirties, and all from different areas of the world. Chandra explained that they were in India staying at another teacher's ashram while Chandra was having her own ashram built. These students were totally and completely dedicated to the spiritual path.

They had abandoned every other aspect of their lives to devote themselves to spiritual practice.

As Chandra praised their purity and dedication, the screen flashed with scenes of this group of men and women clad in white robes sitting around a fire. A large Indian man with a potbelly, no shirt, and white and red paste smeared across his forehead sat with them. They chanted something unintelligible, while repeatedly tossing handfuls of herbs and seeds into a fire.

The scene then flashed to a ceremony. The group sat in a hall with marble flooring. A large crowd sat behind them, wearing regular clothes as opposed to the students' white robes. One by one the pupils walked up to an old man sitting on a chair that looked very much like the satin white Victorian Chandra sat on. He placed his hand on their heads one at a time and again chanted something unintelligible.

"Ah, this is their Brahmacharya ceremony," Chandra explained to the audience, a large smile on her face. "They are being initiated into the monastic path. They have given their lives to realizing enlightenment and to me as their master. They will now live in complete purity and single-pointed focus on becoming masters themselves. They are the first of my Brahmacharyas for my new ashram here in Colorado."

Maji watched with fascination at this special group of individuals. She felt a pull of jealousy at the status they now received and at their freedom to focus only on the spiritual path. She envied that dedication. Looking over at Chandra, she saw pride for them beaming from her eyes. Maji wanted that. She wanted to dive in as deep as she could on this path of enlightenment. She wanted to know she was headed in the right direction. If she made it her only avenue, how could she go wrong? The thought of doing what they were doing was simultaneously exhilarating and frightening. Could she really give everything up? Her job, her home, sexual relationships? She knew with stark clarity that she was being driven deeper and deeper on this path. What was the point in being patient? She could do that. She knew she could.

That evening after the event, she penned a letter to Chandra explaining her desire to take the brahmacharya oath and become a nun at her ashram. Her hands sweat with nervousness as she delivered the letter to the attendant at Chandra's door. She had no idea if the guru would accept her offer. Maybe she would laugh her off. After all, Maji had only known her for four months. Was she being too impetuous? But her heart pounded delightfully at the thought of spending days meditating, exploring profound states of mind, living in a community of individuals that were equally as devoted.

The more she spent time with Chandra, the more she felt alienated from everyday life. Mundane reality couldn't compare to the deep states of bliss, awareness, and spiritual truth she felt during the retreats. She wanted that to be her everyday life.

For the weeks that followed, Maji heard nothing from her mentor about her letter, and resigned herself to unspoken rejection. She felt like a failure and a fool. Maybe the monastic path wasn't for her. Maji knew what a wild child she could be. Perhaps that level of discipline was beyond her. But she also knew her wildness was driven by a search for deeper truth. Surely her devotion was enough to give everything to her quest.

Three weeks after she wrote the letter, Maji resided in a Vail hotel room for another retreat, this time for a whole week. She had taken time off work and used up the last of her savings to pay for the event. Her debt accumulated to pay for these retreats, but she made herself trust it would all work out somehow. As she parted with the money for this week-long journey, every bone in her body screamed that she was doing the right thing. Now she rolled over in her bed on the second morning to see the time flash 6:26 am.

"Oh, shit!" She jumped out of bed. Morning meditation started at 6:30 am, and the doors closed tightly right on time. It was deeply frowned upon in the community to be late. It was considered disruptive and disrespectful.

Chandra rarely showed up for these early morning meditations, but there was a strong expectation for everyone else to be there, especially the "inner circle" students. Maji ran into the bathroom, grabbed her toothbrush and toothpaste, as she plopped onto the toilet and brushed while she peed. The clock now read 6:27. It would take her at least two minutes to get to the hall. She looked down at her white satin pajamas. No time to change her clothes.

"Well, at least they're white. This will have to do."

Maji grabbed a shawl and her meditation cushion and rushed out of the room. She was the last one to enter before the door shut. The only place left to sit was an open spot on the floor in the front of the room by Chandra's chair. Maji blushed, realizing she would have to walk past the entire room in her pajamas. She wrapped her shawl tightly around herself and made her way up the aisle. Some people smiled at her as she passed, but most were already deep in their own inner world, eyes closed. Maji settled herself and closed her own eyes, fighting her lingering embarassment. But she sat up straight, determined to focus.

After about 20 minutes, she felt a swoosh of air next to her and could smell the distinct

135

sandalwood-and-rose blend of Chandra's perfume. She opened her eyes to see her mentor sitting down in her satin chair about 6 feet from Maji. Panic gripped her as she remembered her pajamas. Chandra turned to look at her.

"Are you ready for your Brahmacharya ceremony?" she asked in a whisper. Maji blinked in surprise.

"Oh, wow really? I--I mean yes!" she stammered. "I--I'm in my pajamas..."

Maji blushed, gesturing to her clothes. Chandra blinked and looked her up and down, then shrugged in indifference. Maji could feel the room around her begin to stir as the rest of those present realized Chandra had arrived, a rare treat during morning meditation. One of her attendants rushed over and put a microphone behind the guru's ear.

"This morning I will be initiating one of your sisters into the path of brahmacharya!" Chandra purred over the mic. The room stirred excitedly. Maji felt her heart pound inside her chest. This was happening. This was really happening. And all before breakfast!

"To take this initiation is to dedicate every aspect of your life to realizing your true mastery. The brahmachari surrender their lives completely to the divine! They choose purity. They choose celibacy. They choose discipline to embody the highest vibration of their being! The brahmachari is an example of spiritual dedication!"

Maji felt her palms sweat. Chandra turned to the young woman with a smile and motioned her to come closer. Maji scooted on her hands and knees toward her master and kneeled at her feet. Chandra motioned for her to bend down. As she did, she was surprised to feel her mentor's bare feet rest on the crown of her head.

"The energy of the guru's feet is a blessing to be touched with. Like the sediment in a wine bottle settling on the bottom, powerful purifying energy lives in the guru's feet!"

Maji had heard Chandra speak of this before and saw many students bow to her feet for this reason. This was an ancient tradition in Hindu culture. But she had never seen Chandra place her feet on someone's head. Maji felt a profound sense of gratitude for this blessing. She was being given a gift only reserved for a very special few. Her heart swelled with pride and tears filled her eyes. Then Chandra removed her feet from her disciple's head and replaced them with her hands.

"I'm calling in all the masters, all the angels, and the lineage of my own guru to bless this being on her path of renunciation. As she takes this new path, I will now bestow her with a new spiritual name that reflects the higher vibration she is choosing to live in. She will no longer be known as Maji. She will now be known as Karunamayi Amba Brahmacharini. This Sanskrit name means the Great Mother of Compassion."

Maji swallowed hard. She hadn't realized she would be given a new name, and it was a mouthful! She peered up at her teacher through the spaces in her fingers, feeling the weight of her hands pressing on her head. She felt like both a child under her parents' gaze and a queen being crowned for royalty. The pounding in her chest overwhelmed her.

Chandra released her hands, holding her arms out palms-up next to Maji's face. She looked into her student's eyes with a big smile.

"Bless you, my child!" the Indian woman beamed. "Welcome to the path of Brahmacharya!"

Chandra stood and motioned to one of her attendants. A young man with a long ponytail walked over, carrying a large vase of red roses. He stood about ten feet away from Chandra's chair.

"You will all now bless Karunamayi Amba on her new journey." Chandra motioned for everyone to form a line. She turned and took Maji's arm, moving her into the satin chair. Maji's mouth fell open in surprise. It was strictly forbidden to sit in Chandra's chair. The honor was huge.

"Oh, thank you!" Maji cried to Chandra. A lively song with a woman's high voice singing words of devotion to the divine came over the speakers. Maji looked over to the A/V desk and saw Tye sitting in her regular chair. He winked playfully at her, and she smiled back at him.

Chandra turned to the crowd gathering in a line. With a flourish, she swept her arm in a bow as if she had just performed a magnificent magic trick, then strode down the aisle and out of the room.

Maji sat in Chandra's chair as one by one the line of students approached her and handed her a red rose that had been given to them a moment before by Chandra's attendant. The line of at least two hundred stretched far back into the room.

 As each person offered words of congratulations, tears flowed down Maji's cheeks. She felt as if she sat at her wedding with hundreds of people in attendance. She could not have imagined a more beautiful experience until she looked down at the pile of roses growing in her lap and remembered the pajamas. She began to laugh hysterically, sniffing and snorting through her joyful tears. A woman in her fifties approached to give Maji her rose and paused, a quizzical look on her face. Maji continued to laugh.

"I'm in my pajamas!" she shrieked.

The woman looked down at Maji's sleepwear with surprise, registering what she said. She burst out laughing as well, and their merriment mingled. Maji didn't stop giggling for the rest of the morning until the last person offered a flower and the music faded out. Then she stood from the chair, roses spilling off her lap onto the floor around her. She was born anew, living a new reality. She marveled once again at how quickly identities shift. When she'd awakened that morning, she was Maji. Now as she departed, her head held high, it was as Karunamayi Amba Brahmacharini.

Sometimes I Hate You

It was a blustery Tuesday. The wind blew strong, and the threat of a storm clouded the sky. Justice stood under a tree outside of her middle school, her disposable face mask her only protection as the fierce wind tossed dust in her face. She was waiting for her dad to pick her up after school. Around her, her classmates milled around, laughing and playing, occasionally darting off when they spotted a parent pull up in the car line.

Justice stayed quiet. She felt exhausted. Ever since she'd learned Maji was dying, a heaviness had weighed on her and her family. Going to school with her cheerful friends was a welcome break. She could laugh, goof off, even sit in class--anything to distract her, make her feel that life was normal for a while. But she found herself drained by the end of the day, with no strength left to fight off the creeping sadness. It invaded her mind like a thick fog seeping in the cracks, choking her.

All the focus at home now seemed to be on her stepmother. Every conversation either centered on Maji and how to help her or was interrupted by Maji's forgetfulness. It disrupted Justice's whole world. She was always picking up more chores around the house. Maji just couldn't move like she used to. She was slow and spaced out regularly, forgetting things minutes after they happened, so her stepdaughter had to help more. She wanted to lend a hand, but at the same time, she resented it.

Justice knew her stepmother was trying not to make everything about her. At dinner, Maji and Dad always asked the girls about their day. They laughed and talked like they always had. But it wasn't the same. Even looking at the woman's gaunt face was painful. Death hung over all of them. It made the air thick and heavy. As much as Justice loved her family, she loathed being at that house now, and hated to admit it. They had no idea how much time Maji had left, and Justice just wanted to be far away from her. She was a terrible person.

Now she stood waiting for her dad. Her stomach dropped when she saw Maji's car pull up instead. She tried not to let it show, but she could see her stepmother's face register her disappointment. She had just wanted a few more minutes before she had to face impending death again.

"Hey, kiddo." Maji smiled as Justice climbed in the front seat. "How was your day?"

"It was fine," she murmured.

"Sorry your dad couldn't get you today. His work with a client in Denver ran over. I know I shouldn't drive, but I'm feeling pretty good today, so I thought it was okay! It's you and me, honey!"

"Ok." Justice smiled weakly. Maji pulled out of the parking lot and turned left instead of the usual right that took them home. "Where are we going?"

"I'm starving. Let's grab some grub before we have to pick up the other girls."

Justice's middle school finished one hour before the younger girls' elementary school. Usually, this was her quality time with her dad. She bristled internally at the loss of those precious

141

minutes with him, free from illness and sisters and stepmothers.

They drove for a few minutes in silence. Then Maji pulled into the parking lot of an adorable building with lilac-painted walls and a crisp white trim. It was a small tea house called Blackberry's, and one of Justice's favorite places to eat. It had closed for in-person dining when the pandemic began. Justice's eyes widened.

"Oh my gosh, are they open now? Can we go in?"

"Today is their first day open for in-person service!" Maji beamed. "I thought you would like to go."

Justice turned and gave her first authentic smile of the day to her stepmother. This was a treat! Before Maji got sick, it had been a rare occasion that the two of them ever had one-on-one time together. With four kids and a split schedule, it sometimes seemed impossible. They had gone to Blackberry's together for her birthday three years prior and had an absolute blast. Since then, it had only been trips to the store where she had any solo time with Maji. Now Justice felt her heart lighten at this spontaneous outing.

As much as she didn't want to be around her, she did love Maji. They had good conversations together. Her stepmother was so different from both her mom and dad. Justice grew to appreciate her different perspective on many things in her life.

Sometimes it was annoying how far off-base she could be, how little she understood Justice. But Maji was kind, and in general, an easy stepmom to have. Justice's heart swelled in appreciation as they stepped out of the car. She chided herself for feeling upset.

They walked into the cafe and saw only a few tables and chairs spread widely throughout the quaint space. Only four other people patronized the establishment. Maji and Justice chose a table in a corner by a window, far from the other patrons.

"I do have to be really careful about Covid. I am high-risk," Maji explained.

Justice's heart flipped at the reminder of Maji's sickness. An inkling of anger bubbled up in her. *We couldn't even have a few hours without it coming up*, she thought. She tried to push the feeling away. She just wanted to enjoy this hour.

A petite waitress with bright red braids approached with two water glasses and teacups. They ordered some herbal teas, petit fours, and mini sandwiches.

"I'll go get those for you!" The waitress' smile beamed from underneath her mask, and she rushed off.

"Tell me about your day, honey!" Maji said, leaning back in her chair. Justice smiled, recounting the story of her friend who unsuccessfully tried to take the aluminum lid off his yogurt at lunch until it exploded all over his face and hair. He smelled like strawberries for the rest of the day. She shared with her an account of the choir practice where she and her friend, Alicia, kept singing the baritone notes of the song in deep voices instead of their soprano part and totally confused their teacher for several minutes. Then the teacher, as a joke, made all the boys sing soprano and all the girls sing baritone until the song dissolved into fits of laughter by the whole class. Maji laughed along with Justice, and for a moment, things were light again.

The waitress returned with a tray of tea and food. After she placed everything on the table and walked away, Maji looked at the food in front of them.

"I ordered this?" she asked, confused. "I thought I ordered a hamburger."

Justice's heart sank. "Maji, they don't have hamburgers here. This is the tea house. That's what you ordered."

Maji looked at her stepdaughter, blinking. Sadness pulled down the corners of Maji's eyes. "Oh, right." She laughed, feigning indifference. "You're right. Sorry, a momentary lapse of memory."

The two began to eat, sitting in painful silence for several minutes. Justice picked up a pink, iced petit four and popped it in her mouth.

"I love these," she said, trying to cut through the tension. Maji smiled with closed lips, searching Justice's eyes.

"Honey, I want to know how you are doing with all of this. You know you can talk to me. I know this has been hard."

Justice felt her jaw clench as anger rose in her throat. "I don't want to talk about it." she said heatedly.

Maji flinched, then nodded in understanding. "Ok, we don't have to talk about it."

Silence reigned again. But the dam had been broken. Tears filled Justice's eyes. She quickly stuffed two petit fours in her mouth, as if they could stop the avalanche of emotion that she felt rising inside her. But it didn't work. The tears rolled down her cheeks, round with the cakes in her mouth. Maji's eyes sagged with sadness, and she reached out and took her hand. Justice managed to swallow the cakes, then opened her mouth. Her words burst out of her like a firehose on full blast.

"I just wanted a few moments to be normal! Everything now is about you dying or this stupid pandemic! I feel like none of us have normal lives anymore. I'm just sad all the time. And I have to do so many more chores. I'm so tired. I just want to be happy again. I just want us all to laugh and play again. So, sometimes I want a break! Sometimes I want to get away! Sometimes I just want my dad! When it's just him, I don't have to think about death all the time. It's just easier with him. It was easier before you and Wolf Girl and Star came along. It was just us. But now it's so complicated and really painful! Sometimes I wish you weren't even a part of our family anymore! Sometimes I think I hate you!"

She gasped, shocked at her own words. Yes, it was how she felt, but she never thought she would say it out loud, least of all to Maji. *I'm the most horrible person on Earth.* How could she say something like that to her dying stepmom? Maji's expression didn't change. It was just a quiet sadness in her eyes as she held Justice's hand.

"Maji, I'm sorry!" she cried, now loudly sobbing. She looked around and saw the waitstaff behind the counter staring at them. "I'm sorry I said that. I don't hate you; I promise!"

Maji smiled, a loving smile this time. "Of course you feel that way, Justice. I know how hard this is. I know how hard it is to have a stepmom and stepsisters. Never mind having a stepmom who is dying. It's really normal to feel that way!"

"It is?" Justice sniffed. "Nobody told me that. I feel horrible that I think these thoughts. I don't really want you to go away. I just want things to be easy again. I'm so sorry!"

She choked on her words, blowing her nose into a napkin. Maji stood and moved to the other side of the table, sitting in the chair next to her stepdaughter so she could put her arm around her.

"Justice, I want you to know that you have my full permission to feel what you feel. It doesn't hurt my feelings. I promise. Even though I'm not your mom, I am your stepmom, which means I'm going to love you no matter what. And you want to know something amazing about that?"

"Wha-what?" Justice sniffed.

"With the two daughters that I gave birth to, it's an instinct to love them. I have no control over it. It's a primal force that drives life. It's choiceless. Just as it is for your mom to love you. But with you and Cloud, I chose it. I have had to work with you, like we are right now, to build trust, to build love. And I know you have had to do that with me, too."

Justice nodded, listening, her tears slowing down.

"It's a really powerful thing in life to choose love. Love is the strongest force on the planet. It can be beautiful, and it can be so painful. So, it isn't always easy. And sometimes we just can't do it. Sometimes love hurts too much, and we would rather have it leave than stay and stir up all this pain. So, I get it, kiddo. It makes sense. To be honest, going through all this right now, I feel the same. I wish this would just end."

Maji's eyes filled with tears, and her voice choked on her words as tears began to stream down her face. Justice felt her own eyes well up again at the sight of her stepmother's tears.

Maji continued. "I see how hard this is for all of you. I know I don't have much time left. It feels like torture sometimes to watch you all suffer. I wish I wasn't dying. I wish I could see you all grow up and live the amazing lives I know you are going to live. But I can't. So some days I wish I could just leave now and get it over with and put you all out of your misery. But at the same time, I don't want to, because I want every minute I can have with you! I feel split in two. So, yes, baby, I know how you feel. Don't ever feel bad for how you feel. Life is too complicated to feel bad about our feelings."

Justice listened, wide-eyed, then reached across and hugged Maji tightly.

"I do love you, Maji."

"I love you too, sweetie. I always will."

They held each other close, feeling the great messy complexity that was life and death until the red-headed waitress returned sheepishly.

"Uh, can I get you anything else?" she asked in a quiet voice.

Maji and Justice looked up at her, their faces streaked with tears, both sniffing loudly.

"Maybe some more napkins, so we can blow our noses!" Maji laughed, and Justice laughed with her. The waitress smiled behind her mask, her eyes crinkling. And for the first time in a long while, Justice felt joy in her heart. Even when life was hard, it was always better to choose love.

The Divine Life Of Karunamayi

Maji startled awake to the blaring of her alarm. She opened one eye and saw the red numbers reading 4:30 AM, groaning as she stretched her arms above her head. She could hear the shuffling of bedcovers from across the room as the two other nuns she shared a room with also stirred awake.

"Good morning, sisters!" her roommate Parvati said softly. Maji looked out the window next to her bed. The stars were still twinkling brightly in the dark sky. Maji laughed at their definition of morning.

It was a year after Maji became Karunamayi Amba Brahmancharini. She now lived in Las Altas Ondas, Colorado, a small town of only 1,200 in the Sangre De Cristo Mountain Range. What made this town unusual was the great concentration of multiple spiritual communities that called it home. Las Altas Ondas had three Tibetan Buddhist centers, a Franciscan Monastery, a Zen Buddhist center, a large Hindu ashram, a Shinto organization, a Sufi center, a Kabbalistic Jewish group, and several Native American tribes that had made this town their home for centuries. It was here that Chandra had built her first US ashram. It was here that Maji now lived as a nun. Maji shared the communal living space with four other nuns and six monks, as well as a non-monastic man and woman.

"Can I get the first shower, loves?" Parvati asked.

"Yeah, please!" Maji slurred. "Just wake me up after your three-minute shower. I need to sleep in!" She rolled over, pulling the covers over her head.

Every morning they woke at 4:30 to shower and dress to make morning meditation by 5:00 am. As hard as she tried, Maji could never get used to the early morning schedule. She had always been a night person.

After Maji heard Parvati return, she pulled herself out of bed and headed to the bathroom. As the young woman closed the door, she turned and looked at her tired face in the mirror. Upon arrival at the ashram, all the monastic folks shaved their heads, so Maji found herself bald once again. She ran her hand over the downy fuzz on her skull. *It isn't too long. I don't need to shave it again for a little while.* The nun chuckled to herself. *I stopped shaving my legs, but now I shave my head! Oh, the irony!*

Maji showered her allotted three-minute shower and returned to her room, wrapped in a towel. The other nuns had already dressed and were making their beds.

In the mornings after her shower, Maji performed what was called the "abhiseka" ritual. For this practice, she used a small amount of ash taken from sacred fire ceremonies in India and mixed it into a paste with some water that sat overnight on her altar. She smeared the paste onto three of her fingers, then spread it in three lines at specific spots all over her body that, according to the ancient ritual, were energetically significant center points.

Maji whispered the designated mantras for each spot to create an energetic balance and cleansing in her body, feeling the cold paste dry into a flaky crust on her skin. She completed the ritual with three lines smeared on her forehead and a large red dot in the center of her forehead just above her eyebrows, made from a blend of herbs and spices thought to cleanse the pineal gland, located in the center of the brain. The pineal gland was considered the seat of enlightenment, according to ancient Hindu anatomy. Maji took a deep breath through her nose. She loved the herby smell of the red paste.

The three lines of ash represented the "trifecta" of timeless existence: the beginning, the sustenance, and the dissolution that existed in every moment of experience. The sacred ash symbolized the impermanence of each moment. The lines, worn ornamentally, served as a reminder of these concepts.

Chandra expected the forehead display to look very tidy. So the three nuns crowded together at the bathroom mirror with cotton swabs in hand, and used water to straighten their lines and create an even space between them.

As Maji looked at their three faces in the mirror, mouths stretched open in concentration, she laughed to herself, remembering the days when she was a teenager and shared a bathroom with her older sisters. They had fought over space in front of the mirror to put their makeup on before school. *Is this so different? Girls wear eyeshadow; nuns wear "spiritual makeup."*

Maji performed these rituals with fervor. She was passionately dedicated to this discipline. Every mantra spoken, every brush of her fingers across her skin with ash, every moment sitting in contemplative silence peeled away layers of her own ignorance. One day the effort would pay off and she would emerge into a brilliant state of enlightenment, like Chandra's, where she would finally understand the secrets of the universe. Everything she lived for now was to achieve that.

It would take lifetimes of work to get there, but if she worked hard enough, one day, it would happen.

Maji dressed herself in a simple long white tunic with an ankle-length skirt underneath, as well as a scarf wrapped across her chest or around her head. She had four of these robes made, and they now comprised the entirety of her wardrobe. She wrapped a white shawl tightly around herself as the women left the house, walking across the road to the yurt that was used as the meditation hall.

The monastic community kept a rigorous schedule consisting of almost 14 hours a day of scheduled time. They woke up at 4:30 am to prepare for a group meditation by 5:00, which lasted two hours. Then they shared a communal breakfast, followed by a community meeting to go over the schedule of work projects for the day. They each had their regularly assigned duties, jobs for the community. They also took turns running random errands between their scheduled tasks, beginning at 8:00 am. Once the workday ended at 5:00 pm, they shared a communal dinner, followed by another evening meditation that lasted until 7:30. Six days a week they followed this schedule. Thursdays they took time off from these duties and were expected to fast and stay in silence for the entire day.

Life in the ashram was significantly more challenging than Maji had anticipated. As passionate as she was, Maji found herself increasingly worn out by the rigorous schedule and unrelenting discipline. After several months, she began to question how effective this lifestyle was if it constantly stressed and busied her. It wasn't at all how she had imagined ashram living. But she did savor their meditation practice. The stillness became her resting place.

Maji settled onto her cushion, her legs crossed. Around the yurt sheer white fabric hung down from the ceiling, covering every inch of the walls. The fabric was lit by warm Christmas lights from behind. Colorful round cushions littered the wood floor. At the front of the room were positioned frosted crystal singing bowls of various sizes that surrounded a large altar. On the altar were bouquets of flowers, small statues of various Hindu deities, and a large, framed photo of Chandra that rested on a satin cushion. Vibrant red silk draped around the frame.

One of the monks lit a sweet-smelling stick of incense. He then picked up two small silver cymbals that were connected with a leather rope and dinged them together, causing a high, clear tone to reverberate around the room. This announced the beginning of meditation.

The fire that had been lit in the stove to warm the yurt crackled behind her, and Maji allowed the sound to hypnotize her deep into the colorful landscape of her own mind. Morning meditation began in silence, intended as a practice of mindfulness. She felt herself relax deeply as her mind focused on the rhythm of her own breath. Whenever she became distracted and noticed she was lost in her own thoughts, she labelled whatever was going on in her mind as thinking, and returned again to her breath.

After an hour, Jaiman, the ashram manager, dinged a small crystal bowl to announce the end of silent meditation. The clear crisp sound pulled Maji out of her inner universe. It was now time for their active practice to begin. Chandra had given the monks and nuns a practice to undertake that she considered only fit for those that had awakened their "kundalini" energy, a term used in the ancient yogic tradition. Maji had learned the word from Chandra and realized it referred to the powerful energy she had felt on her vision quest.

Kundalini was an energetic force that everyone had. It lay dormant at the base of the spine. Once it awoke, which could be a slow gradual process or a violent explosion as it was for Maji, it opened up channels in the body to allow spiritual realization to take place. Neither awakening was superior, just different in its experience.

During this meditation, Maji envisioned kundalini energy moving from the crown of the head and base of the spine to meet in the heart's center, then back again. This was done in time with her breath.

Chandra had instructed the ashram residents to speak a mental mantra as the energy met at the heart. Maji usually chose "Om Namah Shivaya," which was a common mantra in Hindu practice. But today, as she felt a deep growling in her stomach, she repeated "toast and tea, toast and tea" instead, which made her smile.

Maji loved this practice. It gave her a blissful feeling throughout her body and swayed her gently as she meditated. Her vision quest and her first retreat with Chandra had given her the same feeling. But now, she had more control of it.

She opened her eyes during the practice to see the other monks and nuns sitting silently, euphoric smiles on their faces as their bodies rocked back and forth. *They're all having partnerless sex!* Maji laughed internally watching their sultry rolls of the spine and hip motions, then chastised herself for such a low vibration thought. They were monastics after all, and sexual energy was supposed to be transformed into spiritual life energy. But Maji couldn't help but feel that this blissful energy was their own sort of cosmic orgasm.

She laughed about it after meditation with Parvati, the nun from France with whom she shared a room.

"Why not call it a cosmic orgasm?" Parvati giggled as they sat together on Maji's bed, savoring a few unscheduled moments before breakfast. The Frenchwoman flung her shawl around her head, her big blue eyes peeking out from underneath, giving her the appearance of the Virgin Mary in a painting. "I feel like I'm fucking God in those moments."

Maji laughed at her brash language. It was frowned upon by Chandra and the community as being "low vibration." Maji found it refreshing.

"I don't think Chandra would agree with your sentiments," Maji giggled.

"Ha! That's because she would be jealous!" Parvati winked at Maji, then her face became solemn. "Do you ever miss it?"

"Miss what?"

"Sex!"

Maji flushed red. "Sometimes, yeah. But then I try to transmute it like Chandra has taught us."

Parvati sighed, staring off into space. "Who knew finding inner peace would be so much damn work."

Maji's heart flipped at her statement. The irony of it turned her stomach. She reached out and squeezed Parvati's hand and leaned into her, their foreheads touching affectionately. "It will be worth the effort one day, right? That's why we are doing the work."

"Hmmm," Parvati mumbled.

Maji couldn't read the tone of her sound.

"Truth be told, sister," Parvati exhaled deeply. "I don't know what else I would be doing if I wasn't here. I don't have anything else left! So, the journey to enlightenment it is for me then!"

Parvati was fourteen years older than Maji. She had been born with the name Dominique in a small town outside Paris, where she grew up as a rebellious punk before storming out of her parents' house at eighteen with a slew of curse words trailing behind her. After getting a taste of the challenges of the real world, she decided to grow her mohawk out and at 19 managed to land a prestigious position as a nanny in the house of a count and countess of the French court.

The count's younger brother immediately took interest in her, and after a scandalous affair that the relatives tried on multiple occasions to end, they married in secret. The family had no choice but to accept Parvati, this "working girl," into their royal fold. She was given a dozen names along with the noble title of countess and suddenly found herself living in a castle in the French countryside with servants.

With untold wealth at hand, no need to work another day of her life, and her face in the newspapers on occasion, Parvati began to feel like a caged bird. The rigid expectation of royal life made each of her decisions a communal family affair. She tried to distract herself from this oppressive feeling by diving into her college education, learning multiple languages, and performing community service.

But then one day everything changed. For years, she and her husband had tried to have a baby. Then, after having given up, she found herself pregnant. She poured herself into her upcoming role as a mother, devoting her entire heart and soul to this new human. Tragically, when she was 30 weeks along, her water broke one night at a restaurant. Her husband rushed her to the emergency room, but her son was born in silence without ever taking a first breath.

As she lay in her hospital bed, she asked to see her dead son between sobs of grief. A handsome Indian nurse with brilliant green eyes and long hair brought in the body. He smiled at her tear-stained face as he passed the still bundle into her arms. Love emanated from him and gratitude for his presence filled her as she said her painful goodbyes to her son.

Later, when she left the hospital, she asked to see the man to thank him for his kindness. When she described him to the other nurses, they looked at her with confusion.

"We don't have any male nurses that work in this department of the hospital," the head nurse explained to her. Parvati was shocked. She became convinced an angel had visited her, a messenger of love and hope.

For Parvati, the death of her son signaled the end of her marriage. She packed her bags, relinquished her title, and found herself again leaving a house with a slew of curse words trailing behind her. Buried in grief, she no longer knew what to do with herself.

It was then that Chandra entered her life. Parvati soon found the guru's promises of personal mastery far more fulfilling than any job or title she'd ever had. The encounter with the angel nurse had prepared her to find deeper meaning in her life. The ex-countess quit her job, sold every last stitch of clothing and material wealth she had, filled just one suitcase, and headed to India to travel with Chandra. She was there for a year before taking the Brahmacharya vow Maji had seen in the video at Chandra's retreat.

When Parvati told Maji her story, the young nun couldn't help thinking how much royal life sounded like ashram life. Only instead of renouncing the world, as royals, they owned it. And that ownership and spotlight were equally disciplined. The only difference was the goal. Instead of enlightenment, they focused on the maintenance of their power and wealth.

Maji and Parvati walked arm-in-arm over to the dining room for breakfast. As they turned to walk in the door, Parvati mimicked the sultry movement used in the kundalini practice in an exaggerated sexual way, silently mouthing "Oh yeah, baby." Maji burst out laughing. As she walked through the doors the other monks and nuns glared at her disapprovingly for breaking the silence. The young nun stifled her laugh, her face turning red.

After the group ate their breakfast in silence and had their community meeting, Maji headed over to the greenhouse. She worked several jobs at the ashram, but above all, Maji's favorite job was in the greenhouse, where she worked for at least two hours a day.

She opened the door and took a deep breath of the humid, earthy air, a smile spreading across her face. The greenhouse became her sanctuary. When she felt overwhelmed by the strict regimen, discipline, and complete lack of privacy that was ashram life, the greenhouse gave Maji a place to let that all go and just be in the simple life flow of flowers, fruits, and vegetables without an agenda.

Resting on the ground were several trays of marigolds waiting to be planted. Their bright orange blossoms burst out of the dirt like tiny suns. Marigolds always made Maji feel happy.

She bent down, carefully working one out of its plastic nest, and dug a small hole with her fingers in the dirt next to a tomato plant. She used a small spade with the other hand to push the dirt to the side. Maji never wore gloves. She loved the feeling of dirt on her hands. To her, it was touching the foundation of life itself. Without dirt, there would be no life. Once life ended, it returned to dirt. And this greenhouse dirt was sacred to her.

The previous owners of the ashram property had put so much care into creating the perfect blend of nutrient-rich soil for life to thrive. They had created a beautifully balanced compost system that returned food scraps and plant waste into the cycle. The compost fed some of the local deer herds. Then it returned to the greenhouse to feed the plants that fed all of them, completing the cycle. The responsibility to maintain that balance continued with her. As she repeatedly plunged her fingers into the dark soil, Maji felt it as an act of worship of the divine life force that moved through them all.

As she planted, Jaiman came into the greenhouse.

"Om Jai Maa, Karunamayi," he said in greeting, nodding his head.

"Om Jai Maa, Jaiman." She waved her dirt-covered hand in his direction.

"Planting marigolds, I see?"

"Yes, they should help with the whitefly issue." Maji smiled.

When they had inherited the greenhouse from the previous owners of the property, it was already a beautifully balanced array of permanent plants that had been tended and cared for lovingly. But in the months between the owners selling the property and the monks and nuns moving in, the greenhouse was neglected, and the fragile ecosystem tilted off-kilter. Plants died, and pests moved in. They now had a rampant infestation of whiteflies and spider mites that were decimating their crops.

Jaiman looked at her blankly, a small note of disapproval in his blinking eyes. He had suggested multiple times to spray the greenhouse with pesticides, but Maji passionately refused. The greenhouse was strictly organic, and being a closed system, the insecticide would have far-reaching consequences beyond taking care of the bug problem. It would throw off the natural bacterial biome in the soil. It would pollute the food they ate.

"I saw you had put in a request for your mother to stay here during the next retreat." He looked with an air of authority at the clipboard in his hand. "You know only monastics can stay here, or people Chandra personally invites."

Maji looked at him in surprise. "But it's my mother, and this is my home. We have the extra rooms for guests."

"Yes, but she isn't a student of Chandra's."

"But she is coming to the retreat, and she can pay for the room."

"Yes, but she isn't a student. Chandra is saving those rooms for students. I'm sorry. She will have to find someplace else to stay."

With that he turned on his heels and walked out the door, saying "Om Jai Maa" behind him as he left. Sadness and anger welled up inside Maji. She had been so excited to have her mother stay at the ashram and experience her new life. As unusual as the young woman's many life decisions had been, her mother always supported her, even if she didn't agree. When she reached out to Maji and said she wanted to visit the retreat, her obvious love and effort filled her heart with appreciation.

She threw her spade into the dirt, closed her eyes, and took a few deep breaths to calm herself.

"You don't need this negativity; this is just because you are so attached to your mom," she said to herself. "Let go of the attachment, and the anger will go."

She closed her eyes and imagined herself severing an invisible cord between herself and her mother. This was a practice Chandra had taught them. The cord represented an unhealthy attachment. To be free of attachment was to love without feeling responsible for the other person or having them be responsible for you. As Chandra explained it, it was freedom in love. The severing didn't mean she couldn't love her mother, just that she was no longer bound by a codependent relationship. The severing was supposed to make the love bigger, a more universal, spiritual love.

She opened her eyes after the practice, expecting to feel better. But all she could feel was disappointment and sadness. She pictured her mom's sweet face and wanted to cry. She felt a sense of betrayal from her community. This was her *mother*.

"I have to work on this more," she muttered, pulling herself upright and wiping her hands on a towel. She walked out of the greenhouse, going past the large compost pile that lived behind the building. A large buck with a round belly stood serenely munching on the food scraps at the top of the pile.

"Hey, Charlie! How you doing, buddy?" Maji chirped. The buck paid her no attention. He was a regular at the ashram and came to the compost pile every day for a buffet, occasionally bringing some does with him. He was so used to their presence they probably could have walked up to him and patted him on the back. But due to his large, ten-point rack of antlers, no one had tried yet. They affectionately named him Compost Charlie. His appearance always brought the young woman joy.

She walked past the buck at a respectful distance, heading up the flagstone path toward the main building of the ashram. She wanted to take fifteen minutes in the meditation hall to sit with her mind and work through her sadness. She didn't want to do that in the greenhouse. The greenhouse was her free zone, which had its own sacred container. That was what the meditation hall was for.

As she walked past the office through the courtyard, Viraj rushed out the door.

"Karunamayi! I was just going to come to look for you!"

"Om Jai Maa, Viraj." Maji smiled weakly, feeling her heart sink at the interruption. *Please don't ask me to do something*, she thought.

"We need to get those posters out about the retreat. I was told you had them done. Can you take the file to the office store and have them print up a hundred of them, please? Gotam is driving to Allensville and we want him to put the flyers up around town."

"Oh, okay. I just need fifteen minutes." She turned to leave.

"Well, he is leaving in forty-five minutes, so you will have to go now to get them done in time."

"Oh, well, okay" She sighed. He handed her the keys to the community van. "I need to go grab my wallet. I'll leave in a jif."

I can take a few minutes when I get back, Maji thought to herself as she walked across the street to the nun's quarters where she kept her wallet. As she walked into the house, she encountered

Annica rushing toward the front door, a telephone in her hand.

"Karunamayi! Thank goodness! I just got off the phone with Marietta. She told me Chandra will be here on Friday!"

"On Friday?! That's the day after tomorrow!" It was always amazing to have Chandra come to the ashram because of the extra time it allowed them to spend with her. But it also meant an incredible amount of prep work. "I thought she wouldn't come for another three weeks. The retreat is a month away!"

"I know, but she changed her mind. She wants to come here for a couple of weeks, then go up to Denver before the retreat. We have to clean her house now!"

Annica's eyes bulged with urgency.

Maji sighed. "Well, I can't now. I have to go to town to print up the flyers. Gotam needs them in forty-five minutes."

"Well, go fast, please," Annica said with an air of slight frustration in her voice. "Tomorrow is Thursday, and I really need a free day. I don't want to be cleaning."

"Neither do I. Ok, I will find you when I get back."

Maji grabbed her wallet and turned to leave. Her heart felt heavy, and she suddenly felt exhausted. As she walked out to the van, her mind drifted to the memory of what she used to think ashram life would be like. She had imagined a slow-paced life filled with hours of meditation.

"Yeah, we have the hours of meditation." She chuckled to herself. "Along with two full-time jobs worth of work with it."

A few hours before Chandra arrived on Friday, the ashram began to fill with students of hers who had driven to the small town to see her. Maji rushed around all morning offering tea and directing people to their rooms. She barely had a chance to use the bathroom.

Maji carried a tray with eight mugs of tea for several guests who waited in the courtyard. She delicately balanced the steaming mugs, carefully keeping her eyes on them as she stepped down the small stone steps from the dining hall. Her gaze didn't move as she zipped around a corner and smashed right into a tall blond woman with a short pixie haircut. The mugs slid sideways on the tray as Maji danced to keep them stable, but the weight flipped the tray out of her hands and the full cups crashed to the ground with a loud shattering sound, splashing hot liquid all over the nun's skirt.

"Oh, shit!" Maji looked up sheepishly at the woman she had smashed into. "Amanda, I'm so sorry! Did I get tea on you?"

Amanda smiled warmly; a pitying look in her eye. She bent down to help Maji pick up the mug shards.

"No, not a drop. I'm sorry, too! It seems we both had our minds elsewhere when we came around the corner."

Maji sighed and smiled at the soft-spoken woman. Amanda served as one of Chandra's personal assistants. She traveled extensively with the guru throughout the year. When she wasn't traveling with Chandra, she worked as a naturopathic doctor. She lived with her wife, Sara, and their two children. The children had come to them as foster kids, taken from their mother as toddlers due to her deep drug addiction. Amanda and Sara adopted them after a year of fostering.

Maji really liked Amanda once she got to know her. She was a very devoted student of Chandra's and a dedicated wife and mother. Maji marveled at how calm and collected the busy woman seemed to be even when she managed so much. The young woman looked up to her as someone who had truly created an amazing life and state of mind.

"I'm happy you're here, Amanda!" Maji smiled, plucking ceramic shards from the stones and dropping the pieces on her tray. "Are Sara and the kids here too?"

Amanda smiled softly, a sadness filling her eyes.

"Yes, they are over there." She sighed. "The kids are so wound up from the long drive. I wish I could send them running up the mountain to burn off some energy!"

Maji looked over to where Amanda pointed and saw Sara leaning against a stone wall on the far side of the courtyard with her phone in her hand. Next to her, a dark-skinned little boy of about nine years with his hair in cornrows tried to climb the wall using his fingers and toes but kept sliding down. To his right squatted a little girl who was the spitting image of her brother, but with multiple braids that ended in colorful plastic balls sprouting from her head. She crouched low, investigating an anthill that she discovered in the crack of the paving stones. She bounced up and down enthusiastically in her crouch, and Maji could see their energy waiting to explode.

"You certainly do have your hands full with them, don't you?" Maji laughed.

Amanda stared at her children, her smile fading a little. "Yes….".

"Amanda, are you OK?" Maji asked. The doctor was usually so cheerful. But Maji could see something was weighing on her mind.

"Oh, yeah, I'm OK. I just have a lot on my mind. Sorry, Karunamayi! It was probably my fault we ran into each other."

"Well, let's just say we both could have paid more attention and share the blame!" Maji laughed. Amanda bent and picked up the last of the broken mug pieces.

Jaiman, who was standing in the middle of the courtyard, raised his cell phone in the air. "Excuse me, everyone!" All heads turned in his direction. "I just received the call from Chandra's driver that she is a few minutes away! Let's all head over to Chandra's house and greet her there!"

The crowd rushed down the street to Chandra's house a block away from the ashram. Fifty people lined the dirt driveway of a majestic two-story adobe home that looked like it had been plucked from a Spanish storybook. Everyone wore white, and as Maji squinted at the gleaming row of devotees in the sunlight, she regretted not having brought sunglasses.

A white Cadillac Escalade appeared over the hill and moved slowly down the driveway. Chandra could be seen through the window, waving at everyone and smiling. As the car proceeded slowly, people reached out and handed the guru a flower or bowed to the car. The scene reminded Maji of the Queen of England driving through downtown London, waving to her subjects.

Once the car parked, a very handsome, tall young man with long dreadlocks jumped out of the front passenger seat. He swiftly opened a white parasol with a lacy fringe before opening the door for Chandra to exit. As she stepped out of the car, the crowd burst into applause. Chandra turned in a circle, slowly greeting everyone, the parasol held above her as she moved by the young man with determined focus. With her hands at her heart, the spiritual leader nodded to people in the crowd.

"I missed you all so!" she gushed, and the crowd responded with loving "Ahhhs." Chandra then turned and abruptly marched into the house.

Amanda stepped forward. "Chandra would like everyone to meet in her parlor."

The crowd filed into a line, one by one, and Maji and the other brahmacharis ushered them slowly into the house. Floor-to-ceiling windows dripping with crystal prisms illuminated the huge room, creating dancing rainbows. Chandra sat on a Victorian chair with a white satin cover, elevated off the floor by about a foot on a wooden stage. Next to her seat stood a small side table. A large bouquet of lilies and roses sat on the other side. The scent of the flowers filled the air, mingling with the odor of the sandalwood oil Chandra wore on her wrists. Two very large Persian rugs laid side by side on the floor in front of her. This was the seating area for the audience, who slowly made their way in and found a seat cross-legged on the floor.

Chandra nodded to Maji, and Maji recognized her cue to get the audio system going. She rushed over to the corner of the room, where a miniature audio panel was set up, and flipped the switches to turn it on. She grabbed Chandra's pink wireless microphone and made her way through the already filling mass of people, stepping over knees and feet carefully, before arriving at her teacher's chair. Chandra tilted her head carefully so Maji could place the microphone behind her ear.

"So good to see you!" Chandra smiled, gently touching the young nun on the cheek. Maji gushed at this gift of grace.

"So good to see you, too!" Maji beamed and headed back to her station at the audio panel.

Chandra began addressing the people in the crowd one by one. Maji sat cross-legged behind the miniature sound system, smooshed into a little ball by the massive number of people crammed into the chamber. She occasionally cued music as Chandra indicated for the group to chant together. Sometimes she would jump up and rush a microphone to someone who couldn't speak loud enough for the others to hear, stepping carefully over legs and heads along the way.

The other brahmacharis waited on the sidelines to bring forward gifts Chandra designated to people or fetch water for their guru. It was a casual gathering, but everyone waited with bated breath to receive direct attention from their leader. For them, it was like talking to God herself. And to receive direct attention spoke to the level of their spiritual realization.

At one point, Chandra turned her attention to Amanda, Sara, and the two siblings. She called the children to sit next to her and gushed as Amanda's daughter presented a drawing she had made of her family with the guru. Amanda kept a sad smile on her face as she watched Chandra pour adoration on her kids.

After two hours, Chandra finally dismissed the crowd. Maji's legs ached from sitting on the floor, so she stood with gratitude. As the last of the crowd ambled out the front door, Chandra called the brahmacharis over to her. The group of shaved-headed, white-clad monks and nuns huddled together at their guru's feet like children around their kindergarten teacher. She had not been back to the ashram for almost five months, so everyone was anxious to hear what she thought of their progress.

Chandra sat in silence for a moment, looking them over with a smile on her face.

"Very good, very good," she said cheerfully. "I see you all have been practicing well. I'm pleased!"

The group all smiled, relaxing a bit in their postures.

"But you can do better." Chandra winked at them playfully. Uncomfortable smiles sullied their faces. "I want each of you to tell me what is challenging you now. Just in one word. I don't need all the story that goes with it. The story is irrelevant."

She turned to Parvati and pointed.

"You! Let's start with you!"

Parvati froze, her eyes going wide as she thought about what to say. She began to speak in French, but Chandra held up her hand.

"No, no *ma cherie*, in English, so everyone can learn from your experience. Now, what is your word that describes your challenge?"

Parvati closed her eyes, squeezing her knees to her chest.

"Freedom."

"Ah!" Chandra shouted angrily. "You feel trapped here, yes?"

Parvati went pale. She shook her head and began to open her mouth to speak, but Chandra held her hand up again.

"I don't want the story or the explanation. No! What I want from you is acceptance. If there is one practice you could do for the rest of your life that would be the greatest practice to achieve mastery, it is the practice of accepting. You love to fight. You are never satisfied where you are. You love to challenge. So now I challenge you! Whatever comes your way, just accept it. It doesn't need to change. Accept, and you will be free!"

Parvati nodded, unsmiling.

Chandra paused for a moment, then her face softened. "You will be free, my love. One day you will be a divine mother to hundreds!"

Parvati's eyes filled with tears, and she finally smiled. Maji knew the Indian woman spoke to the pain of the loss of the nun's son. To be told she would be a divine mother to hundreds had to be a healing balm on her aching heart. Maji felt a stab of jealousy at her prediction.

Chandra turned to Maji and pointed sharply at her. "You! Tell me your challenge! I feel your conflict, so you can't hide it from me."

Maji froze, her mind racing as she tried to formulate a word. She thought of her exhaustion, thought of her nagging doubts about this lifestyle. She was terrified to reveal to Chandra that she questioned the practices. That certainly wasn't devotion, and she didn't want her teacher's wrath calling her out. So, what word would describe what she felt, that kept her cards close to her chest?

"Trust." she met her mentor's eyes.

Chandra stared at her silently, scrutinizing her face, her eyes dancing back and forth between Maji's. The disciple felt her cheeks begin to burn under her gaze.

"Do you know what I see for you?" Chandra asked. Maji shook her head. "I see you one day being like me, a Divine Mother, a guru, with thousands of people at your feet."

Maji sucked in her breath, her heart pounding.

"I see you as a great leader, waking up the minds and hearts of those around you. I need you to be a master like this. To do this, you must simply surrender your doubt. Masters do not doubt. They know! So, my child, know in your heart that you are that. Yes?"

Maji nodded her head, her eyes wide.

"Yes, Chandra!" she gasped. She felt her heart, and her pride, swell. As Chandra turned to the others in the group to discuss their own challenges, the young nun hardly heard a word they said, her heart beating so loudly in her ears. Her mind swam. A guru? Like Chandra? What would that look like? Would she have an ashram? Would she travel the world? Surely she could surrender her doubt, knowing this.

After Chandra spoke to each member of the group, she clapped her hands.

"Now, we must discuss plans. Jaiman, I want you to reach out to Michael, our CFO. There is an adjacent property to this house going on the market soon. I told Hannah, who runs Rolling Hills Realty, to let me know if it ever goes up for sale, and she sent a message this morning saying it is going on the market next month!"

Jaiman picked up his clipboard and began to fervently take notes.

"Yes, Chandra, very exciting! And what would we use this property for?"

"I hope to bring more members to the ashram community. Our ashram is now full except for the guest quarters. We need more space for permanent residents. I have asked Amanda to come to live here, which she could do by the fall."

"Oh, wonderful!" Maji exclaimed in excitement. "Is the house big enough for her family?"

"Oh, no." Chandra chuckled. "It will just be Amanda. I have asked her to come live here as a brahmachari. This is the next step in her spiritual journey. It is time she devoted herself fully to the path."

The room grew very still as everyone stared at Chandra.

"Wh-what about her children?" Maji asked, thinking of the two bright-eyed kids that had sat at Chandra's feet just an hour before. Would Chandra really ask Amanda to leave behind her wife and children?

"Those aren't her real children," Chandra said casually.

Maji's heart dropped into her stomach. Her mind didn't know what to think. She looked around the room and saw blank faces. Suddenly, the sad eyes she'd glimpsed earlier made sense. Her mind filled with the image of Amanda's daughter lovingly giving Chandra the drawing she made of her family with her. A tsunami of horror crashed over Maji. How could Chandra ask a mother to leave her children? Didn't she think about the suffering it would cause those kids? Kids who had already had so much suffering. Wasn't the point of finding enlightenment to keep harm from others?

Chandra moved on to the next business in order and began asking Anicca about preparations for the upcoming retreat. Maji couldn't listen. All she wanted to do was run away. She couldn't get the kids' faces out of her mind. She thought about what Chandra said about her being a guru. It thrilled her to hear those words. It gave her clarity about her choice to be a nun. It filled her with a sense of purpose. She wanted to be a great master and uplift others. But the words "those aren't her real children" smashed that clarity like a hammer, shattering it into razor-sharp shards of doubt and confusion. Maji felt sick to her stomach.

After twenty more minutes, Chandra dismissed the monks and nuns and disappeared into her private room. They all walked back to the ashram in customary silence. The sun was just setting behind the mountains. Jaiman turned to face Parvati and Maji, walking side by side.

"It's a good thing you pre-made dinner, Parvati. With all our guests, if we started cooking now we wouldn't eat until midnight. I am happy to warm up the food, since you did the cooking."

"Wonderful. Thank you, Jaiman," Parvati said softly. Maji couldn't read her emotional state. She hoped it was better than her own.

Maji spoke up. "You know, I think I'm going to fast tonight. I had quite a big lunch, and I don't have any kitchen chores assigned today. I may just read this evening. It's been a busy day."

"Yes, it has, Karunamayi!" Jaiman smiled widely. "Of course. You enjoy your evening."

As the group neared the ashram, Maji saw the guests as well as the rest of the monastics file into the dining hall.

Parvati turned to her and smiled. "I'll see you later."

Maji turned towards the path to the nun's quarters. But then stopped and looked casually over her shoulder. She waited until the last person entered the dining hall, then quickly turned to walk up the road instead. She headed in the opposite direction of Chandra's house and turned at the end of the street up a narrower, less-used dirt road.

The sky was darkening. The night would keep her hidden, so she could be alone with the stars and whatever animals cared to join her on her journey. She wanted to walk, and walk, and walk until she emerged from the flurry of confusion that filled her head.

The trees grew thicker around her as she travelled. The beautiful peaks of the mountain range loomed overhead, a hint of snow brushing their tops. The snow glowed a soft purple as the sun sank lower.

As she stared up at the peaks, the silhouette of a bald eagle flew into her vision. Its sharp cry made her jump in delight as it soared across the sky. There was something in that cry like an offering. It pierced her heart, igniting a light that brought a comforting warmth. A sense of peace grew inside her. She sighed heavily just as the wind gusted around her, and she felt it carry her breath away. This was a force greater than her voice.

Chandra had told her to surrender her doubt. Perhaps it wasn't Chandra or the ashram life she had to surrender to, but to this greater power instead. Maji didn't know exactly what surrendering to a higher power looked like. Did she need to meditate more? Did she need to trust that something else would happen until it did?

Then, suddenly, the absurdity of her own thoughts struck her. Surrender wasn't about doing anything at all or thinking any certain way. It was literally about resting and letting that be okay. She laughed out loud at how hard she tried to make herself and her world perfect.

She sat right in the middle of the dirt road as a self-declaration of her surrender. A fleeting sense of peace washed over her, and she flopped back into the dirt onto her back, staring at the stars. Giggling, she began to move her arms and legs as if making a snow angel.

"Haha, I'm making a dirt angel!" She laughed as the red dust from the ground filled her nose and covered her pristine white clothes. Just as she surrendered, her starchy white robes surrendered to the dirt they collected. Maji laughed louder, feeling joy at the absurdity of it all. At that moment, that joy was all that mattered, and Maji felt grateful for it, even knowing the peace wouldn't last.

175

Will It To Be So

"Mama, what does it mean to pray?" Wolf Girl asked, stroking her mom's face as they snuggled next to each other on the couch. She felt the hollows of Mama's cheeks, her heart aching at how skinny the woman had become.

"Why do you ask about that, baby?"

"Well, my teacher told me she was praying for you. I don't even know what praying is, really."

Mama smiled and stroked Wolf Girl's cheek in exchange, mirroring her movements. Star lifted her head off her mother's chest, listening curiously. Justice lay sprawled on the floor with a book and looked up over her pages. Eamonn and Cloud sat on the other side of the room, lost in play and reading from the phone.

"Ah, my sweet love bug, yes, you do know how to pray. You've been doing it since you were little."

"What? How so?"

"Well..." Mama's brow creased in contemplation. "I suppose I should clarify. You haven't been praying in the traditional religious sense of the word. For example, in Christianity and Judaism, people pray by talking to God. If you were Muslim, you would pray five times a day as a ritual of purification and obedience to Allah. They have specific chants they use for that practice. In Hinduism, there are many types of prayer that are practices of devotion. Pagans pray to invite in the blessings of the gods."

Wolf Girl rolled her eyes in frustration.

"Well, yeah, I don't do any of that. So, what do you mean when you say I pray?"

Mama sat up straighter, disrupting Star's embrace. Her daughter glared at her with a pout.

"So, you know how I say you are really good at manifesting whatever you want? Like all the stuffies you said you would manifest when you were little? Well, you did that by proclaiming to the universe what you wanted; then, you allowed it to happen. You took action but also trusted in some larger power to bring it into existence for you. So, in a way, that's prayer. You aligned yourself with a greater power and trusted, with faith, that the power would deliver. You let yourself feel what it would be like to get what you asked for. It's physics more than anything, which in that sense is a really effective type of prayer. You didn't bother yourself with worrying about whether you were worthy of it or not. You just asked, then expected it with clarity. So, then you received it. Because in truth, our universe is founded in love. And we are that love. So, when we ask for something, the universe wants to give it to us. The trick is in asking clearly, which is the prayer. But most of the time, people don't ask clearly. They mix things up with complicated emotions. But when you were little, you just asked because it was all you knew to do. It worked most of the time, didn't it?"

Wolf Girl stared at Mama, thinking hard. Then realization dawned.

"So that's what my teacher is doing then! She's praying for you not to die and sitting back, waiting for it to happen? And this can work?"

Wolf Girl smacked her forehead, angry at herself for not using her superpower to save her mother. *I'm an idiot! I never even thought of that!*

Maji took her daughter's hand, her brow creased with concern. "Baby, prayer is a very powerful thing. And I'm so grateful for everyone that is praying for me! But just because it works sometimes, that doesn't mean it will work to save my life. I don't want you to think it's a fail-proof solution. Life is much more complicated than that. I don't want you angry at God or the universe--whatever you want to call it--if it doesn't work. There are always bigger things at play we can't see."

Wolf Girl thought back to the election Hillary Clinton had lost. She remembered how she had given up on her method of manifestation then, feeling stupid for even asking for something so big. She knew very well it didn't always work. But surely asking for Mama's life to be saved had to be the biggest, strongest wish any kid could ever ask of the universe, right? Her mother was certainly worthy of being saved.

She felt a deep pull in her chest. Her heart wanted to burst through her rib cage. She had to try! And she had to get as many others on board with her as she could.

"Yes, I know, Mama, but if there is any chance it may work, then we have to try!"

She looked at the other family members, all distracted by something else. Justice was reading, Star was snuggled up next to Maji with her eyes closed, Cloud was on the floor playing with her dolls, and Eamonn was lost in whatever he read on his phone.

Suddenly Wolf Girl grew angry, realizing none of them had been doing anything to stop Mama's death. She wouldn't have it anymore. She was going to pray, and wish, and imagine as much as she could if it killed her! She picked up a pillow and threw it at Justice, knocking her book out of her hand.

"Hey! What was that for?"

"We have work to do! Put the book down! Star, get off Mama! Cloud, put the horses down. Let's talk. Meet me in our room!"

The girls stared at Wolf Girl as if she had gone mad. She glared back, determination on her face.

"Come on, guys! Now!"

The three girls sighed and reluctantly pulled themselves up to meet their sister in the bedroom. When they arrived, she had seated herself on the floor with a whiteboard and marker resting in her lap.

"So why did you make us come in here?" Justice groaned, visibly annoyed.

"Okay, look, sit down," Wolf Girl motioned to the floor next to her, then popped the cap off her marker. The other girls sat down around her in a circle.

"So, Mama said prayer can work. I know it isn't definite, but we have to try!"

"Ok, great." Justice rolled her eyes in annoyance. "So we will pray for Maji. Can I go now?"

"No! Listen!" Wolf Girl leaned in close to the others, as if about to divulge an important secret. "Sure, we could pray and hope for the best. But Mama said it's like physics, right?"

"What's physics?" Cloud asked softly.

Wolf Girl shook her head in frustration. "I don't know, actually. But I do know that if we get as many people as possible to pray for Mama, then it will be more effective, right? That's basic science!"

The girls all nodded in agreement. Wolf Girl got excited.

"So, if it's more effective to have a lot of people praying for her, then it makes sense to assume that it would be even more effective to have people praying who are really close to her! Like, physically close to her."

Star 's face crumpled in disbelief. "So, you mean just put a bunch of people around Mama, praying and hoping she gets better?"

"Yes!" Wolf Girl beamed with pride. "That's exactly what I mean."

The girls stared at her blankly. Wolf Girl rolled her eyes at their lack of understanding.

"Guys, listen. What I mean is that we throw a prayer party! We'll invite anyone and everyone that cares about Mama! Think about it! She'll be surrounded by so many people who'll be wishing and praying for her to get better. How could that not work? Most everyone is vaccinated now, so we don't have to worry as much about COVID."

The girls nodded again, their eyes brightening at the idea.

"Do you really think we can fix Mama?" Star's eyes teared up.

Wolf Girl stared at her baby sister for a moment before pulling her into her lap and wrapping her arms around her. "Baby, I don't know for certain if it will work, but I do know we have to try. We can't just sit around and wait for her to die!"

A sad silence fell over the girls as the thought of Maji's death settled in their minds. A single tear rolled down Cloud's cheek. Justice reached over to her sister, drawing her into an embrace.

"Guys," Justice said, her eyes watering too as she stroked her sister's head. "We might really lose Maji. This might really be the end for her. I think the prayer party is a really good idea. But can we also agree not to waste any moment of Maji's life anymore?"

"What do you mean?" Cloud asked, sniffing.

"I mean, we spend so much time arguing with each other. I know it frustrates Maji and Daddy. And it's usually over some pretty stupid stuff! Can we agree to let it go and just be happy for her? Can we agree to be happy for each other, too? This is so hard. Let's not make it worse. Let's show Maji how much we love her and how much we love each other."

A sad smile crossed Wolf Girl's face. "You're right. Let's promise right now!"

Wolf Girl put her hand in the center of their circle. Justice followed, placing her own hand on top. Cloud and Star sat up and added their hands to the stack.

"We hereby promise to be the best kids to Mama, and the best sisters to each other!" Wolf Girl said with intense formality. "Do you so solemnly swear?"

"I swear!" said Justice, nodding her head firmly.

"I swear!" said Cloud, bouncing in excitement.

"I swear too!" said Star.

"We have all sworn! It's official!"

Wolf Girl smiled, snapping herself out of the melancholy. She picked up the whiteboard and handed it to Star to hold while she picked up the marker.

"Ok, let's make a list of everyone we can think of to invite!"

Thirty minutes later the four girls walked out of the bedroom and marched up to Eamonn. Wolf Girl shoved the whiteboard into his hands.

"What's this?" he asked. The girls smiled at him, pride gleaming in their eyes.

"We want to throw Maji a prayer party!" Wolf Girl beamed. "We want to invite everyone who loves her to come and pray for her to get better! This is the guest list we came up with!"

Eamonn's eyebrows shot up as he reviewed the long list. "I see! Well, this is a very thoughtful idea, but I think we should talk to Maji about it first, don't you think? A party is a big deal. We don't want to exhaust her. But it is a beautiful idea!"

The group brought the whiteboard in the living room where Mama was still seated on the couch, reading. She looked up in surprise.

"What's up, guys? You all look like you have something sneaky going on!"

Wolf Girl sat down next to her mom and laid the whiteboard in her lap.

"We want to throw you a prayer party and invite everyone in the world who is willing to come and pray for you! I hope--no, I *know this* will make you better, Mama!"

Mama looked at the hope dancing in her daughter's eyes. "That's a beautiful idea, Baby. I love it! Let's do it!"

Two weeks later, Maji sat in the same spot on the living room couch. This time, however, dozens of well-wishers surrounded her. She watched the guests laughing and sharing drinks: old friends, new friends, even a few high school friends that she hadn't spoken to in years. The timeline of her life presented itself before her as a rainbow of relationships. She sat quietly, studying each face and reliving the memories, a movie of her life.

Her children had planned this party with the hope it would save her. It was hope that was born from the innocence of childhood, and love, and imagination. This hope filled Maji with a sad sense of the beauty of love. It was beautiful how deeply they could love, and so painful what the loss of that love would bring them.

Her family had hope for her, but Maji knew already that her time was coming soon. It was as clear to her as the love she felt for her family. It was a knowing that came not from the symptoms she was feeling in her body, but from something bigger than any part she identified with as herself. It was as if she was already beginning to touch the other side of the veil. She could feel it calling to her. She pushed hard against this feeling, begging for more time. She wasn't ready to let go yet.

But as she felt the hope of her children, she realized what a gift this prayer party would be for all of them. They saw it as an opportunity to try to heal her. Maji saw it as a chance to say goodbye to all those she loved.

Suddenly, Parvati plopped down on the couch next to her, taking her hand. "Hey, sister!" she beamed.

Maji smiled warmly at her friend. Parvati's long red hair framed her face like a fire, and she was wearing a long tunic-style shirt with a white tiger face emblazoned across the front. Her old friend had softened over the years but never lost that fiery passion that Maji adored so much.

"Isn't this wonderful?" Maji smiled, gesturing around. "I feel like I have a front-row seat to all the memories of my life here."

Parvati smiled, patting her hand. "I see a few of your ex-boyfriends even showed up!" she giggled.

"Shhhh!" Maji laughed. "They might hear you and come over and try to talk to me! Let me just say my dying wish is to be left in peace!"

Parvati burst out laughing, sending Maji into a fit of giggles. The two women leaned into one another affectionately. Maji stared at her friend's face, recalling all the years they spent together as friends. First living as nuns, then being there for one another through marriage and motherhood, divorce, and now impending death. Parvati's eyes saddened as if she could hear Maji's thoughts.

"Look at all these people here praying for you," she whispered, tears watering the corners of her eyes. "It could work, you know. You have to believe it can."

Maji smiled, her throat tightening at her friend's sadness. "It would be amazing if it did, wouldn't it?"

She didn't want to engage Parvati in conversations about whether or not she would be making it through this or not. It seemed irrelevant at this point. And she no longer felt like she could, or should, have any input over the level of hope that those she loved did or did not hold on to. She saw more and more clearly that their paths were their own, including her children's. Whatever circuitous route they would take would be what it would be. As she came nearer and nearer to her inevitable demise, Maji recognized that there was never anyone in control to begin with. Things unfolded as they needed to, for everyone. All Maji could do was love them all and hope they could learn to trust, too.

"I have faith, sister!" Parvati beamed, clearly saying it more for her own peace of mind than Maji's. "I think you need a drink. This is a party after all, and the doctors said a drink or two wouldn't hurt!"

"Sure." Maji smiled as her friend leaped up and headed to the kitchen.

The dying woman returned to reminiscing as she stared at each of her friends, her heart full. Then, as she looked into a darkened corner on the opposite side of the room, her heart stopped cold at the sight of her grandfather--who had passed on twenty years prior. She blinked several times, trying to clear her vision, but he remained, smiling and looking around the room.

I've started hallucinating, Maji thought with dread. *I'm at this stage now.*

She kept her eyes firmly on him, observing his high-waisted tan pants and light blue polo, the style he had worn daily. She remembered his clothes so well. His white hair, which always had a tinge of yellow to it at the tips, was combed to the side as he'd worn it in life. His hands-- the hands that she had always admired for their strength and size--rested on his knees, the veins pronounced.

Her heart swelled with love and longing. She knew her mind conjured him now, in this moment of remembering. But he seemed so real it was hard to believe he wasn't.

Grandpa turned his head, looked her straight in the eyes, and smiled. Maji's heart began to pound loudly in her ears, drowning out the sound of the multiple conversations in the room.

He stood up, his knee jerking a little, causing him to do a small hop as he straightened up, another of his lifelong quirks. Maji held her breath. Grandpa turned and looked back at her over his shoulder, then walked toward the hallway leading to her bedroom. Before he rounded the corner, he turned around and beckoned to her.

Maji felt suspended for a moment, unsure how to act. She wasn't sure if following her hallucination would perpetuate the delusion or snap her back to sanity. But curiosity and longing got the best of her. She pulled herself off the couch, her body protesting the effort.

No one noticed her as she walked through the crowd, as if she moved in a protective bubble. She turned down the hall. She couldn't see her grandfather. *Perhaps he went into the bedroom.* She shook her head at the ridiculousness of the idea that a hallucination could actually go anywhere.

She turned into the bedroom and found it empty. Maji sighed. "Don't be stupid, Maji, he wasn't real."

She walked through the bedroom and into the open bathroom, then stopped in front of the mirror. Her face looked gaunt; her eyes sad. She put her hands to her pale cheeks. She looked closer to fifty. A stab of sadness struck her. *Fifty? I'll never see fifty.* She looked her reflection up and down. Her body was young. But age was not the determining factor of her fate.

She thought of the crowd of people in the other room, people who had featured as characters in the movie of her life. She thought of the various stories their lives wove together. Many of her friends and family had passed on before her. Some of them were quite young. She would be another who passed young.

Anger flashed in her mind, and she closed her eyes tightly, her hands balling up into fists. *No one wants to die young. No one. But for some, that's just their path.* This was Maji's mantra.

"This is just my path," she whispered, trying to focus on the swirling colors behind her eyelids to calm her down. Her anger settled into a dull acceptance. She took a deep breath and opened her eyes.

Standing behind her in the mirror was her grandpa.

Maji yelped in surprise, whirling around. "Grandpa!" she gasped. He stood calmly a few feet from her, a gentle smile on his face. She looked him over in disbelief. A small stain marred the collar of his shirt. His jaw had the hint of scratchy white stubble always present by evening time. She could smell his aftershave. She could see the liver spots on his hands, laid out in a familiar mosaic.

"Grandpa?" she gasped again, tears filling her eyes. "I'm hallucinating? You're not real?" She tried to make her words definitive statements, but the realness of his presence made them come out as questions.

His smile grew wider, and he chuckled lightly. Tears filled Maji's eyes as she heard his laugh, her favorite laugh in the world that sounded like soft rain.

"What is real, Maji?" he asked merrily. His mouth barely moved, but his words were loud and clear. Maji couldn't tell whether she heard them with her ears or her mind. "What is real in this world?" He reached out and took her hand.

Maji's tears spilled freely down her cheeks as she felt the warmth of his hand. Even as a grown woman, his hands were so much bigger than hers.

"Grandpa, you're here!" she gasped. "I feel you!"

She was a little girl again, ready to crawl into his lap and rest her head on his chest. She stepped forward and threw her arms around his neck, sobbing uncontrollably.

"There, there," he said softly, stroking her back. "Why so many tears?"

"I-I've missed you so much!" Maji took in his smell, the feel of his papery skin. "This can't be real, but it *feels* so real."

Grandpa chuckled again, bringing a smile to her lips. Her sobbing stopped. Maji didn't know if her mind was fooling her, or if he really stood here, but his presence filled her with a love and peace. The anger she had felt only moments ago was nothing but a distant dream. His reality or fiction no longer mattered.

Then she found herself asking the same question Grandpa asked her. *What is real in this world?* People claim whatever is real is what they perceive with their five senses. But that reality isn't the same reality for other creatures, such as hawks that can see a hundred times better, or dogs and bears that experience the world through smell, or trees that communicate through the fungal network in their roots. So much that is real to them is not real for humans.

Maji knew she was stepping over to the other side. She felt death pulling on her like a boat set loose from its anchor in the sea. Perhaps as she floated between life and death, her reality, her perception, had opened her to something else.

"Grandpa, I'm dying." Her voice caught in her throat. "Is that why you're here?"

He smiled again, his eyes filled with joy. He cocked his head to the side playfully and reached out, brushing Maji's cheek. "My youngest grandchild. What is it that dies?"

Maji smiled. She remembered how Grandpa spoke with her when she was a child. In his gentle humility, he rarely told her direct answers but guided her to find her own way. Grandpa taught her to probe, to explore as deeply as she could all her curiosities. Here he was doing it again. It brought her more joy than she could ever have imagined.

"I know it's just the body that dies, Grandpa. There is something else, our consciousness, our soul, that remains."

Grandpa's eyes went wide, his smile turning impish. "So, here I am with you! Yet my body died twenty years ago. How am I here?"

Maji thought about standing between life and death. "Is this my mind opening me to experience things on the other side of death? Isn't that where you are?"

"How can consciousness have a 'where'? If all things are of consciousness, how could 'I' be someplace other than everywhere?"

An etheric glow surrounded her, and she laughed. The room around her brightened as a soft light filled it. Maji felt weightless.

"But Grandpa, I do experience you as somewhere. And in this moment, you are here! All through life we experience others as separate individuals, not just nebulous consciousness. My children, oh, Grandpa, I have the most beautiful children, and I experience them as individuals, too! I do understand we are all made of consciousness. So, yes, as consciousness, you, me, them, are everywhere. But as Maji in this body, I am here, and you as you, Grandpa, in that body, you are there!"

She pointed to the floor where he stood. He playfully danced a jig on the spot, eliciting a giggle from his granddaughter.

"So, what is existence, then, that causes you to experience everyone as individuals? What is this thing you feel as so solid, so real? You are Maji, but what is Maji? What is Grandpa?"

Maji paused in contemplation. She looked deep into her grandpa's eyes. His eyes had always turned down at the outer corners, the expression people drew on sad characters. Yet the joy in those eyes contradicted the image. They were the same green she remembered. She saw the blood veins and the tinge of yellow from age in the whites.

The vastness of infinity engulfed her as she gazed into his eyes, as if she could fall into the blacks of his pupils and swim into space. As if she chased the impossible-to-find edges of the universe. A profound sense of awe filled her.

Then all of her perceptions collapsed inward. The blackness of his pupils shrank to pinpoints. Maji felt her sense of self compress into those pinpoints. Her mind folded in on itself, crumpled like a paper bag. All external sensory experiences and physical sensations disappeared. Her thoughts stopped. Everything around her vanished. A moment of panic gripped her. But then that too stopped, and Maji became the singular point in the blackness of her grandfather's eyes. She was stillness. She was void. She was held, suspended in a blank space of nothingness.

An urge to take a deep breath filled her, and she gasped. In one moment, she went from pinpoint small to an explosion of movement, like a star going supernova. She expanded outward, her breath a creative force that unfurled her world around her, a rebirth of the universe.

From her breath swirled out the sky and clouds, the Earth and ground beneath her. The walls and roof unfolded around her. She laughed as each lightbulb popped on to illuminate the room. Her eyes looked down for her body, and it was the search itself that brought it into existence, reformed from her own idea of herself. She turned her gaze upward, back into her grandpa's eyes, where he shimmered into existence once more, a creation of her desire. He smiled warmly, a knowing look in his eyes.

Then she understood. She remembered.

Wolf Girl looked around the house, trying to find Mama. She had seen her sitting in the living room with Parvati earlier, but several minutes had passed since then. The young girl hoped Mama was feeling alright and happy that all these people were here for her, but she also felt a certain sense of responsibility for the guest of honor at the party the girl had devised. *If it's too much, if too many people here have worn her out and made her feel worse...* That was the opposite of what she had wanted to accomplish. She grew angrier and angrier at herself.

"Mama left, and now she is going to get worse because of you, stupid!" Wolf Girl muttered to herself under her breath.

She turned down the hall and saw a light coming from her mother's door, which stood slightly ajar. Wolf Girl carefully pushed it open and saw Mama staring out the nearby bedroom window, eyes unfocused.

Oh my god, Mama is in one of her forgetting places again! This is all my fault!

She slunk over to the woman.

"Mama, are you okay?" she asked timidly, careful to not startle her.

Her mother didn't turn her gaze from the window, but reached back and grabbed her daughter's arm, pulling her around to wrap her in a tight embrace. Wolf Girl laughed in surprise.

"You-you're okay?" she asked again, uncertain. She looked up and saw Mama's eyes glistening with tears.

"My sweet girl, I'm so much better than okay. Thank you!"

"The party hasn't been too much for you, has it?"

"No, sweetheart, the party has been better than I ever could have expected. Thank you so much for thinking of it. It was an amazing idea!"

Wolf Girl perked up. A sense of relief washing over her. She breathed deep and buried her face in her mother's belly, relishing her softness and smell.

"You know what was an even better idea?" Mama asked.

"What?"

"You, Wolf Girl. You were the most incredible idea."

Wolf Girl laughed in puzzlement. Maybe Mama wasn't alright. Was this one of her weird phases again? It didn't seem like it. She wasn't spaced out. She was speaking clearly. "Idea? Me? Are you sure you're okay, Mama?"

Maji bent down and kissed the top of Wolf Girl's head, laughing. "Yes, baby, I'm doing great. Let's go out and enjoy the rest of the party."

She took her daughter's small hand and led her out the door back into the living room. Wolf Girl felt strength and energy in her grip that hadn't been there for some time.

Her heart lifted in hope again. Maybe the prayers were working! She squeezed her mother's hand tight. Perhaps this was a good idea after all.

Freedom

Maji stood in the ashram greenhouse, sweat pouring down her chest, soaking into the fabric of her white tunic between her breasts and down her arms from her armpits. The temperature was at least 90 degrees. She had spent the morning climbing ladders and hanging sticky tape around the high points of the greenhouse walls.

Her insect management was slowly working. But she had learned that an insect problem in a greenhouse is a long, slow marathon to conquer, not the quick sprint of managing an outdoor garden. Slowly but surely, things improved. But she still had some work to do. She mostly had the aphids under control now. The mealybugs and whiteflies were another story. She still had weeks to go of careful spraying with organic solutions, bringing in pest repellent plants, and hanging sticky tape to catch them mid-flight.

Maji looked around the greenhouse, pleased at the sight. Overhead towered the old fig tree that had grown there since the original owners planted it decades earlier. She knew that in its roots it carried the stories of generations of plants that had sprouted, nourished others, and died within this building. It was the mother tree of the greenhouse ecosystem, the foundation. It stood guard as the sentinel of the dome. Maji bowed to it with loving reverence.

Suddenly, Parvati burst into the greenhouse, the screen door slamming loudly with a bang as she ran into the sanctuary.

"Karunamayi, I have to talk to you!" she panted, out of breath. Maji was surprised to see the usually composed Frenchwoman so excited.

"Oh, okay! Is everything alright?".

"Yes and no." Parvati looked around to make sure no one else was within earshot. "Can we go talk in our bedroom? I want us to have some privacy."

"Uh, yeah, sure!"

The two women walked out of the dome and across the street to their house. Parvati followed Maji into the bedroom. The Frenchwoman quietly closed the door, then walked over to her bed and flopped backward onto her back, exhaling in a roar. Maji couldn't tell if the sound was from anger or relief.

"What's going on, sister?" Maji sat on her bed on the other side of the room. She peeled off her sweat-soaked dress, leaving her in just her bra and long skirt.

Parvati stared at the ceiling for a moment, then laughed. "Well, I have been practicing what Chandra told me to practice, which is acceptance," she said, turning her head to look at Maji. "And I have accepted the fact that I am in love with Gotam."

Maji's mouth dropped open in surprise. She never imagined Parvati falling for Gotam, especially not as a nun. She had seemed so dedicated to this path, to attaining enlightenment. Gotam and Parvati were both from France, but that was where their similarities ended. Not only was she ten years older than he, but she also possessed a maturity and sophistication the young monk didn't. While she spent her early adult years living in a castle as nobility, Gotam lived out of a bus, earning money with his guitar on street corners, and kept his hair in long dreadlocks. They couldn't be two more different people.

"Oh, my god," Maji squeaked. "Do you know if he feels the same?"

"Oh, yes." Parvati smiled, her eyes dancing. "Do you remember when he and I took those supplies out to Salt Lake City a couple of months ago for Chandra's retreat? On the drive home, we confessed our feelings for each other. Then, we stopped in a hotel and fucked each other's brains out."

Maji gasped. She couldn't believe it. Parvati spoke those words out loud so casually. The young nun always felt like she was being watched and judged in some way in the ashram, as if Chandra could see everything she thought and felt. Her roommate's confession within the sacred walls of their monastic home sounded an alarm in Maji's head, as if lightning was going to strike with the guru's wrath any minute. She looked around instinctively to make sure no one else was in the room.

"I can't believe that! I don't even know what to say. What does that mean for you both? Are you going to stay in the ashram?"

Parvati sat up, her face turning stone cold. "I feel like I have been living a lie for months now. This lifestyle doesn't make sense to me anymore. Chandra said to practice acceptance. Well, I accept that I don't see the point of renouncing all my desires. Isn't it just pretending? I feel like all we all do here is pretend to be these holy, enlightened beings that never take a shit or want to fuck. It's maddening! Chandra gives us Tantric meditations to do, but Tantra is supposed to be a wild acceptance of everything. So, I've done it. I've accepted it. And now I'm going to leave this ashram and accept those consequences, too!"

Maji stared at her friend, her eyes filling with tears. She felt her own fragile reasons for living this life begin to crack under Parvati's clear and strong declaration. She was right. They all pretended. At least Maji knew she was herself. But isn't that what they had to do before they became enlightened? Wasn't that why it was a practice until they finally figured it all out? And now her closest friend in this life was going to leave and tear a massive grief through her heart. The young woman suddenly felt completely unmoored. She jumped up and threw herself into Parvati's arms, tears flowing down her cheeks.

"Hey, sister." Parvati stroked her back. "It doesn't mean I'm leaving *you*. Gotam and I have found a place to stay in town until we figure out what's next. We can see each other anytime."

"I'm glad you'll be in town." Maji sniffed, pulling herself back from Parvati's embrace. "And I am happy for you, really. It's just confusing. I truly didn't see this coming. And to be honest, I've been questioning this life, too. I've just been afraid to admit it. Hearing you now makes me question it more. You have been an anchor for me. Now you're leaving, and honestly, I'm scared. I don't know what is right anymore. Chandra is our teacher and says this is right, but I don't feel it all the time. Isn't that our ego trying to trick us? Don't you wonder if that's what this is with Gotam? "

Parvati took Maji's hand, her eyes also filling with tears. "Of course, I wonder. But my heart feels clear. And how will we ever be true masters if we can't trust our own hearts? And yes, honestly, I'm scared, too." Her voice dropped to a whisper. "I've had nothing in this country but this ashram. I have no idea what will be next for me. It scares the shit out of me! So, I need you, too, okay? Don't you dare forget about me once I leave."

"I would never do that!"

The two women held each other in a long embrace before Parvati stood up.

"Wish me luck! Gotam and I are going to tell Jaiman right now! I just wanted you to know first."

"Good luck, sister. I have a feeling he won't be as happy for you as I am."

Parvati rolled her eyes. "I have a feeling you are right."

An hour later Maji stood alone on the side of the road and watched as Parvati and Gotam put their bags in the back of a taxi. Jaiman was furious with them and refused to even let them stay to eat lunch with the community. He said they had betrayed Chandra, and their energy would corrupt the sacred space of the ashram. They had to leave immediately.

The other monks and nuns said swift, curt goodbyes to them and disappeared into other parts of the ashram to complete their work for the day. Maji saw the pain in Parvati's eyes as the people she had spent the last year of her life living with dismissed her. *How is this considered compassionate and spiritual?*

Parvati turned to Maji and gave her a long hug.

"We will only be a few miles away. Try to come see me if you can. I know the others will make it hard for you."

"I will. I promise."

She then climbed into the backseat of the taxi with Gotam and drove off down the dirt road. Maji stared after them and watched her last shred of confidence drive away with them.

Weeks passed after the couple left the ashram, and Maji found that her roommate had been right about the others making it hard for her to visit them. She had been forbidden not only by Jaiman to go see them, but by Chandra as well.

Chandra's anger was palpable. She had all the monks and nuns gather in the office for a conference call and explained over the phone with venom in her voice what a betrayal it had been for the traitors to break their vows and leave the ashram. She went on and on about how lost they would be for lifetimes without her as their guru and how they had succumbed to lower vibrational desires.

Maji felt her throat constrict as she listened. Chandra's anger didn't feel like acceptance or compassion. It didn't feel like enlightenment. The young nun knew she had to keep up the expectation of the vows they had taken, but would they really be damned for lifetimes? People choose different paths. *People break vows. Don't half the marriages in the world end in divorce?* Did Chandra think those people would suffer for lifetimes, as well? It felt extreme. It felt like Chandra preached distorted borderline-cultish fundamentalism.

Maji's heart pounded in warning. Her confusion scraped at her insides like a frantic, caged animal. She looked around the room and saw the others with solemn looks on their faces. Many of them nodded in agreement with Chandra's harsh words. Maji suddenly felt extremely alone.

The next day was Thursday, their day of silence and freedom, and it couldn't have come at a better time. She let herself sleep in, then leaped out of bed with enthusiasm. She had a day planned for herself away from the ashram. She didn't care about keeping vows of silence or fasting. She was going to do what felt good for herself.

She went into the kitchen, made herself a sandwich, and packed some fruit in her backpack. She sang a song to herself as she strode out of the kitchen and across the ashram's courtyard. She was going to walk today, maybe even hike up into the hills if she had the energy for it. *I've got to get out of here for a while.* She longed for space where for a few moments she didn't have to be playing a role. She had forgotten what that felt like.

Maji made her way out of the ashram onto the dirt road leading west into the mountains. The day was bright, and the early fall morning had a crispness to it. Maji hiked up and around the winding dirt roads, climbing higher and higher. After about two miles, she headed north toward the Tibetan Buddhist stupa.

A stupa is a large Buddhist monument, built in a very specific pattern representative of enlightenment from the Buddhist perspective. The stupa there in Las Altas Ondas had been built thirty years earlier by a highly respected Tibetan leader and was a pilgrimage place for Buddhist practitioners in the west.

Maji always enjoyed going to the stupa. It had a very different feel from the ashram. Though many stupas were large enough to have rooms one could enter, this stupa was not, so visitors remained outside. The low number of patrons kept the place quiet. The building stood high on a hill and overlooked the entire valley. From one of the benches, one could see for at least 80 miles across the valley to the next mountain range. The stupa itself was clean and simple, painted a crisp white. Colorful prayer flags of white, red, yellow, blue, and green hung from poles and trees surrounding it. Maji felt both enlivened and serene there. The vast view of the valley and the open expanse of the sky gave her the sense of spaciousness she craved.

As she huffed her way up the hill and through the parking area, gratitude filled her at the place's emptiness. A soft breeze caused the colorful prayer flags to dance and wave a welcome to her. She waved back, giggling at her own silliness.

Upon arriving at the stupa, it was customary for visitors to perform the mindfulness practice of walking meditation by circling the stupa in silence. Maji had no interest in practicing that day. Every moment of her life felt like a practice. At that instant, she wasn't going to practice anything; she was just going to live.

She trotted over to the bench and chucked her backpack underneath it, her metal water bottle inside ringing from the impact like a gong. She flung herself onto the bench on her back and stared up at the clouds peacefully drifting through the bright, blue sky. She sighed heavily, her lips flapping noisily. The relaxed nature of the noise her lips made felt almost rebellious to the pure, pristine ways of a nun, and she liked that. She brought her forearm up to her mouth and began blowing loud, wet raspberries, letting the farting sound echo around her. She laughed delightfully as her fart symphony grew louder and louder. A small finch in a tree overhead cocked its head at her, and she turned towards it and blew as hard as she could on her arm, startling it away.

Maji laughed, feeling free for the first time in a while. She reached down for her backpack and fished inside for her sandwich. As she pulled it out, she noticed the colorful reflection of the prayer flags glinting off the plastic bag it was wrapped in. It swirled colorfully as she moved the bag. She paused for a moment, looking at the colors. The shine, the rainbow effect, like a work of art. An accidental mosaic. Maji wished she had a camera to capture it and preserve the beauty of it.

Then the flaws in that idea struck her. What was beautiful was the perfect mingling of light and color in such a simple everyday object as a plastic bag to create something so beautiful. It was spontaneous and uncontrived. Trying to preserve that would be like trying to capture the wind in a bottle. It was the happening of it that was miraculous. It was the noticing of it that made it astonishing.

Maji looked up from her colorful plastic bag and considered everything around that she could see as spontaneous and uncontrived. The gnarled branches of the trees that reminded her of old man's arms, the random cracks in the paving stones that looked like a river map, the synchronized way the flags blew like a wave from the rolling breeze--all of this spoke to her of unplanned in-the-moment occurrence. The synchronized chaos of it all struck her with an ironic sense of dichotomy. Random perfection.

Suddenly, in a blink, as her eyes landed on a scrubby bush fifty feet away from her, she lost all sense of her localized self. In a moment, Maji as an individual completely disappeared. Her five senses lost all meaning. She experienced herself as everything. She was the grass she looked at. She was the sky and the clouds. She was the stupa. The feeling differed from her vision quest, when she had merely experienced feeling and connection to everything. No, this went beyond that. This was stepping outside of anything whatsoever she could identify with and becoming the entire universe. She went beyond feeling and seeing. Her conscious awareness encompassed existence as a whole, and both her body and the intangibility of its borders joined in her awareness. She had gone from being the wave to being the ocean. The dichotomy of chaotic perfection she had recognized became clear and simple in that it was all one and the same. It was her, as all of existence. It was perfection. It couldn't deviate from that, because it was all that existed.

Maji hovered in perfect calm in that state, being the all. There was no other way to exist. Then, as she took a breath, her awareness compressed back into a localized sense of individual self, as quickly as a camera angle changes in a movie. Maji looked around, feeling the shift, registering her body and the "otherness" of everything else. It was so simple, the shift. So subtle yet so profound, another dichotomy that existed in this all-encompassing whole of creation. She had no idea how long the experience lasted. It didn't matter, because in that state time didn't exist as anything other than another experience of the senses.

Maji laughed as loud and hard as she could. She fell on the ground and rolled back and forth, gripping her tiny individual body in a glorious, outrageous hug until tears flowed down her cheeks. Unbelievable calm and joy filled her.

The nun looked down at her white robes and felt the emptiness and meaninglessness of her holy uniform. She realized she didn't even care that it was meaningless. It was what it was. She felt a simplicity to being alive. All the struggle, the trying, the pretending, the ritual, the clothes, the names, the fights, the ways she tried to bend herself into some preconceived idea of enlightenment, were completely unnecessary. Because when she experienced herself as all of creation, she recognized there was never anything else she had to be. She was the all. And as the all, she played a delightful game called "Maji." In this game, she searched and bent and conformed herself to the idea of a thing called "enlightenment", but that, too, was just a concept. She could never be anything more or less than the perfection of the all.

She laughed at the irony of it. She had worked so hard and did all the things she thought would get her to a certain state of spiritual development, when the fact was that she never needed to do any of it. The circular nature of it all was so ridiculous, so hilarious, that she split her sides laughing.

Maji sat up, feeling more relaxed than she ever had in her entire life. All she had to do was relax. She looked down, noticing the sandwich still in her hand. She unwrapped it and took slow bites, savoring the beauty of taste in her mouth and the feeling of the bread between her cheeks. She felt utterly delighted to be alive, experiencing the world through her senses.

After she finished her sandwich, she stood and walked back to the ashram. She had taken a journey across the universe and back. In temporal reality, she knew she had only been gone a little more than an hour. But her quest was over. She no longer had to seek. She had become Dorothy in the *Wizard of Oz* realizing she had the power to return home at any time. It just took the journey to get to that place.

After that day, Maji no longer felt confused. She felt startling clarity and calm in everything she did. She went through her daily routine, observing herself. Like an audience member at an entertaining interactive play, she watched the troubling emotions of confusion, annoyance, anger, and sadness pop up from time to time in her psyche. But she remained a detached witness to the experience. Her life was nothing more than a line of dominoes. One moment fell into the next, and the next, and the next. There was nothing to hang on to because each moment would end and each new one would occur. She didn't have to worry any longer about what would come, because it would come no matter what.

She watched herself go through the motions of the meditation practices, of the rituals of the ashram. She no longer felt that they were a thing she had to do to accomplish something. There was nothing to accomplish. So, she watched the show unfold in the awareness that she was the one creating it. She knew Chandra had built the ashram for people to practice and strive and try to reach enlightenment. Maji almost laughed out loud sometimes during the practices when she saw the amount of striving within the community. She wanted to tell everyone that all they had to do was relax. There was no place to go. But in her experience, the ashram life was the opposite of relaxing.

Several weeks after her experience at the stupa the day arrived when Maji realized she could no longer stay. She had spent the morning finishing up office work and headed over to the greenhouse to plant some lettuce seeds.

She walked through the door of the rounded dome, and she stopped dead at what she saw, a wave of horror and confusion crashing over her. The entire greenhouse was empty. All the plants had been ripped out and lay withered and dying in heaps on the floor. Her tomato plants, kale, chard, spinach, and beans. Someone had knocked down the rows of corn. The cucumbers, cabbage, and carrots had been yanked out before they could grow to maturity. Even the nasturtium and marigolds were pulled out by their roots. The only thing left standing was the giant fig tree. It towered over her, naked around its trunk where the other plants had once been.

The soil looked wet and angry, and a stench of chemical pesticide hung in the air. To Maji, it smelled like death. All around her, the last year she spent tending, balancing, listening, and nurturing, was destroyed. The plants she had grown in harmony, the delicate ecosystem she nurtured, lay dead at her feet. A tsunami of sadness crashed over her, and she fell to her knees, tears spilling down her cheeks.

"I'm so sorry," she sobbed to the greenhouse. "This shouldn't have happened."

Wiping the tears from her face, she turned and marched solemnly to Jaiman's office. He turned to her with a smile as she opened the door.

"Hello, Karunamayi! Om Jai Maa!" he spun his chair back to face his computer screen.

"Jaiman, I was just in the greenhouse." Maji crossed her arms and waited for an explanation.

Jaiman registered her anger and turned his head slightly to give a phony smile of placation. "Ah yes, I meant to tell you earlier and it completely slipped my mind! I spoke with Chandra about the insect problem in the greenhouse. She told me we should just take everything out, spray it down with pesticides, and start over new. Two of the visiting community members were looking for some volunteer work this morning, so I sent them over there to take care of it.

They did a very thorough job."

"You do realize that thirty years of organic care in that greenhouse was just destroyed? The soil is most likely ruined now and certainly filled with poisons." Maji's voice stayed flat.

"Yes, but it was what Chandra wanted, and she knows best."

"I don't think she does know best!" Maji barked. Jaiman's face fell in confusion. Those words were practically blasphemous.

"Karunamayi, well…" he stammered. "It's a new start, a fresh beginning. Just imagine the possibility now of starting over! You can create whatever you want now without any hindrances. Chandra knew that."

Maji thought about his words. Maybe Chandra did know that. This was the game, she remembered, playing out in front of her. The destruction was a message. The greenhouse had been her attempt at creating an enlightened ecosystem while simultaneously trying to enlighten herself. Now it was over, and the message was loud and clear.

"Jaiman, it's time for me to go."

"Yes, alright. I knew you would understand. I will see you at lunch."

"No, Jaiman, I mean it's time for me to leave the ashram."

He whirled around in his chair and stared at her in shock.

"Because of the greenhouse? Don't you think that's extreme? You're just reacting from an emotional place."

"It isn't because of the greenhouse, Jaiman. The greenhouse just pointed me to the right time."

Maji wanted to stay honest with herself. The nun lifestyle, the ritual, the spiritual name, the hours and hours of meditation no longer held deep meaning or value to her. And the young woman knew it wouldn't help her or anyone else if she stayed. The message was clear. It was time to create something new. "I don't want to anger anyone, not you, not Chandra, but this doesn't make sense to me anymore." She sighed.

"Karunamayi, I can't support this decision. You took a vow and made a commitment to Chandra. This is out of integrity and is coming from a lower vibration. I suggest you really reexamine your choice here."

"Thank you, Jaiman. I appreciate your perspective. But I disagree. To stay would be out of integrity with myself. I'm sorry. I will go pack my things."

Jaiman's face grew red with anger and embarrassment as Maji stood to leave. She stopped before walking out the door.

"I will write Chandra an email. Thank you for everything, Jaiman. I really do appreciate it."

An hour later, she went to Parvati and Gotam's small apartment. They welcomed her with open arms and offered to let her stay until she figured out her next steps. She remained only a few days before she found a free place to house-sit for a few months in Boulder.

The transition wasn't as easy as she expected. As she'd suspected, Chandra's entire community ostracized her. The guru was beyond furious and refused to speak with her again. Maji only learned this from community members who went out of their way to contact her and

208

tell her how disappointed in her they were. Despite their harsh words, she saw clearly why she made her choice and still was able to laugh at the game.

Though she knew she was playing the game called "Maji," it took her two more years to figure out how she wanted that game to continue. She had played the role of Karunamayi Amba Brahmacharini so well, she didn't remember who Maji was before. But she also knew she couldn't be the Maji she had been. The dominoes in the line of her life had fallen, and now she had to follow this new path.

The twenty-seven-year-old decided to go back to school and finish her degree. She had a new future to create, and education would help her piece together her life in a way that could aid others. Maybe Maji could reinvent herself through intellect and academia.

While at school, she met a handsome man who shared her passion for nature and the spiritual path. A friendship began between them as they shared several classes, and soon Maji found herself spending almost every day with him.

Together, they spoke about freedom and practicing wild acceptance. They made passionate love and took long hikes. They read ancient books on cosmology and philosophy. They studied and shared epiphanies of profound insight. She told him about the game, and how they were all players, how they were all one. He listened, and she felt like he understood. She fell completely, totally, utterly in love. She had never felt such a delicious, amazing, romantic adoration before. He was a gift. She could build a life with him. She gave herself to him completely.

But he didn't want all of her. The intensity scared him. He pushed her away. He grew angry at her for no reason, saw her as the source of all the pain in his life. Maji didn't understand why. She gave more of herself. He pushed her away harder. Then he pulled her back in, hungry for love but unsure how to receive it. She didn't know herself anymore. She remembered this was a game, but the game was no longer clear. It was painful and confusing.

After a year of this painful dance, he finally pushed her away for good. One week after he broke her heart and told her it was over, Maji found out she was pregnant. The birth control had failed. This part of the game became serious.

She marveled at the miracle she felt growing inside of her. She felt it there before she peed on the pregnancy test. It was as if a lightbulb turned on inside of her. She knew it was a girl. A powerful love grew inside her. A protective instinct rose, and at the same time, an incredible sadness. She didn't know how he would react.

He was enraged when she told him. He screamed at her as she cowered on the couch, her hands wrapped protectively around her belly. He punched the wall above her head repeatedly until she agreed, through tears, to get an abortion. How could she bring a child into the world alone? She was a college student. He would make her life a nightmare. She didn't want this part of the game, but here it was.

At the clinic, her stomach fluttered with the nausea of morning sickness. The little life inside her flipped and twirled, a warm light pulsing. She broke down in tears and sobbed in the nurse's arms.

"You don't have to do this," the nurse said calmly, patting Maji on her back. She looked over the nurse's shoulder at her ex-boyfriend, sitting there in the chair next to her with venom in his eyes. She was terrified. She felt like she had no choice. He didn't want to give her one.

"Yes, I do," Maji whispered.

On the table, the doctor spread her legs and shoved the cold, hard metal scapula inside of her.

"Take a deep breath. This will only take a minute."

The nurse who held Maji while she cried now squeezed her hand tightly. Searing pain ripped through her, and Maji felt all the muscles in her abdomen seize up. Violence raged inside her. Her body screamed in horror. The light of the tiny life went out like a puff of smoke. She felt death inside of her. Her body shook uncontrollably for several minutes, the nurse squeezing her hand tightly as Maji sobbed through deep, racking breaths. A deep blackness impressed itself on her mind. The protective instinct inside of her wailed in agony and failure. Sadness filled the empty space in her womb and consumed her.

It was then that Maji forgot it was a game.

<u>Expatriate</u>

After the abortion, pain filled Maji's shrinking being. She became the embodiment of failure, forgot perfection, and spent most of her days trying to remember why being alive was a good thing. She desperately tried to recall what hope felt like, the knowledge of the game. She failed. She woke up in the mornings to flashbacks of that ripping feeling in her womb, of death inside her body. It haunted her throughout each day.

Maji had always been pro-choice, and she still was. But she no longer felt that when the subject was raised, she could thrust her fist in the air in feminist solidarity. Instead, she could only offer a bowed head and hand on her heart in recognition of the complicated, painful experience of choosing the life or death of your unborn child.

Meaning vanished from her life. She continued with her studies because doing so was the only thing that made sense anymore. But she had become a walking, hollow shell, blankly going through the motions.

When graduation came a year later, she celebrated with relieved accomplishment, and also the realization that she could now escape the place that reminded her of her ongoing pain. She found a new purpose, which was to run, to go someplace as foreign and strange to her as anything she could imagine so she could wipe the slate clean and start a new life. She wanted to exist in a new universe. She wanted to be a new Maji.

The new graduate found a job teaching English to business professionals in Santiago, Chile. She didn't speak a word of Spanish but didn't care. In her mind, the more foreign to her, the better. She would reinvent herself through learning a new language.

She found herself once again selling almost everything she owned, keeping only what would fit in the two suitcases she would bring with her on the plane. She found a host family with an adult son who spoke English and was willing to be her guide for a while until she learned enough Spanish to get around. The school that hired her had an English-speaking director who dealt with foreign teachers regularly. That was all the preparation she needed. She trusted everything else would fall into place, but didn't care much if it didn't. All she knew was that this was what she had to do.

The morning she got off the plane in Santiago after more than 16 hours of flights and layovers, she was met by her host's charismatic son, Alfonso. In the sea of dark-skinned, black-haired Latinos that surrounded her at the airport, he stood out with his flaming red hair and neon-colored shirt.

"You're Maji, yes?" He rushed up to her and kissed her on the cheek before she could answer. "Welcome to Chile!"

"Thank you, Alfonso!" She smiled, flushed and surprised.

"Oh, everyone kisses hello here in Chile--you'll see. It's very different from the US." He tossed these words over his shoulder as he turned to rush out the doors of the airport, both of her suitcases in his hands.

"Have you been to the US before?"

"Oh, yeah, I lived in Vermont for two years. I was a videographer at a ski resort up there. It was great! But it took a little getting used to. *Gringolandia* is a cold place, and I don't mean the weather!"

"Gringolandia?"

"Yeah, you know." Alfonso laughed. "Where all the Gringos live!"

Maji chuckled in response. Alfonso brought her through the parking lot to a small car that looked, to Maji, to be the size of a roller skate. Her two bags took up the entire back seat. Looking around the parking lot, she noticed that all the cars were significantly smaller than the ones in the US.

On the drive to her new host home, Alfonso talked her ear off about Chile, and specifically Santiago. She learned about the current government, the economy, and the methods to navigate the complicated bus and subway system of the sprawling urban metropolis. The largest city Maji had lived near was Denver, and Santiago was at least four times the size of it. She gazed through the window in awe as the buildings went on and on. Most impressive were the towering mountains that surrounded the city, dwarfing the peaks that formed Denver's backdrop.

They arrived at the apartment in the affluent section of the city to find it empty. Alfonso said his parents would arrive later in the day, then told Maji to change into a swimsuit.

"Let's take a swim. The pool is on the roof. It's fucking hot!"

Maji was sweating through her jeans and a swim sounded nice. It was a bit of a shock to her system, given that there had been snow on the ground in Colorado when she left. But it was a different season there in the southern hemisphere. She smiled. *I'll get two whole summers here.*

Maji slipped into her bikini and met Alfonso by the front door. He led her up the elevator and through a door onto the roof patio. As he opened the door, they were met with cheers by a group of perhaps fifteen young men and women who appeared to be in their late twenties. They all relaxed around the pool, beers in their hands. Alfonso laughed at Maji's look of surprise.

"I called all my friends and told them a Gringa was going to be living in my apartment. They all want to check you out!"

Maji felt her face turn red as one by one each of Alfonso's friends walked over and kissed Maji on the cheek with the words "*mucho gusto.*" She soon learned that almost none of them spoke English. Alfonso informed her that the language wasn't as necessary down in Chile. People studied it in high school, but they were so far from any English-speaking countries that it wasn't as common as it would be in Spanish-speaking countries that shared a border with the US, such as Mexico.

Her guide and his friends chatted happily around the yankee as she sat in silence, unable to understand much of anything. Her silence held a sense of relief. She didn't have to answer any questions about who she was. She didn't have to show up and be anything other than herself, in her own skin, sitting there as something to look at. She could relax in her foreign solitude.

After about thirty minutes, a young man with a round nose and kind eyes walked over and sat next to her by the side of the pool.

"Hello, I'm Xavier," he said in a thick accent. "It's nice to meet you."

"*Hola, Xavier,*" Maji said in slow Spanish. "*¡Mucho gusto!*"

Xavier laughed at her attempt to speak his language but continued in his own broken English.

"I hope you will like Chile. It's a good country. We have good wine and good people. You see!"

"Well, I've only been here for a few hours, and I feel so welcome already!" Maji smiled, looking around at the spontaneous party going on around her. "I haven't tried the wine yet, but I hear it's nice."

Xavier laughed out loud, slapping his knee.

"Oh, you are in Chile. You try it!" He turned to the others close by and said something in a flurry of Spanish which caused them all to burst out laughing. Maji looked at Xavier in confusion.

"Ah, no worry," he said. "You try wine tonight!"

After the pool party, Maji met her host parents. They didn't speak even the most basic English, but were very warm and welcoming to her through Alfonso's translation. They showed her to her room and left her to rest for a short while. Maji lay on the bed, and after what felt like just a few moments, she heard a gentle knock on the door.

"Maji!" Alfonso sang through the closed entryway. "It's dinner time! Time to come out and meet the rest of the family!"

Maji blinked, bleary-eyed and exhausted. She didn't know there was a "rest of the family" to meet. When she walked out the door and down the hall to the dining room, she was surprised to see eight more people in the room besides Alfonso and his parents. Alfonso introduced her to his older sister, her husband and two children, two of his cousins, and an aunt and uncle.

"Did they all want to meet me, too?" she asked him after the customary kisses were exchanged.

"Of course!" he said. "And we always get together for weekend dinners, so you aren't the only reason."

Throughout the meal, Maji sat in silence as the conversation carried on in Spanish without her. Occasionally, Alfonso translated, and sometimes one of the family members asked her a question through Alfonso for translation. But mostly the "Gringa" kept quiet and watched everything from a distance, her mind savoring the opportunity to watch it all, like a movie. It was much easier to be emotionally detached from all these strangers and foreign conversations. She felt relieved.

After dinner, Maji returned to her room, aching to rest. Just as she was about to change her clothes, Alfonso knocked on the door again.

"Maji! It's time to go!"

"Go? Where are we going?"

"To meet our friends! It is Saturday, you know! That's one of the best nights of the week in the city."

Maji sighed, shaking her head to wake up. She already felt drained from all the newness of her situation and the jet lag, but she didn't want to be rude. She quickly brushed her hair and grabbed her purse.

Her guide drove her only a few miles to an even more affluent part of the city. The houses were still much smaller than what was normal in the US, but the quality of the landscaping and decor marked them as high-end.

Alfonso walked her through the door of a modern two-story house. Through the entryway, Maji could see a pool lit up by blue light in the backyard. Alfonso explained that this was Margarita's house, a long-time friend of his. She lived there with her parents and brother.

Almost all of Alfonso's friends live with their parents, just like him. This realization gave her a first taste of culture shock. As someone in her late twenties, Maji could never imagine living with her parents. She had left home when she was eighteen years old after graduating high school and never looked back. She valued her alone time and freedom far too much. But from what she gathered, none of these people had ever left their parent's' houses. They slept in the same beds they had been in since they were kids. It boggled her mind. Didn't they feel oppressed? Didn't they feel like children? But if it was the cultural norm, who was she to judge?

When they walked into the house, the same group of friends that had partied at the pool gathered around a large dining table on the porch. They all held filled wine glasses and smoked cigarettes. The air was thick with tobacco smoke. Maji coughed as she entered.

Margarita jumped out of her chair and rushed over to Maji, her long, blond-streaked brown hair bouncing across her shoulders. She kissed her guest fiercely on the cheek before saying in a heavy accent, "Welcome to my house, Gringa!"

Maji laughed as Margarita took her by the arm and ushered her to a chair. She then placed a wine glass in front of her and filled it to the top.

"Now, wine!" Margarita laughed.

Xavier sat a couple of seats down from Maji. He leaned forward with a broad smile. "I tell them you try Chilean wine tonight! There is many bottles for drink!"

Maji blushed as all eyes were on her. She picked up the glass, careful not to spill, and took a small sip. The room was silent as they waited for a reaction from her. "It's delicious," she smiled.

Alfonso said some rapid words in Spanish, and everyone cheered. He patted the Gringa heartily on the back. Then the room erupted in conversation, and Maji was once again left with her thoughts.

After a few minutes, Xavier pulled his chair close to Maji. His kind eyes and warm smile put her at ease. After speaking with him for about twenty minutes, she realized he knew even less English than she had first thought, but his effort to understand and communicate charmed her.

"I have a motorcycle," he said. "I drive you already city?"

"What?" Maji asked, giggling. The wine was going to her head, and Xavier's broken English grew more difficult to understand. Alfonso had been eavesdropping and leaned over to elaborate.

"He wants to give you a tour of the city on his motorcycle," he said, his words slurring with tipsiness. "I would say no, that I wouldn't allow it, but he is my best friend, so I approve."

"You wouldn't allow it?" Maji asked in disgust, her eyebrows shooting up. "Excuse me?"

"It's a joke, girl! Don't worry, I know you are a strong, independent woman, blah blah blah. We aren't so machismo here in Chile. Don't confuse us with Mexican men."

Maji laughed at his jab.

Margarita stood, grabbed a wine bottle, and filled Maji's glass to the top once more. "*Mas vino*, Maji! *Tienes que celebrar como un Chileno*!"

The group cheered again, clinking glasses as Maji raised hers to her lips once more. She had never been much of a drinker, and she really hadn't had alcohol at all since before she had gone to live in the ashram. The effects were intense, and she felt her head beginning to spin.

Well, when in Rome!

The evening went on, and as the group drank more, she noticed they grew more outgoing in their attempts to speak to her in broken English. Maji, in turn, found herself more open to trying what little Spanish she knew. They all spoke haltingly with one another and erupted into laughter often at their failed communication. Every time she emptied her glass, Margarita cheered and filled it to the top again, the group cheering with her for Maji to drink more. As they all laughed and dissolved into uninhibited merriment, the yankee began to realize drunkenness was a universal language within itself.

By midnight, Maji's vision doubled. She felt herself swaying in her chair until she realized everyone was getting up around her.

"Is it time to go home, Alfonso?" she asked, her words badly slurring.

"Home?" Alfonso guffawed, his eyes unfocused. "No, the night is just starting! It's time to go out! This was just a warm-up!"

Maji groaned. She couldn't believe the amount of social energy the Chileans had. Already, on her very first day in the country, she had engaged in more social events than she usually would in weeks back home in the US. To everyone around her, this seemed perfectly normal. Maji was dragging, aching for bed.

"Alfonso, I don't know if I can do it."

He took her arm, swaying with her in drunkenness. "It's all good, Maji. Some dancing will straighten you right up."

Maji didn't know whose car they piled in. The streetlights blurred outside the windows as they drove. All she heard was slurred, drunken Spanish. Her eyes began to close until finally the car came to a stop, and they all stumbled out into the parking lot of a club. Alfonso grabbed her arm and dragged her through a bright red door surrounded by flashing neon lights. Inside the club, reggaeton music blared over the speakers. Bodies swirled and jerked in a flurry of movement on the dance floor.

Maji didn't remember putting her purse down. All she knew was that at some point she was spinning and twirling along with Alfonso and Xavier at her side. At another point in time, she looked down and saw another wine glass in her hand. Her lungs burned from the heavily smoke-filled air.

Does every person in Chile smoke? she thought, coughing.

The night pulsed with blurred colors and pungent smells of sweat, smoke, and alcohol. The sounds of music and Spanish melded together into a thunderous drone in Maji's head. A penetrating sense of fatigue overwhelmed her. Her legs wobbled and her muscles ached. Eventually, she sat in a chair and put her head down on her arms on a table. Then everything went dark.

The next day the Gringa woke up in her bed, still dressed from the night before, reeking of stale cigarette smoke and sickeningly sweet wine. Maji's head rolled and pounded like thunder. Her stomach lurched, and she thought she would puke. She stumbled to the bathroom and landed on her knees in front of the toilet. Her stomach surged, and its contents spewed into the bowl. Her body ached all over. She felt sicker than she had in years. Her throat ached and her voice rasped from all the cigarette smoke she'd breathed the night before.

She looked across the room at the clock on her bedside table. It was 1:18 p.m. After less than thirty-six hours in Chile, she was already wrung out and hung up to dry. *What have I gotten myself into?*

All she wanted to do was curl up in bed and watch a movie. Then she remembered all the movies there were in Spanish. She also realized she couldn't hide from her host family. They would be expecting her to eat dinner with them.

Maji felt exhausted physically and emotionally. Tears filled her eyes. She took a deep breath, calling on her inner reserves for strength. "You signed up for this, so you make the best of it!" she scolded herself. Then, she curled up in a ball on the bathroom floor and fell asleep.

After a few weeks, Maji began to feel more settled in Santiago. She began taking Spanish classes at the school where she taught and slowly became more comfortable in trying to speak and understand this new language. She made it a priority to learn how to politely turn down a drink in Spanish. She started her job and found she really enjoyed teaching adults. Commuting around the city, however, was a different experience altogether.

In the morning, Maji had to take a bus to the subway, then take the underground train for twenty minutes, then take another bus to her school's headquarters. Once she picked up her curriculum for the day, she would take yet another bus or subway ride to a different part of the city where her class would ensue. She often felt like a sheep being corralled into different pens as she went from bus to train to bus again. The endless commute stretched her workdays into ten- and eleven-hour days. Maji found herself getting home well after 7:00 p.m, completely exhausted. Thankfully, the Chilean custom was to eat dinner at 8:00 or later, so at least she was able to have a hot meal.

The sheer amount of people who surrounded her at all times overwhelmed her. She often looked longingly out the bus window at the mountains, wondering when she would get a chance to hike. But no buses went to the rural mountain trails, and from what Maji could tell, hiking wasn't as popular of an activity in Santiago as it had been in Colorado. When she asked her host mother about it, she laughed.

"Why would you want to go into the mountains? They're too tall! The weather gets so extreme!"

Finally, after a month, Maji took up Xavier's offer of a city tour. She had spent time with him on weekends while out with Alfonso, and often her new friend showed up unexpectedly for dinner on weeknights. Alfonso and his family seemed accustomed to this, and always welcomed him with casual familiarity.

Maji and Xavier found a natural rhythm of communication, alternating between his broken English and her broken Spanish. He was very patient with her and helped her find words she didn't know. He ended up being one of the best Spanish teachers she could have, and was patient and kind, a true friend that she could rely on in this strange country.

On this sunny Saturday, Maji trepidatiously climbed onto the back of Xavier's brown Yamaha motorcycle. He assured her he had been driving hogs since he was a kid, so she was in safe hands. But she soon learned that driving a motorcycle in Chile was very different from in the US.

Xavier spent more time driving up the center line of lanes than he did in the lanes themselves. He navigated between the cars with ease, despite the stop-and-go traffic. Chileans used their horns heavily, so a constant drone of honks formed the background of their rides. Xavier followed suit and hit his horn at least a dozen times per minute announcing their presence. Maji clung tightly to his waist, holding her breath as he zipped through the city streets.

Besides the white-knuckled driving, Maji thoroughly enjoyed her days with Xavier. In one day he took her to Santiago's Contemporary Art Museum and the Arts District, they had lunch at a delicious Peruvian restaurant, and Maji learned that Peruvian food was far more interesting than Chilean cuisine. Then after lunch, he told her to hop on the bike for a surprise.

They began to make their way through a part of the city Maji had never been to before. After about 45 minutes, they pulled into a parking lot and Maji saw signs for a hiking trail.

"Are you taking me hiking?" Maji asked excitedly.

"Hiking?" Xavier asked, not understanding the word.

"Trekking," Maji said, remembering the Spanish word.

"Yes! Trekking! You say you trek *mucho.*" Xavier pulled the bike to a stop.

A man in an orange vest walked over to them, and Xavier handed him some pesos.

"It costs money to hike?" Maji asked.

"Yes, it helps the economy. Good jobs and pays to protect the land."

Maji clapped her hands, a wide smile on her face. She breathed a sigh of relief at the near-emptiness of the parking lot. The Gringa still struggled with the amount of extroversion required in this country, so every break she could get was welcome.

Maji, who was used to climbing thousands of feet in altitude in Colorado, found the hike effortless .. *There have to be more difficult hikes here. The mountains are so tall!* But the amount of exertion on Xavier's face coupled with his heavy breathing showed he hadn't "trekked" much. *What a sweet guy, to do this!*

After that day, Xavier began driving Maji to work almost every morning. This saved her almost a half hour in commuting time. The happy conversation with Xavier was much better than a silent bus ride.

After two months, Maji's time at her host family's home ended. She found a shared house in a nice neighborhood a little closer to work. She had two roommates her age who spoke a minimal amount of English. None of them saw each other very much. They all worked incredibly long days in the city, which was the norm. But for the first time since she had arrived, Maji finally felt like an adult again, with her own space. She was able to relax and try to create some sense of home. Everything was still so new and foreign, and Maji realized much of her identity had now transformed into Maji the Expatriate, a unique Gringa unicorn with all sorts of philosophies and cultural norms strange and exotic to the locals.

The yankee had learned to love many things about Chile. She loved everyone's warmth, though it exhausted her. A sense of community prevailed here that she'd never experienced in the United States, a culture focused on individuality and personal freedoms. The connection between friends and family inspired her. She learned to love Chilean wine and found herself drinking a glass of it almost every night at dinner. And she learned to love speaking Spanish. It forced her to use her brain in a way she never had before. The sentence structure, descriptions, expressions, and heavy Chilean slang challenged her to see the world in a new way.

She appreciated that in every upper-middle-class family, like Xavier's and Alfonso's, housekeepers called "nannies" did all the cooking and cleaning five days a week. Her roommate, who owned the house she lived in, came from such a family and happily paid for this service. Having lived on her own since she was eighteen, Maji found it downright luxurious that she didn't have to worry about the next meal, vacuuming the house, or even doing the dishes. In this one way, she lived like the American upper class–a great irony given her meager teaching salary.

But there were also many things about Chile she didn't like, as hard as she tried. The food tasted bland, except for empanadas. Those little meat-filled pastry pockets had their own category of deliciousness. But everything else had all the flavor of generic white bread and instant coffee. They tended to overcook the vegetables, when they served any at all. Chileans followed such a meat-heavy diet she wondered how there weren't mile-long lines outside the hospital for people to get angioplasties.

She deeply resented the smoking. Chileans could smoke indoors almost everywhere. Between that and the heavy pollution of the city, Maji's voice had developed a permanent raspiness that constantly tickled her throat.

And she learned she especially didn't like living in a city. She felt a constant state of claustrophobia and ached for a spacious, natural landscape to breathe in, but being dependent on buses or friends to drive her around, it rarely happened. Maji knew she wouldn't last too long living in Santiago. Her body and soul ached for the simplicity and stillness of nature.

She wasn't sure when it happened, but she realized one day that she and Xavier were now dating. She had grown more comfortable with him and her ability to communicate with him. They spoke more and more about deeply personal matters. He shared with her his longing to leave Chile and experience another part of the world. He had tried to get a visa to New Zealand, but it hadn't come through yet. He admired her bravery for coming to Chile when she didn't know anyone or the culture.

She told him about living as a nun in the ashram and her multiple spiritual experiences. He listened in awe. She wasn't sure if he understood what she described, but it fascinated and intrigued him, nonetheless.

Then, in a profound act of vulnerability, Maji told Xavier about her abortion. She hadn't been sure if she would ever tell anyone in Chile about it. Across the board, everyone she'd talked with about women's rights there was vehemently opposed to abortion. In the almost exclusively Catholic culture, there was a broad cultural agreement that the practice equated to murder. Maji learned quickly to hold her cards close and never disclose her secret.

With Xavier, she would finally let her guard down. She wanted to trust him, and she knew he wanted to trust her. If she was truly going to let someone know her, they would have to know all sides of her. She was ready to do that with Xavier, and let the outcome be what it might. The loneliness of the secret drained her. She wanted to let him in. Perhaps his curiosity and excitement about other cultures would keep his mind open.

She explained to him what had happened with her ex, how in love she was, and how devastated she had been to find out she was pregnant only a week after the relationship ended. She told Xavier how he had screamed at her and pounded the wall next to her head. She told him how she had been in a living nightmare and felt like she had no choice. She told him how she felt like a failure, and she could no longer be the same person she was before, so she came to Chile to reinvent herself.

Xavier listened, his mouth open in shock. When she finished telling her story, she waited for the hammer of judgment to fall. Instead, his eyes filled with tears, and he pulled her in close to him, wrapping his arms around her.

"I'm so sorry," he said softly in Spanish, tears spilling down his cheeks. "No one should feel that pain. I would never do that to you. I would give you a child whenever you want!"

Maji's heart melted at his compassion. His words of giving her a child were a healing balm on a raw wound. She cried tears of gratitude in his arms.

He kissed her a week later. They spent the night together a week after that. He told her he loved her two weeks further in. Xavier's adoration filled in the empty spaces that had been left in Maji's heart. They talked about having a baby together. Maji's heart ached at the thought of being able to actually feel a child grow in her womb and replace the haunting feeling of death left there.

Four months into their relationship, only half a year after Maji had arrived in Chile, Xavier proposed to her. They sat at a dinner table at an upscale Italian restaurant in the heart of the city. As Maji ate her ravioli, she looked up to see the server standing next to her with a red velvet box on a silver tray. She looked over at Xavier, his face red with anxiety.

"I want to…. will you think about…maybe can we…" He stumbled on his words.

"He wants to marry you!" the waiter burst out in English, causing Maji and Xavier both to laugh. Xavier stood and grabbed the box, then dropped to his knee before Maji. When she said "yes," the entire restaurant burst into applause.

Maji accepted his proposal with joy, but even more with relief. It was as if a knot in her shoulder was finally being massaged, and she could release some of the pain and guilt of the abortion. She knew the relationship had moved lightning fast, but she trusted they would be able to navigate their future obstacles. She had to.

Two months after their engagement was announced, Maji sat on the toilet in her bathroom staring at the blue lines on the tiny stick in her hands. Joyful tears filled her eyes. Her heart fluttered. Finally, the miracle she had snuffed out in death would flourish and bloom within her.

A powerful, primal instinct rose inside her, and suddenly her life was no longer just hers. All her faraway dreams, desires, and fantasies took a backseat to a small cluster of cells growing within her. In that moment her identity shifted once more. Now, instead of Maji the Expatriate, she was Maji the Mother.

Maji floated through her days with a life inside of her bridging the sacred and the mundane. She marveled at the things she knew without any physical or medical confirmation. She knew without question the baby was a girl. She felt a strength and ferocity in the little creature, an energetic imprint forming the core of her being. No outward signs of pregnancy had shown yet. The knowledge was just that clear.

The challenges of pregnancy hit her hard. She laughed at the term "*morning* sickness" because the nausea and weakness she felt were with her twenty-four hours a day. She couldn't get through an hour without feeling the need to vomit unless she constantly ate. She taught with crackers stuffed into her cheeks to keep the queasiness at bay. The simplest smells, from car exhaust to someone's cologne, sent her running for the restroom.

Maji experienced a level of exhaustion she didn't know was possible. She moved in slow motion. The pregnancy kept her constantly drained, and she fell asleep on the bus between classes almost every day. One day, she woke up twenty minutes past her stop, and had to make a humiliating phone call to the school..

Xavier and Maji decided to have their wedding sooner than later due to her pregnancy. Her fiance's parents owned a lake house a few hours outside the city in the wine country. The couple decided to have a small ceremony with just a judge and those closest to them.

Maji refused to wear a white wedding dress after wearing that color for so long as a nun. The tradition of the "pure white bride" was outdated and didn't apply to her anyway. She chose a simple green lace cocktail dress that brought out the color of her eyes.

On the day of the wedding, her morning sickness assailed her worse than ever. She lay in bed up until moments before the ceremony with her head on her arms, taking care not to disturb her carefully styled hair. Shoving a cracker in her mouth, she stood and descended the porch stairs to the waiting participants outside.

The judge was a kind, round woman with oversized eyeglasses. Her broad smile warmed Maji's heart. But when she approached and greeted the bride, Maji was struck with the worst breath she had ever smelled. The judge spoke to them in hurried Spanish, leaning in close to the Gringa so she could understand her words, but Maji hardly heard a thing she said. She concentrated all her energy on keeping the sickness away. To the pregnant woman's heightened sense of smell, the odor of her breath reeked of just-eaten tuna and garlic and onions, all in one steaming pile. The overwhelming smell of her breath filled Maji's entire experience, and it took everything in her not to turn around and run into the restroom.

When it was time for her to repeat her vows after the judge, she missed her cue, and her groom elbowed her. Maji said the words as fast as she could, holding the vomit down. When the judge finally announced them as husband and wife, she kissed her lover aggressively, turned, and ran for the bathroom to the background of her new family's laughter.

After the wedding, Maji moved into Xavier's parents' house with him. They made plans to eventually move out and get their own apartment in the city. But over the next couple of months, the bride found herself increasingly missing the United States. She wanted to be close to her parents. She wanted to be somewhere people around her weren't smoking all the time. And as her growing child demanded more from her body, she wanted to be somewhere with food she liked.

The cold winter months moved in. Maji had never experienced such a miserable winter in her life. Deprived of central heating, she slept under piles of blankets to keep warm. Portable kerosene heaters warmed individual rooms. The smell of paraffin permeated her clothes, and the chill never left her body.

In the winter, low pressure pushed the pollution further into the bowl-shaped valley, concentrating it into a dark brown smog all around them. Even her white clothes started to take on a grey color. The locals called this seasonal phenomenon "the ashtray." Every breath she took was a toxic blight seeping through her body to her unborn child. It terrified her. What if this unhealthy environment caused her baby harm, or worse, led to a miscarriage?

Maji walked into their bedroom one night after work. Xavier sat on the end of the bed, untying his shoes. The smell of cigarette smoke seeped into the room. Xavier's father was a heavy smoker but had kindly chosen to smoke only in his bedroom with the door closed and the window cracked due to Maji's pregnancy. But the stench permeated throughout the house, and it threatened the unborn child in Maji's womb like a creeping perpetrator. Maji felt her stomach flip with nausea. She moved to open the window of their bedroom, but stopped, remembering the cold air and the pollution.

She sat down next to Xavier with a huff, tears springing into her eyes. "I miss Colorado! I miss the fresh air. I miss the healthy, hippy restaurants of Boulder. I miss open nature. I miss my parents." Tears flowed down her cheeks. She spent so much of her time crying, moved to tears by the smallest provocation. Pregnancy was a roller coaster of emotion.

Xavier put his arm around her. "I'm sorry, Maji. I know you don't like living in Santiago."

"W-would you ever consider living in the United States? I know your family is here, but you wanted to leave Chile before we met."

Xavier stared at the floor for a moment. "I'm ready for a new adventure," he said in Spanish, nodding his head. "I admit I do feel stuck here. But my English is so bad. How would I ever get a good job?"

Maji's eyes lit up. "I could get my old caregiving job back and that could float us for a while. And I know we could find you something. There are many opportunities there! And you would learn English quite fast, being immersed. Look how much Spanish I've learned!"

Xavier smiled and squeezed his wife's hand. "It's a big step, Maji. You're asking me to give up my life here."

"I know. If you need to think about it, I understand. If you want to talk to your parents about it, I understand that too."

He blinked several times, then slapped his knee. "No! This is our life and family now, so we make the decisions. It's a great opportunity. I say let's do it!"

Maji squealed in delight and threw her arms around his neck.

КУРА

234

The Birth Of A Mother

Maji was indeed able to get her job back. They welcomed her with an enthusiastic email. She found an amazing apartment for them in Boulder through a friend. So, when she reached her twentieth week of pregnancy, they boarded a plane and flew back to her familiar home.

Maji realized before they left how difficult it would be for Xavier to adjust to living in a new country. Her own difficulties living in Chile motivated the move, so she expected him to need an adjustment period. Would it be weeks, months, a year before he found his way? She didn't know. But she accepted that things would be out of balance in their household for a time and faced that responsibility with determination.

Soon after they arrived in the States, Xavier connected with a local Chilean community found through a friend of Maji's. One of the older gentlemen in the group, a contractor, found Xavier a construction job making $10 per hour.

Her husband was elated, but Maji panicked at the minimal salary. It was far from being anything they could survive on, especially while she would be on maternity leave after the baby was born. She knew teenagers who made more money.

"It's just for now until I can find something better," he promised. But as the months rolled on, Maji never saw her husband looking for other work. She never saw him do much of anything other than go to work and watch TV at home.

One day Maji returned home from work to find the apartment completely messy. Dirty dishes filled the sink and clothes covered the floor. Her ankles had swollen from being on her feet much of the day. Their unborn daughter rolled and kicked in her belly. She was exhausted.

"Xavier, can you please do the dishes and pick up? I really need to rest." She plopped onto the couch with a tired sigh. Xavier looked over at her angrily.

"What do you think I am, the nanny?" he snapped.

Maji looked at him in shock. "Xavier, there is no nanny. This isn't Chile, so yes, we are both the nanny here. It's not going to get done on its own."

He sighed and pounded the arm of his chair as he stood. A warning siren went off inside Maji's head. But she squelched it and dismissed his behavior as culture shock. *He's never had to handle any housework before.* He always had a nanny at his parents' house who did it for him.

As her due date neared, Maji's anticipation grew. She and Xavier agreed on the name Cecelia. The future mother created sweet lullabies and sang to her unborn daughter as often as she could, stroking her belly. She imagined all the different things her daughter might become. Maybe she would be a singer or an artist. Maybe she would find passion in the sciences. Maybe she would have a great sense of humor like her dad, or a more serious and contemplative demeanor like Maji. She did know with clarity that Cecelia would be strong, and fiercely intelligent. She could feel it in her energy.

Maji marveled at how clearly she could sense the child's essence. As adults, we take for granted that we generally judge who people are based on their looks or how they speak and act. She didn't know any of that with her baby. But she could feel who she was as one feels the rays of the sun on a hot day. It reminded Maji of something bigger, something majestic. She couldn't quite put her finger on what it was, but it felt miraculous.

Maji had decided she wanted to give birth in the comfort and sanctuary of her own home. She thought hospitals too often resorted to unnecessary medical interventions during childbirth. The more stories she heard, the more she felt the medical system didn't trust a woman's ability to do what she was physically and instinctually designed to do. Women were often encouraged to take painkillers even when they said they didn't want to. And if labor was taking too long, often a doctor would opt for a C-section just to get it over with. Maji didn't want anyone taking her choice away when it came to how her body wanted to handle the delivery of her baby. Hence, she found the midwife Elizabeth, who had an impeccable record of successful home-birth deliveries.

One evening, Xavier and Maji had finished watching a movie. Maji went to the bathroom to get ready for bed. She sat on the toilet, releasing the pressure of the constant urge to pee. The relief was always a very temporary feeling. She had spent so much time in the bathroom during the past few weeks.

Maji stood up from the toilet and walked over to the sink to brush her teeth. She suddenly felt a popping feeling inside of her and looked down to see a pink-tinged liquid dribble onto the floor.

"Xavier!" Maji yelled in surprise. "The baby is coming!"

Her husband rushed into the bathroom, his eyes bulging in excited anxiety.

"Oh, my, god, what do you want me to do?" he asked in Spanish, repeatedly brushing his hair from his forehead.

Suddenly, a massive wave of pain ripped through Maji's body, starting from her belly button and rippling down to her pelvis. She gripped her belly and dropped to her knees. Her breath caught in a loud moan. Such intensity! A powerful outside force had possessed her body, and all she could do was breathe. The contraction lasted a full minute, an eternity to Maji.

"Holy shit!" she panted as the wave passed. "Oh, my! Wow!"

Suddenly, Maji realized why so many women opted to use painkillers and epidurals during labor. The closest thing she had ever experienced to the contraction was the existential experience of her vision quest. But this time, the feeling wasn't ecstatic and blissful. It was pure power pulling her open to be a doorway to new life, and every muscle in her body wanted to fight it.

Xavier helped her off the floor and over to the bed. He kissed her forehead with nervous excitement, then ran to get his phone. Maji heard him speaking his broken English over the phone in the other room.

"Here, the midwife wants to talk to you," he said.

Maji took the phone, still panting.

"Hi, Maji, how are you doing?" asked Elizabeth, a soft-spoken woman with gray hair. "How far apart are your contractions, hon?"

"I don't know. I've only had one so far. But my water broke."

"Ok, so, you are on your way. But true active labor doesn't really start until the contractions are regularly at least five minutes apart. That could be hours from now, even into tomorrow morning. I want you to call me back when–"

Another contraction hit her hard. She dropped the phone onto the bed and fell to the floor onto her hands and knees, a low guttural sound rising from her throat. Every muscle in her body squeezed and pulsed. This time the contraction lasted more than a minute. Xavier rubbed her back furiously as she took deep breaths.

When it subsided, she sat on her knees, sweat beading on her forehead, and picked up the phone.

"Are–are you still there?" she asked, gasping.

"Yes, honey, I'm here!" said Elizabeth excitedly. "That was a big one, wasn't it? And only a couple of minutes after the first one! Wow, Maji, this baby is determined to make it into this world quickly! You may be in active labor after all! I want you to hydrate and rest as best you can. I will get my equipment and be there as soon as possible, in about forty-five minutes. Hang tight, Mama! Your baby will be in your arms soon!"

After she hung up the phone, Maji's contractions came more and more quickly. She soon discovered that the best way to ride their wave was to drop to the floor and relax her body as much as possible. With each breath, she repeated "opening, opening, opening," and imagined her body blossoming like a flower to allow her child into the world.

The contractions came closer and closer together. Maji fell into a trance-like state. She didn't remember lying down on the bed, but at some point, she realized she was on her side. She didn't know when Elizabeth arrived, but she opened her eyes when she heard her voice. The midwife leaned down close to her ear and asked if she wanted her to put on the music playlist Maji had created for the labor. The laboring mother laughed out loud at the absurdity of the question. She could barely register what room she was in, let alone what kind of music that was playing.

"If you need music, you are more than welcome to!"

Maji's experience transformed into a series of physical sensations that went above and beyond anything she had felt in her body before. She fell so deeply into each contraction that pure power replaced the pain. She felt as if lightning bolts could shoot out of the palms of her hands. Through the power of her body's activity, she was capable of anything. The force of the universe stood right there with her.

"I feel like Wonder Woman!"

Soon, a deep pressure began to build inside her, and she knew it was time to start pushing. She surrendered to a higher power, to the force of creation itself moving through her, making her into a divine goddess of life and fertility. But she also felt like she was trying to take a giant shit. At some point some of it came out of her as she bore down hard on her bowels and the midwife had to wipe it away.

The juxtaposition of the sacred experience with such a gross feeling brought a memory back to Maji. The revelation at the Buddhist temple surfaced in her mind, when she'd seen all of manifest reality as one beautiful expression of the eternal self, creating a finite view so it could experience itself. The poop, the divine goddess surrender, was all one and the same. *All of it is a game*.

At the end of the bed the midwife crouched, ready to catch the baby, and Xavier helped support Maji's legs as she delivered on her side. They stared with puzzled expressions as her laughter filled the room. She pushed, and surrendered, and laughed.

"Oh, she's crowning!" Elizabeth said joyfully. "I see her head!"

Tears filled Xavier's eyes. He said something in hurried Spanish. Maji realized he was praying. She felt the pressure build inside her, and a surge of power moved through her being. Her mouth opened and she roared with a ferocity she had never experienced before. She bore down as hard as she could and felt Cecelia kick up hard inside of her, trying to push herself out. Maji groaned at the gut punch her unborn child delivered her.

Suddenly, a high howl filled the room, and the midwife jumped in surprise.

"Oh, my gosh! Her head is out and nothing else, but she's already crying! In all my years, I've never seen that before!" She laughed.

But her cry didn't sound like a baby's cry at all. It sounded like a small wolf puppy howling for its mother, high and long and clear. Maji felt her kick two more times inside of her, eliciting a gasp in pain.

Okay, baby girl, I get it! You want out! she thought, and she pushed as hard as she could. A great pressure released, as if the universe released Maji from a massive bear hug, and the baby slid out right into Elizabeth's hands.

"What a perfectly beautiful baby girl!" she cooed, laying her on Maji's chest.

The new mother looked down at her newborn daughter. A full head of dark brown hair rested against Maji's sweat-covered skin. Out of a red and crinkled face she continued to howl, her mouth in a perfect tiny little "o". Her cries sliced through the long, lingering pain that had been with Maji ever since her abortion. It tore it to shreds, and freed her heart into a wondrous joy, a profound, unconditional love she'd never known possible

"It's you!" Maji laughed, tears filling her eyes. "It's my little Wolf Girl!"

Wolf Girl stopped her howl at the familiar sound of her mother's voice, and stared up at her with big, dark eyes. Pure curiosity filled her tiny expression. Her glassy eyes reflected Maji's joy-filled face back to her, a mirror of mother to daughter to mother.

It was then Maji knew. All the pain she had felt--the heartbreak, the abortion, the horrifying feeling of death in her body, the forgetting, the sense of failure--all was perfect, divine, and immaculately ordered to bring her to that moment, right then and there, where she would remember again. And Maji saw that this, too, was the game. *We forget so we can remember again!* When she looked at her newborn daughter, she gazed at the most beautiful, perfect version of the divine she could ever imagine. She was looking at her eternal self.

"Thank you, my little Wolf Girl!" Maji cried, tears spilling down her face as she lovingly wiped her daughter's wet head with a soft pink blanket, pulling her close. "And welcome to the world."

243

<u>Goodbye</u>

Maji didn't know when it began exactly, perhaps when she found she could no longer get out of bed without help. But she soon realized her reality had become a series of blurry, disjointed experiences punctuated by moments of clarity and waves of emotion. She remembered a few visits from the doctor, his hand on her head as she lay in bed. Eamonn peered over his shoulder, his face full of concern. They had discussed sending her to the hospital but agreed to have hospice care come to her at home instead. Maji knew she didn't want to die anywhere else.

"The most important thing now is that you're comfortable, Maji," the doctor said softly.

"I'm lying in bed 24 hours a day, Doc. I couldn't be more comfortable if I tried," Maji joked back, bringing large smiles to both men's faces.

Several days passed in which she found herself fading back into clarity as if waking from a dream, to find one of the girls curled up next to her in bed, stroking her arm, or her face. One day Wolf Girl sang a love song to her that Maji had always sung when her daughter was a baby. Maji opened her eyes and sang the song with her. Wolf Girl's eyes filled with tears, and she wrapped her arms around her mother as they sang the song together over and over.

Another day, Cloud and Eamonn sat on the bed with Maji. She faded in and out of conscious awareness, her eyes half closed. Tears rolled down Cloud's cheeks as she turned to her father. "Maji is going to die soon, isn't she Daddy?" she whispered. Eamonn's eyes flowed over with tears as well, and his words choked in his throat.

"Yes, sweetie, she is."

Maji's eyes shot open, a rush of sadness filling her at the sight of their tears. "My loves, no. No. No." she sobbed.

Eamonn reached out and took her hand, kissing it gently. "It's okay, my queen," he said through tears. "It's okay."

But Maji didn't feel okay. She wanted to take all their sadness, bottle it up, and throw it far away. She wanted to explain to them what she knew death actually was. She had found peace with it. But she had not yet found peace with their pain.

Maji pushed herself to a sitting position.

"Cloud, honey, what do you think happens when we die?" Maji asked softly, her voice cracking with the effort. Cloud sniffed loudly, wiping her nose.

"I don't know. Maybe everything goes dark?"

"You mean like going to sleep?"

"Yeah, I guess."

"But then what happens? We don't just stay in the dark forever after that."

"We don't?" Cloud asked, her face surprised.

"Oh, no, sweetie, we don't. This I know for a fact. Think of it like this. Our bodies are like these boxes that hold the essence of who we are inside of it while we are alive. Our essence can do everything the body can do, but while it's inside of it, it can't do more than what the body is capable of. Once we die, our essence is free to do whatever it wants, since it is out of the body—whatever it can, which is a lot! It's whatever we can think of with our imagination."

"Really? Whatever we can think of?" Cloud's eyes grew wide.

"Yes!" Maji smiled, her breath wheezing with the effort of speech. She reached out and took Cloud's hand. "So, what do you think will happen to me after I die? I need your help, Cloud. You have one of the biggest imaginations of anyone I know. Can you help me think of it now, so I can remember it after I die and have a really good time?"

Cloud smiled and shifted herself into a cross-legged position on the bed. Eamonn and Maji listened intently.

"Well, you definitely will be able to fly!" She beamed.

"Oh, absolutely! I'm really excited to do that!" Maji smiled.

"And you definitely will have a pegasus as a pet. And you won't even have any allergies to it like you do to horses now!"

"Oh, my gosh, that will be amazing!" Maji laughed. "What else?"

"Well." Cloud crossed her arms over her chest and brought her finger to her chin, contemplating. "I think you will be able to see everyone you have ever known that has died. And you all will throw a big, big party! And you'll be able to dance for as long as you want, Maji, without getting tired. For days or even weeks, if you want!"

"Oh, I love dancing! I can't wait to do that!"

"Also, you will have magical powers to paint anything anywhere! If you want a rainbow in the sky, you will paint it right in the sky! If you want a flower on a plant, you can paint it right then and there! If you want to change your outfit, then whoosh, you can paint a new one right onto yourself! It will be your artist's superpower!"

Cloud began to bounce with excitement, her imagination running wild. Maji and Eamonn laughed at her joy.

"This sounds amazing, Cloud!" Maji said. "I think I'm going to have a really good time!"

"I think so too, Maji!" Cloud shifted onto her knees to bounce even higher.

"I want you to remember that sweetie, when you get sad. Remember what a good time I'm having and that you helped me imagine it!"

Cloud stopped bouncing, her face falling.

"I'm going to miss you, Maji." Tears filling her eyes.

Maji stared at her stepdaughter, her heart aching. Though their relationship had always been peaceful, Cloud had the greatest difficulty of all the girls in letting Maji in emotionally. She had always put up an invisible wall between them, an unspoken reminder that Maji was never her *real* parent. Now as they sat there together on the bed with death so close, the wall had vanished. Cloud had torn it down.

"I'm going to miss you too, Cloud," she said softly. "I want you to know that I love you, and I always will."

"I love you, too, Maji." She lay her head down in Maji's lap, reaching out for her dad's hand. Eamonn bent down and kissed his daughter, then looked into his wife's eyes. They smiled at each other while Maji stroked her stepdaughter's hair.

Star was the one who clung to Maji's side the most. Many nights the dying mother awoke only to find her youngest child next to her in bed, her face pressed against her mother's chest, dried tear streaks on her cheeks. Maji looked at her round, cherub face and felt a sense of dread. Would Star even remember her when she was grown? Would she be forever scarred by the absence of her mother? Already, she felt the world with more intensity than anyone Maji had ever known. Would she be okay?

One day, Maji woke in bed to find Star with a bouquet of flowers in her hands. She sat next to her mother, placing petals one by one all over the covers and around Maji's head on the pillow.

"Whatcha doing, baby?" Maji asked.

"Well…" Star sniffed, a look of happy determination on her face. "I know how much you love being in nature, and all the plants and stuff. And I know you can't really go outside much anymore. So, I wanted to bring some of it to you, Mama. And the petals are so bright and pretty, and you're so pretty, I just thought it would be nice to dress you up like a bouquet of flowers, too!"

Maji's lips spread wide in a smile, and she pulled her daughter close to her, kissing her on her cheek. "You are just the sweetest, baby!" Then she had an idea. She pushed herself up to a sitting position. "Star, I think there is something very important we should do. Can you please go get my tin box of seeds from the back of the refrigerator?"

Star's eyes grew wide. "Oh, okay!"

She hopped off the bed and ran out of the room. A few moments later she returned with a small, lime green metal box with a handle on the lid. She carefully placed it in her mother's hands. Cold from being in the refrigerator, the container sent a chill down Maji's arms. She opened it up and thumbed through the small envelopes stacked inside. They were labeled with a name and a roughly drawn picture of a plant on each tan packet. Finally she stopped, seeing the one she had been searching for.

"Look!" Excitement laced her words as she drew out the envelope. She tore open the flap and grabbed Star's hand, turning it so her palm was up. Then she carefully turned over the envelope, dropping a small seed bundle that looked like a helicopter propeller into Star's hand. Two bumps fused together with rounded wings like those of a dragonfly coming off the sides. It was a maple seed. Maji had collected it a year ago during a family walk. She'd seen a beautiful tree with leaves turning a brilliant red. She loved the color so much that she snatched one of the little seed pods that whirled through the air when the wind shook them loose, hoping to plant it. She had completely forgotten about it until that moment.

"This is a maple tree seed!" she explained as Star picked up the little winged packet of life with her other hand, turning it to see it from all sides. "And you and I are going to plant it!"

Maji began to move slowly out of bed, spilling flower petals onto the floor. Star panicked, taking her hand.

"Mama, wait! Should you get up? Is that okay?"

"For this, you bet I can get up!" Maji laughed. But her body felt like it was made of stone. Each movement left her breathless. Star stayed close, her face crumpled in concern.

She made her way carefully to the front door with Star holding her hand tightly. The other three girls peeked their heads out of their rooms.

"Maji, what are you doing?" Justice asked in surprise, rushing over to her side.

"I'm heading out the front door. Can you girls help me? We have something we need to do!"

Wolf Girl laughed nervously, fear in her eyes, and took Maji's other hand. Cloud ran and opened the front door.

"What do we have to do, Maji?" Cloud asked.

"Well, kiddo, I need you to go get a shovel out of the garage. And Wolf Girl, I need you to go grab whatever is left of the topsoil we have out there. We are doing some gardening!"

The girls exchanged looks in concern, unmoving, until finally, Star barked, "You heard her! Go get what she asked for! Jeez!"

Maji made her way slowly through the doorway, then down the two front steps. She paused for a moment, looking around, before selecting a spot to plant the little maple seed. It would be in the corner of their yard, undisturbed by mowers and pedestrians.

Maji ambled to the spot and lowered herself to the grass. Soon, Cloud and Wolf Girl returned with the shovel and dirt. Maji instructed her daughter to dig a small hole, and the young girl rolled her eyes at what she perceived as a chore.

Then, Maji had Star present the seed. She held it up in the air ceremoniously, as if holding a grand prize.

"Look!" Star grinned and tossed the seed up into the air. It twirled in a fast pirouette and fluttered to the ground. Cloud picked it up, laughing, and did the same. Finally, Maji instructed them to place it carefully in the hole. She bent forward and shrouded it with dirt. The five of them stared silently at the small mound for a moment before Maji took a breath.

"I'm not going to be here much longer, girls." Her voice wavered as her eyes brimmed with tears. The four children stared back at her, their eyes wide, their faces melting into sadness. "I want to plant this so you always have someplace to go to connect with me. We are planting this tree together. This tree will grow and change just like you girls. When I'm gone, you can always come to this tree to talk to me. I promise I will always be listening."

A tear rolled down Maji's cheek. She wiped it with her finger. Then, seeing the drop resting on her skin, she flicked it onto the mound of dirt where the seed had been planted. Maji reached over to Star and caught her tear as well, flicking it onto the dirt. The other girls watched Maji, then repeated the gesture with their own moisture.

"You see, babies? Our tears, our sadness, are still going to bring new life. Even in the hardest times, there is always something new being born!"

Maji looked at each of their faces, resigned, sad. *They've finally accepted that I'm going to die.* They were no longer trying to save her. Something settled inside the dying woman. The time had come to say goodbye.

"Girls, I want you to know that I have lived an amazing life. I have no regrets, other than I wish I had more time to be with you and watch you grow. You have truly been the greatest gift of my life."

She took Wolf Girl's hand. "My first-born baby, I want to thank you for showing me what true unconditional love is. I didn't know what that was until you were born. My life could never have been so rich without you in it. I'm so proud of who you are. I will never worry about you, because you will always find your way. You always do! Remember that you can have and do whatever you put your mind to! Stay brave, my Wolf Girl. You will never be alone. I will always be with you."

Wolf Girl looked at her mother with big, glassy eyes. She breathed heavily, visibly fighting back her tears. Maji squeezed her hand, then turned to Justice and Cloud.

"Do you know what you two girls have given me? You have shown me the power of choosing to love you. I know having a stepmom hasn't always been easy. I have tried to be a good bonus mom to you. And sometimes I failed miserably. Sometimes, it felt like we were aliens to each other, I know! But despite that, I have woken up every day and seen the beautiful people you two are. I have learned so many new ways to be in this world by watching what is so unique and amazing about you two. Choosing to love you has been such a new and profound way for me to love! My life has been richer, and I'm a better person because of you."

"We're better people, too, because of you, Maji," Justice whispered.

"I love you both so much."

Cloud burst into tears and threw herself into Maji's arms. The hugs she had shared with her stepmother over the years had always been guarded. This embrace, however, was a full surrender, a full expression of love. Maji's heart burst with joy at this beautiful gift. She held her stepdaughter close and stroked her hair while she sobbed.

"Cloud, never lose that beautiful imagination of yours and that kind heart. Keep building magical universes, and don't forget that there is magic in this universe for you, too. I promise. Your kindness is an inspiration to me and a gift to this world."

"I'll miss you, Maji!" Cloud cried.

"I will miss you, too. But you know what? I really won't be gone. This body will be gone. But I will always live in your hearts and your memories. When you think of me, I want you to remember how much I love you, how much fun we have had together, and what a happy life you have given me. I want you to know that with that one thought, that one feeling of my love, I will be right there with you. There is no other place I could be!"

Maji looked up at Justice. Her oldest stepdaughter had a stoic look on her face, but tears flowed freely down her cheeks.

"You, young lady, are going to set this world straight, I believe. Your ability to draw the lines around what is important to you, what isn't, and what you will create has been amazing to watch. You have so much more clarity and confidence than I had at your age. I'm so proud of you, Justice. Thank you for letting me into your life. You have been such a gift to me."

Justice smiled a tight-lipped smile, her face a mix of love and pain. Maji turned finally to Star, whose face was red with emotion.

"My youngest baby. You are the most passionate person I know. Remember what I told you about that? About living such a passionate and intense life?"

Star sniffed, lifting her head.

"You said it was my superpower."

"That's right! And don't you forget it! Whenever it feels hard, just remember you are in training. You are going to do amazing things, Star. You are going to light up this whole world with your passion. And you know what? Your passion has always shown me what it means to be unafraid of living life at full blast. Thank you for inspiring me, baby. It has been such a gift to watch you grow. Being your mama has been the most amazing adventure of my life. Even though I'll be gone, I will be right there with you, watching you as you grow. I will be cheering you on the whole way, because I believe in you."

She watched as an intense wave of emotion passed through Star, her eyes squeezing shut, her fists balling up. Maji held her breath, expecting her daughter to explode, to drop on the ground and scream. But to Maji's surprise, Star took a deep breath, relaxed her hands, and opened her watery eyes. She reached out and took her mother's hand, a small, calm smile on her lips.

"I love you so much, Mama. You are the best mama in the whole wide world. Thank you for the tree." She choked, then continued. "I will always come and sit by it to find you."

"You're welcome, baby. I love you. I love all of you. And that love will never die."

After that day, Maji never got out of bed again.

She knew she was beginning to die a few days later. She spent most of the day in a state of blurry awareness, then opened her eyes in the evening to startling clarity. The kids and Eamonn sat in the room with her before bedtime, in the middle of a conversation about Justice's volleyball team.

"Coach had told us to rest, but Adrienne kept running up and down the hallway, squirting Julia with her water bottle. It was hilarious!" Justice laughed, and Maji smiled at her joy. There had been less and less of it in the house lately, and it was a welcome feeling.

"Then, when we had to start the match, she was already out of breath and Coach had to tell her to….."

Without warning, Maji's hearing faded out, as if someone had turned a dial. Justice's voice sounded like a channel was missing on a stereo recording. All the dying woman caught was the low bass tones. Everything inside of her slowed down. Turning her head and her eyes, she watched the faces of her family blur. She blinked to try to clear her vision, but to no avail. The power was slowly shutting off. It was then she realized Eamonn had been gently stroking her hand, but she hadn't felt it. She took a deep breath.

This is it. Here I go.

Should she tell them it was time? But she didn't want to interrupt their casual levity. She had no idea how long it would take. So, she watched them through blurred eyes, taking in what she could.

I love them so much. Please let them be okay without me. Please let them find joy and peace and always feel my love.

After several more minutes, the kids began to depart for bed.

"Please say goodnight to me before you go," Maji croaked through her failing voice. The girls paused, startled by the serious tone in Maji's voice. They exchanged looks. Star jumped forward and began covering Maji's face with kisses.

"I could never leave without saying goodnight to the best mommy ever!"

Maji chuckled, her heart swelling, a deep sense of peace spreading through her. One by one the girls hugged and kissed her. Wolf Girl was last, and as she pulled away from the final hug

255

with Maji, she paused, looking her mother in the eyes.

"I love you so much!" she whispered, stroking Maji's cheek with her hand. Maji felt the faint brush of her fingertips and the slight pressure on her cheeks. Love overwhelmed her.

"I love you so much, too!"

They all left the room, and Maji rested for a moment in the silence. She began to feel very heavy, as if her entire body was made of stone pressing down into the earth. She desperately wanted to roll onto her side to fight the deepening discomfort, but when she tried, she found she could no longer move.

Come on body, just roll, she thought. But nothing happened. Her body could no longer hear her mind. She felt herself sink deeper and deeper into the bed as if a giant boulder had been rolled on top of her.

Eamonn came back into the room and sat next to Maji. His face blanched as he looked at her.

"Maji, what's happening?" he gasped at her pallid face, panic in his voice.

"Please, can you roll me over? I can't move," she asked, barely a whisper.

A small sob sounded in his throat. *He knows*, she thought. He gently moved her onto her side, fluffing the pillow under her head.

"Should I get the kids now?" he asked.

But Maji couldn't hear him. She saw only a dim outline of his form. In her vision, the world began to warp and shimmer, as if she watched a mirage in the desert. Its beauty struck her and reminded her of the day at the stupa. The colors in her plastic sandwich bag flashed before her. A raspy giggle escaped her lips.

"What do you need, Maji?" Eamonn asked, desperation in his voice. This time Maji heard him.

"Don't worry, my love. I have everything I need," she whispered, a smile on her face. Sleep overcame her.

The next morning, Maji awoke, and the world remained a shimmering mirage. She lifted her head, as heavy as a bowling ball, looked around, and saw the blurry outlines of her family sitting next to her.

"She's awake!" someone said, but the voice was so hollow and distant, Maji didn't know which child it was. She tried to say something, but her swollen tongue refused to move in her desert-dry mouth. A soft moan escaped her lips, causing her blurry family to move around like fluttering bird's wings. Maji's eyes felt incredibly dry. She tried to blink to moisten them, but it didn't help.

A shadow moved in front of Maji. She felt a straw touch her lips. With a tremendous effort, she was able to wrap her lips around the plastic and suck. Relief washed through her as the cool liquid slid down her throat. But only seconds after swallowing, she felt as parched as Death Valley. Her nostrils stuck together like glue.

In a bizarre contradiction, the dry feeling was accompanied by a sensation that she was being carried away by a huge body of water. Her body thrashed around under the waves of the ocean. And yet, at the same time, she remained motionless on the bed, except for the occasional twitch and jerk. This contrast between dry and wet, stillness and uncontrollable movement overwhelmed her faculties. Maji wanted to cry in frustration but had no tears.

One of her kids approached and stroked her face. The touch felt like a distant memory. Her body trembled.

"It's okay, Mama, it's okay."

It was Wolf Girl. Maji recognized her voice and could even faintly smell her scent. She turned her eyes to gaze into her daughter's face, but it appeared as a dull shadow. All around the girl swirled a vision of swirling smoke, as if Wolf Girl was a ghost about to vanish into the ether.

No, don't go, she thought. Then, she realized she was the one departing, and she wheezed out a small giggle at the momentary delusion. It sent a ripple of pleasure through her body, almost like a tiny orgasm.

But the pleasure was fleeting, and soon the delightful ripples turned into waves of pain, crashing through the dying woman without mercy. She whimpered, wanting to squeeze her daughter's hand, but still she had no control over her body. Fear took her, and the sensation of spinning wildly out of control. She wanted to thrash and run and jump away from the feeling, but she couldn't. She wanted to roar, but nothing remained in her to make the sound. Her hand twitched in Wolf Girl's grasp.

Stop, Maji! she told herself. *There is nothing to fight. Just surrender. Just relax. There is nothing left to do.*

She went utterly still. A coldness started creeping through her body, starting at her feet and hands, then slowly moving up. Maji opened her eyes again, looking into the blurred and distorted faces of her family. She reached deep into her mind, wanting to see their faces once more, wanting her vision to clear one last time. But it wouldn't. She couldn't remember their names. What was the name of the daughter that was holding her hand?

Someone in the room spoke, and the incomprehensible words jumped into her vision as colors and movement. She cast her eyes at each distorted figure, watching the forms morph and change, a distinct high-pitched hum sounding from each figure as it moved. Maji's vision and hearing scrambled in her brain. The world vanished into the swirling smoke.

A loud roar sounded in her ears, like a roaring bonfire. She stood in the middle of a massive flame, and all the water, all the cells in her body were being consumed in the fire, yet she felt no pain. She was dissolving into smoke.

Maji struggled to breathe. Each inhale was a monumental, rattling effort. Each time she took in a breath, it seeped out invisible holes along her throat. She couldn't get enough air. Her eyes closed, and the bed beneath her vanished.

Maji stood in dim sunlight, a soft, red glow surrounding her. She blinked her eyes and thought she saw the silhouette of trees swaying in the gentle breeze that lifted her hair. She felt a profound sense of peace. She wasn't sure where she was or how she got there, but it didn't matter. All was simple, peaceful. In the distance, the outline of a figure approached. As it neared, she recognized the tell-tale white hair and gentle gait of her grandfather.

"Grandpa!" Her voice echoed. He strode up to her, a soft smile on his lips. She vaguely recalled seeing him recently, though the exact time eluded her.

"Grandpa, am I dreaming?" she asked.

He reached out and took her hand. "Sweetie, we are always dreaming." He pulled her arm after him as he walked back in the direction from which he'd come. Their feet made no sound as they walked.

In the distance, Maji saw soft yellow points of light emerge into view until hundreds dotted the horizon. As she drew closer to the lights, she recognized them as small candles, nestled into the center of large flower blossoms, floating peacefully on a slow-moving river.

Grandpa led her up to the river's edge. Small, translucent pebbles lined the length of the shore. Maji pushed some with her toe. She looked up and pointed to the floating blossoms with the lights.

"What are these, Grandpa?" she asked.

He reached down and gently scooped up one of the blossoms, the small flame dancing gently in the center of the large pink petals. "This is life," he said, his smile beaming.

"I don't understand, Grandpa. What does that mean?"

"This is life." He nodded towards the flame.

As Maji gazed at the flame, its color began to change. The yellow deepened first into orange, then into a soft red. The woman looked up and saw all the lights in the river make the same transformation. The breeze that had blown gently started to strengthen, spinning the flames wildly on their wicks. The sky deepened to a darker red as well, until all around her, everything had a deep rose glow. The wind whipped around her, throwing her hair in front of her face. Grandpa smiled broadly at her.

"Grandpa, what is happening?"

Even through the wind, an overwhelming sense of peace prevailed, but she was confused. She looked into the old man's smiling face. He acted as if nothing was happening. Maji looked out across the water. One by one the dancing flames flicked out, extinguished by the gusting wind. It howled in her ears. She watched in awe as the wind picked up each blossom and carried it off beyond her sight. Then the wind grew into a swirling tornado, a whirlwind sucking the water from the river. Maji reached out and grabbed her grandfather's arm.

"Grandpa! Do you see this?! Grandpa! What should we do?" she yelled, but her words were carried away by the storm. He still smiled at her peacefully, the blossom he had plucked from the river still resting undisturbed in his hands. The small red flame twirled excitedly in the wind.

"Maji, honey, I told you. This is life." His voice sounded loud and clear despite the wind. "And this one, this one right here, this is your life."

He smiled wide again, then gently leaned forward and blew the small flame out.

In her bed, Maji sucked in air, then exhaled long and slow. She inhaled once more, her waxy cheeks pinching inward. There was a five-second pause before she let the breath out. Then another seven seconds before she inhaled again. After one last long pause, Maji exhaled the last wind from her body. Her heart went still.

Maji was dead.

262

The In-Between

A giant monster burst into the room. It ripped the roof off, smashed through the walls and began shredding Star to pieces. But it didn't make a sound as it decimated her. It couldn't, because the monster was the silence and stillness at the end of Mama's last breath. It strangled her. She couldn't breathe. It blackened her world and ripped from her everything that felt like love.

She'd watched in horror as Eamonn stroked Maji's face, tears streaming down his cheeks, and Wolf Girl held their mother's hand. Her voice cracked and trembled as she sang the same song Mama had always told them she'd sung to her sister as a baby. Justice and Cloud hugged each other at the end of the bed, sniffling loudly. Star watched all of this as if from a distance, until finally, Mama breathed her last breath.

Then the monster came. It ripped her apart from the inside and pushed down on her from the outside, crushing her until she couldn't breathe. The pain--oh, god, the pain! --was so unbearable. She didn't know if it was her body that hurt or her mind or her heart until she realized it was all of them.

Around her, she heard the sobs of her family. Was the monster attacking them, too? She didn't know, but she knew she couldn't help them. She had to run to save herself. She had to escape this unbelievable pain before it destroyed her.

Star screamed as loud as she could and threw herself off the bed. She clutched her knees tightly to her chest, a defense against the monster. But it did no good. The pain didn't stop.

From the floor, she saw Wolf Girl collapse onto their mother's lifeless body, and the monster's claws dug deeper into Star's flesh. Star rolled onto her knees and scrambled as fast as she could to the wall. Then she pulled herself up and ran. With all the strength she had, she ran.

Behind her, Wolf Girl called her name. Eamonn told her to let Star go. She burst out the front door and was struck by the sun's utterly inappropriate brightness. Hadn't the monster destroyed all the light by now? It had destroyed everything else. Surely now it would follow her outside and gobble up the clouds and sky, too.

The grieving girl sprinted down the sidewalk, her feet pounding as loudly as she could make them, tears streaming off her face behind her, her ongoing scream roaring with each thundering stride she took. She ran until she felt like her lungs were going to burst, and then she ran more.

Finally, after several minutes, Star reached a large grove of trees on the edge of a park several blocks from her house. It was dark there. She could hide from the monster there. Maybe the pain would stop.

She leaped into the grove and fell to her knees onto the soft carpet of pine needles, breathing hard. She waited, catching her breath, to see what would happen. Her heart pounded in her chest. No sound but her own breathing reached her ears. No one was chasing her. No one was coming to find her. Usually, it would be Mama who would come. Now Mama was gone.

Star pulled her knees close to her chest, a long wail escaping her throat. How would she be able to go on living? How could she face this big world without her mommy there to protect her?

She thought about what Mama had told her, that the bigness of everything she felt was a gift, was her superpower, and that she was in training with this power. What was that word Mama had used to describe what she had? Courage. She'd said Star had the courage to feel so much. Yet now here she was, cowering in the trees, running from her pain. Where was her courage now? Mama had always made her safe with her feelings, reminding her, holding her, telling her how amazing she was. Now no one protected her, and Star had to face the monster by herself. And it was the biggest monster she had ever faced.

Shame overcame her in her dark hiding place. What would Mama think if she were there now? This was the biggest test of all, to face the experience of her mother's death without running. That would be true courage, wouldn't it? Could Mama see her now, hiding? Would she be angry at her? *But if she can see me now, she can see if I'm brave, too.* Star took a deep breath and roared.

She stood up, brushing the pine needles off her pants. She stepped out of the trees and trudged down the street toward her house. The heavy air around her pulsed with darkness despite the sun. Sadness and dread bubbled up inside of her like a pot boiling over. She gritted her teeth, fighting the urge to run again, and steadily made her way back through her front door.

She slogged down the hall toward the room where Mama lay lifeless. Her fear grew at the thought of looking at her mother now, unmoving, still as marble. God itself lay dead in that bed.

She remembered her superpower. She had to face this fear for Mama.

She shuffled into the room. Eamonn and Wolf Girl both lay on the bed with Mama's still body, their cheeks glistening with tears. Cloud lay curled up in a ball at Mama's feet, her back to Star. Justice sat on the edge of the bed, her head bowed low. They all looked up in surprise as Star came into the room. Wolf Girl gasped and jumped off the bed, throwing her arms around her sister.

"Where did you go?!" she wailed. "I need you right now, Star! I need you!"

Star blinked in surprise. All she had thought about was running from her pain. She didn't think anyone else had needed or wanted her there. How could she be of help to anyone? But as she felt her older sister's arms holding her tight, her weight leaning into her for support, she realized that courage meant making space for other people, too, when life was hard. She felt Wolf Girl's tears, but she also felt her love. This miserable experience had somehow magnified their bond. Star's heart opened. They held each other for quite some time, swaying together in their mutual embrace, finding comfort in their shared love.

Star pulled away from Wolf Girl and forced herself to look over at Mama. She hadn't known a human body could be so still. Mama looked like a wax statue. Star stepped over to her, her heart pounding in her ears. Calling on courage, she reached up and touched the waxen face. The cold of it sent a chill through her body. Tears were flowing freely down her cheeks. When had she started crying again? Star ran her hand down Mama's neck and over her shoulder, her fingers trembling. So cold. She laid her hand over Mama's heart and gasped in surprise.

"Mama is still warm here!" She pressed her hand on her mother's chest. "Why is she still warm?"

"I think it means there is a bit of Maji still with us," Eamonn said softly, placing his hand on her chest next to Star's. "It takes some time for someone to completely cross over."

Star placed her left hand on her own chest, still feeling the warmth of her mother's heart with her right. The warmth brought comfort. A memory surfaced: Mama extolling her courage and pointing at her heart. *That's where courage lives. In the heart.* And now Mama was sending Star a message through that warm heart center.

"I will have courage for you, Mama," Star whispered. "I promise!"

Maji felt her last breath as one feels a leap off a cliff. Her candle blew out. She expected a tremendous fall. Instead, grace infused the process, as if she slipped into a warm pool. It was floating. It was surrender.

A broad sense of freedom came over her with her last breath. Her physical senses gone, she perceived now through consciousness itself. A deep sense of stillness pervaded her being. She rested in a state of pure potential, a witness to the universe right before the Big Bang. Something swirled within that stillness, but never burst forth to become something tangible or witnessed. Maji herself felt the absence of any sense of Maji. She was spaciousness, stillness, and conception before the first cell split. She was pre-breath. She was the line between awake and asleep. She was resting in the ground of existence.

Maji stayed in that place for some time, floating in non-conceptual awareness, until her sense of self and of abandoning it floated into her awareness. Forms appeared, first hazy, then with greater clarity, until she recognized her own body laying on a bed in front of her, still and lifeless. She saw her family gathered around her. Wolf Girl lay on Maji's unmoving chest, crying. She saw Justice and Cloud. She saw their tears and felt a deep pain for being the cause of them. But where was Star?

As soon as the thought came to her, Maji found herself next to her youngest daughter, sitting in the shadows of trees. She recognized the place a few blocks from their house. Star hugged her knees close to her chest, rocking back and forth, sobbing loudly. Grief wrenched Maji's soul.

She tried to say, "I'm sorry I left you, baby," but had no voice. She wanted to reach out and hug Star, but she had no arms to wrap around her. Instead, she sent her love. Deep, profound love.

Star looked up as if sensing her mother near. She turned her head and rested her gaze near Maji. She wiped her snotty nose on her sleeve and brushed the tears from her eyes. With a ferocious roar, she stood up and began to walk back towards the house.

Maji thought again of the other family members with her by the bedside. In an instant, she was with them by her body. At the same time, somehow, she walked with Star back to the house. *With no body, I'm no longer limited. I can be many places at once.*

She thought of her mother and found herself by her side. The woman stood at the kitchen sink, washing dishes. A surge of love rushed through her as she looked at her mother's face. How unfair that she outlived her daughter! It was every parent's worst nightmare. Mom didn't even know yet that she had died.

Her mother paused and looked up, setting the dish she was washing in the sink. Her eyes filled with tears.

"Maji?" she whispered. "Honey? Maji?"

Tears spilled down her cheeks. She turned, wiping her hands on a towel, and reached for her cell phone. She called Eamonn. Maji watched him, back in their own home, reach over and pick up the phone, standing to exit the room as he spoke to her mother. Her mother's face crumpled as she received the news of Maji's death.

The pain of everyone who loved her hit her like an icy blast of winter wind, and she wanted to take it away. She wanted to undo her death. She felt pulled in multiple directions as her awareness spread to all those she loved, and their sadness overwhelmed her. She was pulled under the tide of so many others' emotions. She couldn't stand being the source of so much suffering. She felt helpless, unmoored, like she was drowning. She wanted the peace she had expected in death, but the experience of her family's pain was so far from that.

Then she saw Star moving close to her body. The little girl touched her face and shoulders. Her hand rested on her mother's chest.

"Maji is still warm here! Why is she still warm?" Maji came close to her child and sensed the warmth in her own chest, as if she still inhabited her body.

I'm here, baby. I'm here!

"I think it means there is a bit of Maji still with us. It takes some time for someone to completely cross over."

269

Star put her hand on her own chest, and Maji felt the warmth pass between them, between life and death. An ocean of love swelled around her.

"I will have courage for you, Maji. I promise!"

A small smile shone through her daughter's tears.

A wave of relief washed over her. Some great restraint upon her released. The peace finally came. And as she let go and relaxed into peace, her awareness began to fade, and Maji slipped into dark unconsciousness.

Unraveling Mindscape

After Maji died, her awareness flickered in and out over the next three days, from sleep into wakefulness and back again. She saw the moments of mourning her family and friends experienced as her death became widely known. Unable to touch them, she watched each ride a rollercoaster of grief and shock. Sometimes they sensed her presence, and recognition flashed across their faces, but for the most part she was just a whisper in the wind to them.

As the days passed, her connection grew fainter. Her ability to perceive their faces, the rooms they were in and the words they said deteriorated. It was as if the lights were dimming in their world.

At one point, Maji watched Eamonn alone in their shared room. He lay on the bed, his arms wrapped around her pillow. Tears flowed down his cheeks, and he kept taking long, deep sniffs of the pillow. It took her a moment to realize why, and to remember that she had ever had a scent. She no longer remembered what her body had looked like. A moment of panic hit her with the realization that she was, at last, leaving this world behind.

"Eamonn," she tried to say, wanting desperately to touch him. "Eamonn, I'm going."

He lifted his head, looking into the distance. "I love you, Maji," he sniffed.

Darkness filled her vision. His face disappeared into it, and Maji found herself in a lightless, vast space once more.

This time she was fully awake in the darkness. She was aware she was someplace, but she didn't know where that "someplace" was. She sensed her own movement. Had she regained form? A soft glow emitted from her. She had become a point of light herself.

All around her, the darkness dissolved into a gentle luminescence that shimmered like a mirage in a desert, growing brighter and brighter until her vision filled with light wherever she looked. A myriad of colors swirled and danced in that light. Before she could focus her awareness on any one part of it, it would morph, so the moment Maji was able to identify a specific color, it shifted to another one. Forms took shape but changed as soon as she began to recognize them.

She was perceiving the materials of reality. A profound sense of awe filled her. They were utterly intangible, lacking in anything solid whatsoever. She had stepped inside a cosmic microscope, and she perceived things smaller than the smallest subatomic particles.

A revelation hit her: the lights changed and swirled in cadence with her thoughts. When she remained still, the colors slowed their swirling motion, and rippled and danced like light reflecting off a lake's surface. Whenever she analyzed what she perceived, the motion intensified, the colors changed more rapidly, and the light crashed and moved like violent waves in the ocean.

So, this is the after-life, she thought. *Is this a place? Is this my soul, here?* The idea of dying brought thoughts of the life she left behind, of her family and friends. The colors and light violently jerked and danced in her vision.

She couldn't remember the names of her family members. She had four daughters. She knew that. She had a partner. But what were their names? She knew she was dead, but she didn't remember dying.

Something inside her released its grip, and Maji's attention drifted away from the life left behind. It was over. She had to let go of it. But even if she couldn't remember their names, the love she felt for the people that had given her life meaning stayed strong. *That, at least, I must not forget.*

The colors swirled in a beautiful circular pattern all around. Maji watched as the light drifted into various spherical shapes. These shapes held a perfection that lent Maji a peaceful equanimity. She watched in a space of stillness, wondering at their shifts.

The spheres glowed at varying degrees. Some shone blindingly bright, while others appeared to be mere suggestions of a sphere, like the burned shape of the sun when one looks away after staring directly into it. Some were more solid than others, and Maji felt she could reach out and take them, bouncing them like balls. Others were just whispers, suggestions that faded away on the edges of her awareness.

Not only did her visual awareness expand, but her mind as well. When in her body, she had perceived the world through the limitations of human eyes. Her peripheral vision was narrow, her depth perception limited. Now she could see for an infinite distance in all directions.

The spheres coalesced and formed small geometric groups of colors in an unending display. Maji's vision became the depth perception of an eagle, the thousand eyes of a fly, the sonar sense of a narwhal. She no longer perceived as a human, but as a being of creation itself. In this bodiless state, Maji was freed from the conditioned perception of life.

Soon a great thunderous roar sounded all around her, rolling in from all directions and back out again, like a thousand trains all barreling through a station simultaneously. The light around her grew sharper, and fine shafts like laser beams shot around her.

The perception and awareness she experienced at that moment overwhelmed her, so much bigger than anything she had known in life. The booming barrage blared louder than any decibel she could have heard in life, yet caused no pain. It deluged and confused her, and fear bubbled in her mind.

What is this place?! What is happening to me!?

As her fear grew, a form shimmered into shape in front of her. The spheres of lights coalesced into the figure of a small child. Her brown, pigtailed hair tickled Maji's memory. She stared hard into her face as the little girl stared back, unmoving. And the recognition dawned.

That's me! That's Maji! Maji!

It was herself when she was just a child. It was her ten-year-old self. The girl smiled, reached down to her feet, and plucked a small flower that appeared as she reached for it. All around her, the forms of trees took shape, and soon the two Majis stood together, face to face in a forest. Iridescent trees quivered between solidity and swirling light. The roaring sound faded to nothing.

The little girl Maji smiled at her. "You tried, Maji," she said with a sympathetic tone.

"I tried? What do you mean?"

"You did the best you could, but in the end, nothing can be saved from death. It's all a part of the game."

Maji frowned, an unsettling feeling welling in her mind. Little Girl Maji turned her gaze over Maji's shoulder. Her eyes grew wide, and she inched backward as a look of terror filled her face. She let out a blood-curdling scream.

"Run!" she shrieked. Maji whirled around to see a massive tsunami of pure fire barreled toward them at breakneck speed. Trees exploded into bursts of flame before being consumed and overtaken by the wave of fire.

Pure terror overtook her. She screamed and ran, following her younger self. The thunderous roar of the fire chased them. Trees exploded like fireworks behind them as the inferno gained ground.

With her younger self, Maji ran as fast as she could. Sticks and twigs scraped her legs as she sprinted, then disappeared into a swirl of colored light.

Her vision expanded once more beyond human limitations, and she beheld the entire planet. As far as she could see in every direction, there was nothing but fire. Every forest, every mountain, burned. Animal and human bones littered the landscape. Across the entire Earth, the oceans steamed as fire and lava poured into them, turning them into clouds of vapor. It was the apocalypse everywhere she could see.

We failed, Maji thought as she ran. *We killed the Earth! We failed!*

They burst through a grove of trees and the woman stopped dead in her tracks in shock. In front of her, laid out in blankets on their bellies in the grass, were Star, Cloud, Wolf Girl, and Justice. A flash of memory flooded over Maji.

My children! Maji remembered. *Oh my god, I have to save my children!*

"Girls!" Maji screamed. "Run, girls, run!!! There's a fire!"

The girls looked up at Maji's words, smiles spreading across their faces as they saw her.

"Maji!" Cloud exclaimed, jumping up and running over to her. "Come play with us!"

"No! Girls! We have to run! There's a fire!" Maji looked behind her and saw the great blaze grow closer. The heat pulsed against her back. A tree a few feet away from her exploded, sending pieces of flaming wood sailing through the air and falling all around them.

Cloud pulled on Maji's arm to lead her over to the blankets. The girls smiled at her, oblivious to the fire that was almost on top of them. Maji reached out for them, grabbing their hands, trying to pull them to their feet, but they laughed and wrenched their hands away, rolling into the grass.

The fire began to circle them. Maji looked around for her younger self but didn't see her anywhere. She screamed as loud as she could at the girls to run, but they just smiled and laughed. She grabbed their arms, legs, and feet, and tried to drag them off their blankets, but they laughed and rolled away from her or knocked her over with a playful kick.

Tears began to stream down Maji's face as she watched the fire burn everything around them. Waves of heat distorted her vision. She screamed in a panic, tried shaking them to wake the girls up, but they ignored her, and laughed and talked among themselves.

Maji screamed in terror as the flames licked the edges of the girls' blankets. She watched Star leap to her feet, dancing joyfully as the flames circled around her. The flames emitted a sound like the combination of wood cracking and a high tea-kettle screech. Star did a playful twirl on one foot, then landed squarely in the center of a flame. Her face morphed into terror, and she screamed at the top of her lungs when her pant legs caught fire.

"No! *No!*" Maji screamed and leaped forward toward her daughter, wrapping her arms and legs around her. But the flames consumed her relentlessly. Maji's flesh burned as the raging fire enveloped her youngest daughter. The desperate mother tried to smother the fire, but a sense of helpless horror mocked her vain efforts. Star's screams echoed all around them, combining with the echo of Maji's own wails, until the worst sound of all took over– silence. Maji watched impotently as her daughter's body disintegrated into ash.

The other girls looked around as if awakened from some trance, registering what was happening. They screamed in terror at the sight of the pile of bones and ash that had once been their sister's Star's body and clung to each other in the middle of the circle of blankets.

"Save us!" they cried.

She was failing. She had to save her children, but she was failing. The emotion weighed on her body like a suit of lead. She tried to move but could only do so in slow motion. As hard as she tried, she couldn't get her legs to move faster than a slow drag.

In desperation, she flung herself as hard as she could toward the other three girls as the circle of fire moved closer. They all smashed together in the center of flaming wood and smoke. Screams filled the air around her. She wrapped her arms around them, hoping she could protect them from the inferno. But the roar grew louder. The heat began searing their flesh. The flame consumed them all. Her mind became pure heat and terror.

Then everything went startlingly white all around her, and the cacophony stopped, leaving only the sound of Maji's own gasp in a vast void. She tried to adjust her eyes to the brightness. The swirling-colored light appeared all around her once more. Mixed within it, swirling in and out of form, was the flaming, burning wasteland of Earth's landscape. On the ground in front of her lay four blackened skeletons, the bones of her children. Maji wailed in despair.

I couldn't save them! I failed. I failed!

With her vast vision, she looked around and saw the fire no longer burned. Instead, she saw skeletons of forests, smoldering and black. Her soul had taken on that same dark color, and around her, the swirling light dimmed. Maji wanted to run from the vision, to close her eyes against it, but she couldn't. Nothing could remove the horror. It was everywhere. She couldn't escape.

She sank into despair, into the void, the feeling of sinking continuing on and on. After a time, the motion shifted, and she was being rocked gently over rolling waves. Maji's crying softened.

The swirling lights began to come together into a form all around her. As it took shape, Maji looked up and realized she was cradled in the arms of a massive figure, a woman. Her form never completely solidified but remained partially ethereal and shimmered in and out of sight. Her kind eyes looked down at Maji, and in her face the confused woman saw her mother's. Then it shifted and became her grandmother. Then, a breath later, it morphed into Chandra's face. The woman's face never stopped changing, but always stayed on the edge of recognition.

Behind this great mother figure, the lights swirled together into another form. This figure was male, and he gently wrapped his arms around the great mother, holding Maji as well. With the same semi-transparency as his mate, his face morphed from her grandfather, to Eamonn, to Xavier, to her father.

"My child, it's all okay," both figures cooed, speaking with one voice. Their voice came from all directions, a symphony of flutes, harps, and bird songs. It was one of the most beautiful sounds Maji had ever heard and filled her with a deep love. "There is nothing to save. Trying to stop change is like trying to catch the sky in a jar."

"But my babies!" Maji cried. The great mother and father smiled and pulled Maji closer, nestling her against the great mother's breast.

"They are our babies, too," they said, and both sets of eyes looked up over the scorched landscape. Maji followed their gaze to the charred death in all directions. Her worst fear had come true. Mankind's greed and arrogance had won and taken all life on Earth with it, including her own children. Humanity had failed.

But then her pain turned to awe as she watched the smoldering trees sprout leaves. The blackened ground transformed into a carpet of green, with tiny green shoots pushing through the ash. A sweet smell filled the air as the smoke dissipated, and the sound of birds singing began.

The bones of her children stopped smoking, and with a soft glow, transformed back into the four girls lying naked in the grass. They sat up, rubbing their eyes as if waking from a deep sleep.

Maji gasped in surprise and wanted to leap from the arms of the great mother and run to her children, but she had lost the ability to move. As if sensing her desire, the great mother pulled her even closer to her. The strength she felt in the great mother's arms caused the woman to pause, and her urge to run after the girls faded. Instead, she wanted to cry with relief.

"They are our babies, too," the great mother and father said again. "Nothing really happens in death, other than what is always happening, which is change. Creation itself is constant change."

"I saw them die," Maji whimpered. "I saw the Earth die. Have we failed? Have we killed our planet? Will my girls be okay? Do they have any future?"

The great mother and father both smiled lovingly at Maji.

"Death is not a failure, Maji. And change is only hard when we refuse to accept it. Humanity is an expression of intelligence, creativity, and evolution. But much like light cannot be seen unless it is in contrast to darkness, so too humanity is an expression of greed, arrogance, ignorance, and selfishness. They exist simultaneously and define the other. Right, wrong, failure, success…these are just ideas created to give meaning and purpose to the human mind. It helps the mind organize the larger whole into ways it can understand within its own limitations, much like yours is doing right now."

Maji gasped. *Is this all in my mind?*

"There is no failure," the great mother and father continued. "There is only pure creative expression that cannot die. The future of the planet and your children is completely unknown, dear one, because there is no future. There is only an eternal now. But we can promise you that it is always within perfection that all of creation unfolds."

Maji stared at their luminescent faces, changing again and again into people she had known, loved, and admired throughout her life. She turned her gaze to the morphing landscape, filled with growing, changing light.

The four girls leaped to their feet, brushing the last of the grey ash off their bodies.

Laughing, they turned and ran into the iridescent forest, disappearing into a newly formed forest. Maji watched them go, her heart light. An urge to follow them flickered inside her. But then Maji paused. She couldn't follow them. She wasn't sure why, but she knew that she couldn't and that she didn't need to. Everything was okay. As the great mother had said, there was perfection in this, even if Maji didn't fully understand it or see it. There was renewal.

She looked around, uncertain as to where she was or what was happening to her. She moved in a dream, without dreaming. Only the deep sensation of love and nurturance was certain. The fear was gone. Maji nestled deeper into the great mother's arms, allowing herself to rest in a state of peace. Her mind settled. Her awareness expanded beyond thought.

As her being spread, she noticed small details she had not been able to before. Beautiful streams of light left her heart and connected with those of the great mother and father. They swirled slowly in the shape of a double-helix, wrapped around itself. The balls of light coalesced into groups, and within each of them, Maji saw an infinite number of great mothers and fathers. More shafts of light sprang from her heart and connected to the endless parents networking Maji in a vast web of love-fueled light.

As Maji witnessed this, she realized she was no longer being held by the great mother in her arms. Her own body had dissolved into swirling light and mixed in with the light of the great mother and father. They were now the same body. The same voice. And with startling clarity, Maji saw that they were the same mind. She experienced with wonder the feeling of holding herself in her arms. And she felt an unending love that felt like the seed of creation itself.

She had become the Great Mother Maji.

Her mind merged with all the other great mothers and fathers, and Maji saw and thought with an inexhaustible awareness. Within each sphere, and within the belly of each great mother in that sphere, Maji beheld a vast array of worlds unfolding. She saw Earth and witnessed the lives of billions of people. Each life played out before her, rainbow lights dancing through a prism. They were distinct in color, expression, and form, born from the singular rays of lights emerging from the hearts of the great mothers.

She witnessed the lives of animals, centered on die-or-survive instinct and the primal urges of procreation and fear. She experienced the lives of insects, flat and unemotional, driven by chemical reactions that propelled their lives forward.

She touched the lives of plants and marveled at the sentience of the trees, who spoke to each other through their root systems and sensed the world in a slow-motion dance where breaths were seasons long and lifetimes stretched through centuries. Maji saw the world as they did, without eyes and ears to hear, but through the wisdom of the seasonal changes, the gentle touching of the roots, the interconnected community built in their forests.

Within the bellies of other great mothers, she witnessed horrific visions of burning hells and creatures trapped there within endless repetitive cycles, mental prisons. She saw deformed, headless creatures spinning in endless confusion, and others with mouths so small they could never eat or drink enough to sate themselves. These creatures lived in an unending cycle of suffering that unfolded over and over before her eyes. Her heart ached in compassion for them. She wanted to scream to wake them, but could do nothing

High above in other bellies of great mothers, Maji saw God-like creatures that existed in parallel dimensions to humans. These beings sat suspended in states of pure power and bliss, unaware that anything existed outside their own pristine experience. They clung so tightly to euphoria that they ceased movement for fear of disturbing their delicate equilibrium, and lived for centuries before decaying into death, unaware they had ever lived to begin with.

As Maji watched endless lives commence, live, and die before her, she became aware of the timeline of her own lifestream. All of linear time collapsed into one sustained "now", and she experienced every life she had ever lived in a single instant.

Maji saw herself live as an amoeba, floating in the muck puddles of early Earth when the air was mostly methane and carbon dioxide. She experienced her life as a dragonfly, a lizard, a bear, and an early Australopithecus. Her mind evolved to form language, create ritual, and place her red-dyed handprint on the stone caves to declare the world, "Yes! I exist," humanity's first declaration of self-awareness.

She witnessed the lives she had lived as *Homo sapiens* before she was Maji. Each had shaped and informed her life as Maji. The patterns repeated over and over again in each life, with slight variations. Her last two lives before she was Maji had informed much of who she had become.

In the early 1900's, she had been a monk in Tibet named Samten. She experienced herself as a boy sent off by her family to live in a monastery at the age of seven. She felt sad and alone, missing her parents. She felt Samten's deep jealousy of his four sisters, who got to stay home with their parents. As he grew into a young man in his twenties, Samten struggled to find his place in the monastery.

At age twenty-five, he grew infatuated with a young woman who lived in the village near his monastery. His heart broke a year later when she married another man. Frustrated and discouraged by the monastic lifestyle, Samten vowed to be reborn as a woman so he could experience the householder life and free himself from the responsibility of being the family's honored monk.

As he grew into middle age, he finally accepted his life as a monk and began to embrace the Buddhist teachings. Maji experienced his peaceful years, where his mind rested. Maji experienced Samten's moments of touching enlightenment, when he saw the game, and then forgot again.

But when China invaded Tibet in 1950, Samten's experience changed. He and his fellow monks lived in fear. His anger grew as the Chinese army came and burned their monastery to the ground in the name of cultural cleansing. She felt his horror as he watched them burn thousand-year-old sacred Buddhist texts. Samten ran out into a field during the uprising, rifle in hand, filled with fear as he saw the angry faces of the Chinese soldiers aim their weapons. She felt the bullet rip through his side and heard his voice as he screamed in pain. He fell to the dirt. His last thoughts were of anger at the injustice he and his people had been served.

He went through the afterlife, just like Maji. His visions unfolded, and Maji experienced his view of the infinite within her own view of the infinite. She experienced his awe and fear as he, too, was held in the arms of the great mother and father. But he turned his focus to his anger. He channeled his energy, and like a ball rolling downhill, it became a powerful attracting force he couldn't resist. This karmic momentum focused Samten's stream of consciousness toward another rebirth. The violence and anger he'd died with, combined with his desire for justice and peace, created the perfect conditions for rebirth in South Africa at the height of the political unrest of the Apartheid. Samten became Ayize, a little girl born in Soweto, a sprawling shantytown outside of Johannesburg.

Ayize grew up in the shadow of loss and poverty. Grief was the caretaker that flowed from her mother's milk into her body. Anger surrounded her, and she woke most mornings to the cries of her people demanding justice in the streets. Sickened by all the suffering she witnessed, Ayize learned to abhor violence and chose to live a life of peace.

Ayize had a grandmother who became more of a caretaker to her than her own mother was. She was a wisened, wrinkled woman that seemed to live outside the happenings of the world. She was a Sangoma, a traditional Zulu healer, and understood the workings of the natural world.

At the age of fourteen, Ayize grew ill. As she lay on her bed, her grandmother and fellow healers sang songs to her. Ayize experienced a profound awakening and felt the "umbilini" power rising through her body. It was the same kundalini power Maji experienced on her vision quest. The umbilini healed her.

At sixteen years old Ayize fell in love with a young man of twenty. Her mother slapped her hard across the face when she told her she was pregnant. Her boyfriend punched the wall next to her head and refused to acknowledge he was the father. Ayize found the herbs her grandmother kept to induce a miscarraige, but her ignorance betrayed her. She took too much. As she lay dying from loss of blood her grandmother found her, and with tears told her to help their family from the spirit world.

In the afterlife, Maji witnessed Ayize's experience of the infinite within her own. The woman's compelling regret, her sense of justice, her familial loyalty—all of these merged to be reborn in the form of Maji.

Maji experienced her own life in that eternal now.

She was born and found joy in her mother's love, healing the pain carried into that life from Ayize. Maji lived her childhood again and the happiness of her time with her grandfather, so similar to Ayize's grandmother in her former life. She once again experienced sadness and anger at the destruction of the natural environment and injustices of the world through greed and power. Once again, she walked away from the political battle to choose peace, simplicity, and harmony with nature. Maji saw both Samten and Ayize in that choice.

Then came her vision quest and the powerful force of energy that opened her to profound interconnectedness. She lived again in Chandra's ashram and felt again that oneness with everything at the stupa. She remembered the game.

She also experienced the trauma of the abortion, the feeling of death in her body, and the feeling of failure. She forgot the game. She lived through her time in Chile, meeting Xavier, and their wedding, then moving back to Colorado. The incredible birth of her daughters once again fulfilled a desire that lasted lifetimes.

The years of marriage to Xavier, and the slow disintegration of their relationship. The exhaustion of doing it all in the relationship. His resentment at being stuck in a country he didn't like. Her painful choice to end their marriage, and the pain and heartbreak it brought both of them.

Her time meeting Eamonn. Her initial distrust. That first lightning kiss that changed everything. Excitement and novelty. Fear and the certainty of failure. She experienced the healing of their mutual love and devotion. She saw the end of a karmic cycle of heartbreak that lasted lifetimes.

She saw her relationship unfold with Justice and Cloud into the unique form of love that could only exist between stepparents and stepchildren. She watched their family grow and change together, learning to love in awkward yet beautiful ways.

She experienced all of this–her past lives, her life as Maji, and all the lives lived by so many different beings–in an instant. All these moments she lived not as individual, separate experiences, but as one vast blanket of manifestation, each moment a gentle fold within eternal timelessness.

But for all the vastness and infinity Maji was able to perceive through her multiple lifetimes on Earth, there was one singular experience that narrowed her focus into a single flash of startling clarity. It was the moment, as the just-born Wolf Girl was placed in Maji's arms, her small howl wailing through the night, that Maji looked into her child's dark eyes. She saw her own reflection there, her own face staring back at her. In that reflection shone numerous reflections of all the lives she had ever lived, and all the lives Wolf Girl had ever lived. They melded into that one moment as a unified whole. A profound wave of unconditional love for her child, and for all their past lives, washed over her. She saw all the lives that played out in the bellies of the great mothers as one and the same as her own. She remembered the game again. And there, in re-experiencing that one unique moment in all of infinite experience, Maji recognized her true nature.

All of it, from the amoeba in the sludge to the great fathers and mothers and their bellies of infinity, formed the great dance of her own mind. No physical place existed here. The visions of her burning children and the scorched Earth had been projections of all her worst fears. The warmth she felt in the arms of the great mother and father had been her own endless resource of love presented in a way she could process.

This was not new. Maji, as a being, had never existed anywhere other than her own consciousness. Her recognition of the game within several lives, her experience of it now in her journey of the in-between–all was a beautiful dance that spanned millennia, a singular experience of one moment that the illusion of time turned into many, spread out as a whisper of an idea from a vast consciousness that was her, that was everyone, that was everything.

As Maji's consciousness recognized this, her small sense of self vanished. Maji was the All. The cycles of her lifetimes had reached a conclusion. Maji was free.

<u>Painting Rainbows</u>

It was two weeks after Maji had died. The funeral had passed, and the meals dropped off by loved ones had all been eaten. Star and Wolf Girl had spent the better part of a week at their dad's house but were now back with Eamonn and Cloud and Justice. Though Eamonn had no biological claim, Xavier agreed to a shared custody of his daughters, for their sake. They were still family, even if it was now a fragmented one.

The girls felt pressured to resume some sense of normalcy in their lives, if only for a way to distract themselves from their grief. They all decided they wanted to go back to school that week. It was better than sitting home, wallowing. They wanted to think about something else, be around friends, and move on from Maji's death. But as they walked one by one through the front doors at the end of the school day, the silence that met them instead of Maji's lilting "hello" was a stabbing reminder.

Wolf Girl had cried so much over the past ten days that no tears were left in her body. She dropped her backpack on the floor and trudged to the couch in the living room to flop down, exhausted. Star followed and snuggled up next to her on the couch. She had hardly left her sister's side since their mother died. Wolf Girl didn't mind.

Cloud and Justice followed them into the living room, and both girls sprawled out on the floor. In the past, they would have jumped on the TV to play video games, or call friends, or grab some dolls and go outside to play. But none of them had any motivation to do anything. Sadness weighed them down.

"What do you think Mama is doing right now?" Star asked.

"Maji is dead, Star. She isn't doing anything," Justice said curtly. Star turned her head and buried her face in Wolf Girl's side to hide her emotion, but her sobs betrayed her.

Wolf Girl frowned. "She isn't completely gone!" she said to Star. "I feel her sometimes, I swear. Some part of her is out there. Her soul, or something."

Justice sat up, sighing. "I'm sorry, Star. I shouldn't have said that. I agree with Wolf Girl. I know there is some part of her out there."

Justice crawled across the floor and wrapped her arms around Star and Wolf Girl. Cloud jumped up, running over to join them. The four girls held each other silently for long moments, filling the open wound left by Maji's loss with love for each other. All the silly arguments over dolls and dishes and messy rooms no longer mattered. Only love mattered.

"Maji told me she could do whatever she wanted after she died," Cloud piped up. "I think she's flying around in heaven somewhere. Maybe on the back of a butterfly!"

The four girls all smiled at that thought, imagining Maji riding on a creature with beautifully painted wings.

"Maybe she found the most beautiful mountains in the universe to hike in!" Star smiled. "You know how much she loved the mountains. I bet she's just hiking and flying!"

Inexplicably, a soft glow began to fill the living room where the girls sat.

Wolf Girl sat up tall, her eyes big. "You guys," she whispered. "Do you feel that?"

The four girls sat in stillness, listening. The energy in the room shifted palpably. They remained intently still.

"It's Mama!" Star shouted. "She must've heard us talking about her!"

A comforting warmth spread through them. It reminded Wolf Girl and Star of their mother's arms wrapped around them. Cloud and Justice felt the comfort of their own mother combined with the undeniable energy of Maji. The room hummed and filled with Maji's scent.

A glorious vision of creation's perfection enveloped them, and with it, a revelation of the interconnectedness of all life. Gentle waves of energy moved through them, a vast web connecting every living thing.

Star lifted her hands and turned them over. Ripples of light emanated from them. Wolf Girl touched her cheeks, tears spilling over them from the awe and beauty of the vision unfolding within her mind, her mother's presence more clear than ever. Justice looked at the other three girls, her eyes wide and mouth open in wonder. Cloud cried softly, overwhelmed and overjoyed.

Within their minds, they stepped beyond the immaturity of children and their undeveloped view of the world into vast wisdom. They experienced, for a brief moment, the vision of the infinite that Maji had. Billions of lives unfolded, more varied than they could count. They touched the very particles of the universe and saw the vast web of which they were a part. They each had a glimpse into their own past and future lives and saw how time collapsed into one singular present moment. They witnessed Maji wake up to her true nature and felt her merge into the vast consciousness that was everything.

As they sat in shocked awe and wonder, the gentle glow in the room shifted slowly until it had transformed to a myriad of colors wherever they looked. They all reached up, touching the bands of color in amazement. Tears flowed down their faces.

"Maji is painting rainbows!" Cloud laughed. "We said she would be able to paint rainbows when she died. Look! She's painting rainbows for us!"

The girls laughed and stood, twirling and dancing in the multicolored light, glorying in Maji's freedom with a joy that transcended cognition.

After several minutes, the vision and the rainbows faded. Their past lives vanished. Their minds receded to the finite. But the profound love they felt ingrained itself on them in that moment. For that moment, they were all free.

Author's Note

At the age of thirty nine, after dealing with several mysterious health issues, I was diagnosed with early cognitive decline leading to Alzheimer's Disease. My doctor discovered I had two of the "Alzheimer's genes", which put me at a sixty to ninety percent chance of contracting the disease later in life. But my body aches and gaps in memory confirmed the process had already begun for me.

There was irony in that diagnosis. Having spent my entire adult life practicing "mind training" as it is defined in Eastern religious philosophies, here I was facing losing my own mind. It terrified me. And the possibility of my family watching my slow decline terrified me more. So I turned to my spiritual practice once again.

In Tibetan Buddhism there is a practice called Chöd which involves putting yourself in uncomfortable circumstances to cut through fear and attachment. Imagining your own death is one way to do this. This story is my Chöd practice. I have been told numerous times over the years by people that know me that I should write a book about my life since it has been such an unusual one. I never felt compelled to just tell a story. I wanted to convey something more meaningful. When I received my diagnosis, I realized this was not only an important time for me to grow spiritually, but that I could share this journey with others in a way that would be meaningful to them as well. Maji's life, as experienced through the flashbacks in the story, is based on my own life. Her journey and spiritual realizations are my own. Though I was unable to include all of the amazing adventures and journeys I have lived, the ones presented here were based on the experiences that were most impactful to my spiritual growth. Maji's present day timeline of facing her own imminent death was my practice in choosing to die well and imagining what that would be like.

Her journey through the afterlife was inspired by the teachings of The Tibetan Book of the Dead. Over the centuries, Buddhist practitioners who learned to be masters of their own consciousness discovered how to remain completely aware through dying, the afterlife, and rebirth. They brought back with them detailed accounts of the "bardo", which literally translates to mean "the in-between." They offered detailed descriptions of facing aspects of their own consciousness in the afterlife. They explained how most people experience it as a dream. The few who are able to recognize this experience as a projection of their own mind wake up to their true nature, and are freed from the karmic cycle of rebirth. Much of the Buddhist practice of learning to recognize this in death is actually a journey to free one from fear and live a good life. They are inextricably linked.

I'm happy to report that through the wisdom of amazing doctors and cutting edge science, I am keeping Alzheimer's Disease at bay. I live an extremely healthy and happy life. This diagnosis has been a true blessing, and I no longer squander any moment of my life or take for granted the love and relationships I have. I savor every moment with my four daughters and my partner. I have no idea what the future may hold, but I'm no longer afraid of it. I don't want to waste any moment living in fear. I have realized, as Maji did, that it is all perfect. My hope is that Maji's story can inspire you to live your own life this way. Thank you from the bottom of my heart for joining me on this journey.

Acknowledgements

Thank you to everyone who believed in the vision of this book. Thank you to my partner Robert, my best friend Priya, and everyone else who encouraged me along the way. Thank you to my editor Paul McLerran for doing such an amazing job and pushing me to be a much better writer than I had known I could be. Thank you to Christopher and LuAnne Hormel for the incredible investment in this project and my art in general. Thank you to my children for riding this emotional rollercoatser with me.

Thank you to everyone who contributed to the initial investment of this project. Thank you to the Boulder County Arts Alliance for awarding me the Martha Kate Thomas Fund to complete this project. Thank you to Beads On One String for awarding me the Connections Grant to create this book.

Thank you to all the contributors of the crowdfunding campaign: Matthew Mendez-Vanacore, Annette Jones, Brandi Mason, Christa Cooper, She-Fi Show, Kate Jean, Lori Morris, Haley and Luis Ibarra, Karen Davis, Joseph B Callahan, Ryan Howard, Jen Jackson, Victoria Wagoner, Leanne Fenton, Kent Bernhard, Dave Mayer, Rivkah Bacharach, Max Gibson, Emma Tummon, Erin Siepker, Vladimir Fleurima, Erin Siepker, Jeremy Bruce, Sandy Harold, Brianna McGeehan, Stephanie Danyi, Jeff & Jill Groves & Family, Eileen Rogers, Brianne Langille, Jeff Johnston, Travis Pierce, Jacque Wedding-Scott, Lauren Zablotny, Linda Larsen, Farrah Greatbatch, Kirsty Spraggon, Shelley Brown, Sara Jordan, Dove Weissman, Selena Lael Magram, Deborah Kerrigan West, Christopher B Martin, Lucy Walker, Larry D Goyda, Diane Pappas, Katya Slivinskaya, Shelley Harris, Tracy Grant, Melissa Ashton, Susan Gohr Preiss, Susan Martin, Stacy Burgess, James Willhour, Glennis Smith, Sky Canyon, Kindra Greentree Berv & Peter Berv, Lisa Secco, Sreedevi Bringi, Raymon and Cathey Valdez, Paal Joachim Romdahl, Jamie E. Hamilton-Jurkovich, Glennis Smith, Jenevieve Russell, Jared Stokes, Lary Vongsavanh, Annamaria Laverty, Corin O'Connell, Michael Faulkner, Sara Hopkins, Jeffrey Vander Clute, Mary Huron Hunter, Marilee Talkington, Collardson Family, Midge James, Gwenn Seemel, John

Mercede, Jeff and Tammy Thramann, Mary Hostetter, Rashida Bell, Terry Braun, Matthew Melton, Paulette Schneider, Vera Berv, Frank Berliner, Daniel Schuring, Kim L Regan, Danae Shanti, Mary Evans, Glenn Weissel, Dennis Runge, Rochelle Walden, Heather Rose Stegman, Ashara Morris, Ana Medina, Anne Alexander, Priya Laasch, Barbara Jane Walters, Colby Cooper, Kathleen Lawson, Adina Winfrey, Hugh and Patty Josephs, Matthew Henry, Constance J Leshin, Lisa Torick, Kristen Kardos, Artamis Parsi, Rhonda Cooper, Keesha Saunders, Diane Thoms, Kristin Flood, Jonas Magram, Lisa G Kral, Leyla Sarper, Heather Phillips, Keith Percy, Elizabeth Dayton, Christopher Waterman, Cameron Ring, Paul Lawson, Thiago Leao

And thank you to you, the readers, for being a part of my creative world!

<u>About The Author</u>

Award-winning artist and author Kyra Coates studied at the Corcoran School of Art and the Maryland Institute, College of Art. She had her first publication in 2000 and began showing her art professionally in 2001. After a spiritual awakening in her twenties, Kyra became a Hindu nun devoted to a path of enlightenment. She went on to receive a degree in Religious Studies and Psychology from Naropa University, where she focused her studies on the psychology of enlightenment. When she left her robes behind, her professional focus returned to her art, writing, and non-profit work. Kyra has received numerous awards and grants for her creative work addressing both spirituality and women's empowerment. She lives in Colorado with her partner and four children.

Artwork

Printed in Great Britain
by Amazon

24603904R00176